# Trail of the Outlaw

**Books by James Duermeyer**

Flint Bluff
Market Time Conspiracy
Singing Creek
Heroes in Obscurity
The Capture of the USS Pueblo; the Incident,
the Aftermath, and the Motives of North Korea

# Trail of the Outlaw

James Duermeyer

SPEAKING VOLUMES, LLC
NAPLES, FLORIDA
2020

Trail of the Outlaw

The views expressed are solely those of the author. The work was designed, produced, and published in the United States of America.

ISBN 978-1-64540-366-1

# South Central United States

# Chapter One

## San Antonio, Texas - 1809

Lily had sternly warned her only two years before when the same thing had occurred. Sissy had been told in no uncertain terms that she would find her "cowboy-pleasing pink rump on the street" if it ever happened again. Yet here she was, almost two years to the day later, in the dark shadows just prior to dawn, skittering through black alleyways and streets, making her way to the gates of the Mission San Francisco de la Espada.

Miss Lily, in reality, was the high and mighty Lillian Fontleroy, formerly of the New Orleans Fontleroy family, which had been highly regarded in the social circles of that city. That is, until Lily was seventeen years old, when her father had managed to extract a considerable sum of money from several of his friends under less than honorable conditions. When this was discovered, the family was forced to hurriedly leave New Orleans during a pitch-black night. The disgraced family headed west to San Antonio. It was shortly after this fateful move that both of Lily's parents contracted the flu and died. With meager funds at her disposal, Lillian Fontleroy began earning money using a skill that she had learned in the fancy horse-drawn closed carriages of the young wealthy suitors with whom she had consorted in New Orleans. By sheer guile and self-promoting fortitude, she began earning a handsome amount of money by accompanying wealthy cattle ranchers to their hotels when they came to town. In her prime, she had been a favorite of several of the wealthy cattle barons who visited San Antonio and, in time, her monetary assets grew proportionately. With her earnings, she was able to buy a worn property that was soon grandly refurbished and expensively bedecked in the finest furnishings, including a stable of young, comely women for the pleasure of the San Antonio male clientele.

***

Just six hours before, Sissy Amos had been lying on a hard, dirty, blanket-covered pallet in her friend's one room shack, located within spitting distance of the Mission San Antonio Valero, the mission that the Spanish soldiers were now calling Alamo. Sissy Amos, with the help of her friend, had just birthed the caterwauling, blood-flecked baby boy that she now carried wrapped in soiled rags. Other soiled rags were tied tightly to her legs and groin, making the walking possible, but painful. A note had been hastily scribbled with charcoal on a piece of butcher's paper and placed inside the wrappings on the baby. The note simply said, "The name is Vogler."

Her mud-edged skirt dragged on the hard-packed caliche clay path. As she made her way through the night, she kept thinking about how she had gotten into this predicament; not once, but twice with the same man. Sissy had been a prostitute for nearly ten of her twenty-five years. Of all of the men she had been with, only one, the same, damn, low-life drifter who had fathered the previous baby had ever gotten her pregnant. His name was Vernon Vogler, himself the product of a carnal union unsanctified by any hint of marriage between those responsible for his birth. Sissy had fallen for his grease-slick sweet-talk as he had told her how he was making a good living and that he wanted her to be a permanent part of his life.

The forever-glib Vernon Vogler's idea of making a good living was to hang about at gaming and drinking establishments, sidling up to strangers and meticulously picking their pockets. While it was true that he made enough cash in his endeavors to manage a modest living, women, in his estimation, were only a means for sport and satisfaction of his manly desires. Having a woman as a permanent life partner had never been in his plans, even though he had told a goodly number of short-term female companions that they were to be in his future, happily-married life. The line seemed to work well when it came time to lure them abed for a couple of nights of pleasurable debauchery at a reduced monetary rate, or better yet, for no fee at all. Sissy Amos was only another in a long line of whores to whom he had alluded marriage.

Two years ago, Vernon Vogler had arrived in town nearly penniless, and with the talk of a snake, he had cajoled Miss Lily Fontleroy, owner and proprietor of one of the town's largest sporting houses, into bedding one of her stable of whores under the guise that he would pay at the end of the week; not the way Miss Lily normally did business. But even she had been the recipient of Vogler's oily charm and grudgingly assented to his wishes.

The unlucky woman of pleasure assigned to him that evening two years ago had turned out to be Miss Sissy Amos. The beguiling grifter had spun his web with Miss Amos to the point that she had freely entertained him for two days, and even staked him to a cash purse so that he could visit the gaming tables in the city. Vogler had successfully increased the stake and lifted a few valuable baubles and trinkets from the unsuspecting gambling clientele. But none of the ill-gotten gain had been repaid to the starry-eyed Miss Amos. Knowing he had latched onto a girl with a steady income, and a not-so-steady intelligence level, Vernon was not eager to leave town. Twice a week, he paused in his illegal ventures to visit Sissy. At this point, he was appropriately paying Miss Lily for services received, and all participants were happy.

3

But the easy life-style of Vernon Vogler would soon come crashing against stark reality. Young Miss Amos informed him that she was with child and would like to begin making plans for a visit to the priest to conduct and bless their marriage. The ever-smiling Vernon Vogler, in his most syrupy manner, brought tears to the eyes of Sissy Amos as he informed her that he would be unable to carry out any wedding plans, as he could not afford to get married on his meager income, the same excuse he had been using for weeks to explain why he had not paid Sissy back for the initial monetary stake she had provided.

While the smile was still pasted to his face, Vogler was subsequently confronted by Sissy's employer, the formidable Miss Lily and one of her male, peace-making associates, who ever-so-gently informed Mr. Vogler that he needed to begin making monetary restitution to Sissy and plans for the wedding. Ever undeterred, that same evening under a pitch-black sky, Vernon Vogler rather permanently "borrowed" an old horse from the back pen of the livery stable, where he could not be readily observed, and slowly and stealthily made his way out of San Antonio. He was also clever enough not to leave town on any main road where Miss Lily had posted two of her most trusted "peace makers" to intercept any attempt by Vogler to skip out on his matrimonial and monetary responsibilities. As a result, after hours of diligent observation, Miss Lily's associates were confident when they returned at dawn to report to their employer that Vogler had not left town by way of either of the two main roads they had been watching.

For the next two days, however, there was no sign of Vernon Vogler, and he did not keep his usual appointment with Sissy Amos. It was then that Miss Lily knew the rooster had flown the coop. In her twenty years of experiences dealing with lusty cowboys, bald-faced liars, and grifters, she had seen this scenario play out several times. And each time it had happened, no wedding vows had been exchanged. In addition, in each instance, she had taken no pity on the poor girl involved. The pregnant prostitutes had all been summarily sent packing. Lily was not completely heartless, however. Two of those women previously discharged had been rehired after they had shed themselves of any lingering responsibilities, namely their unwanted offspring.

But just as in most of life's circumstances, there is usually an exception, and that had been Sissy Amos. Lily had taken pity on the poor girl, as Sissy was one of her favorite girls and a real money maker for the business. And in some ways, Sissy Amos also reminded Lily of her own younger days. So Lily bent her own principles and allowed Sissy Amos to remain in the house. She would continue to entertain and service clients until even the rowdy cowboys wanted nothing to do with the girl with the protruding belly. At that point, Sissy was banished to her room and would remain there until the birth of the child.

While Sissy was out of action, so to speak, Miss Lily kept diligent notes on the expenses for feeding a non-productive employee. Sissy Amos would be expected to work off these expenses as soon as she was able to return to work. For four months, Sissy Amos was not seen outside her drab room in the sporting house. At the end of those four months, one of Miss Lily's house servants unceremoniously placed the baby outside the large wooden gate of the Mission Espada, where it had been retrieved by the good friars. A scrap of paper with the word "Vogler" written on it had been pinned to the small blanket wrapped snugly around the baby.

***

Two years later, Vernon Vogler sashayed down the wooden sidewalks of San Antonio, once again frequenting the gaming establishments and slowly lining his pockets with the stolen belongings of others.

Sashay was not a misnomer. Vernon Vogler was vain to the point of being quite the foppish dandy. For the past two years, he had taken up residence in a small rooming house on the banks of the Colorado River in Austin. He indulged in the very latest men's fashions and loved to display his wardrobe while traipsing from gambling houses to sporting houses throughout that city. His thin, short stature did not contribute to a masculine appearance, and often his gait almost made it appear that he was walking on his tiptoes. His thin black mustache and hair were always neatly trimmed and oiled. He bathed regularly and smelled as good as any woman. It was because of these mannerisms that behind his back, and yes, sometimes to his face, he was scorned and jeered at by the other male clients in the locations he frequented. It seems that the other men kept a rumor alive concerning Vernon's manliness. If they only knew, of course, this was certainly not true. The number of illegitimate children fathered by Vernon Vogler in central Texas would have amazed his male, rumor-mongering acquaintances.

But as strange as the man was, women loved to be around Vernon. They found him charming, witty, attentive, and eager to develop a more physical presence with each and every one of them, from women of modest means to those who occupied positions of higher social standing. It was this animal magnetism from the opposite gender that led Vernon to seek a hasty retreat from Austin. It seems that a private investigator working for a local judge had discovered that the judge's wife was not above slipping from the house during court sessions to clandestinely fall into the accommodating embraces of Vernon Vogler. Just prior to the judge correcting this impingement on his honor's honor with a shotgun, true to form, Vernon had beat a hasty retreat from Austin in the wee hours of the morning, making a return trip to San Antonio.

Upon reaching San Antonio, Vogler knew where he could find warm creature comfort. But he knew he could not simply walk into the establishment of Miss Lily, so he did the next best thing. In the hours just past the closing of Miss Lily's establishment, he climbed into the window of Sissy Amos's bedroom. And poor, simple-minded Sissy welcomed him to her perfumed bosom as if he had never been away. With his ever-present slick vernacular, Vernon Vogler could have probably sold three-legged horses to cowboys. It did not take anywhere near that much effort, and with very few words on his part, he soon had Miss Amos spread-eagled in his web. The periodic window entrances lasted several weeks, and once again, after an untold number of clandestine meetings with the ever-so-slimy Mr. Vogler, Sissy Amos's natural monthly cycle ceased. For the second time, she found herself carrying the illegitimate offspring of Vernon Vogler.

If these details had been known at the local betting establishments, a standing bet would have soon arisen. It would have been a fool's bet as the odds would have been quite uneven. The fictitious wager would have been a simple bet; would he or would he not flee the banal encumbrances of fatherhood? The outcome was that as soon as Vernon Vogler noticed a rise in the smooth belly of his paramour, and she was forced to confess, he fled, this time on a slightly better horse that he purchased at the same livery stable where he had stolen a steed two years prior. Vernon Vogler would never be seen in either Austin or San Antonio again.

Sissy Amos was now on her own. She knew that Miss Lily would bounce her if she found out that she was pregnant a second time, especially if she knew that she had allowed Vernon Vogler to be entertained. Sissy kept working, but gave Miss Lily notice that she would need to leave for a time to visit an ailing aunt in St. Louis. But in fact, Sissy Amos had no aunt and no money. Vernon Vogler had once again relieved her of any spare cash she had accumulated. So, for the past five months, Sissy Amos had lived in the dirt-floor shack of her friend, another lady of the evening who worked at an establishment of lesser repute than Miss Lily's, waiting for the birth of her baby. She passed the time staring out of the dirt encrusted single glass window of the shack, periodically cursing the ground on which the Mr. Vernon Vogler walked.

\*\*\*

On this evening, Sissy herself was at that same mission gate which had been visited by a servant on Miss Lily's staff two years ago. Sissy Amos did not care a whit for the precious life she had just produced. She only wanted this unnecessary burden out of her life, and that was her present task. Approaching the darkened gate of Mission Espada, she looked carefully in all directions. Not a soul was on the street as she carefully placed the burden on the ground outside the gate. Looking around on the ground, she found what she needed, a large round stone. She lifted the stone and began pounding it on the gate. The large wooden gate echoed resoundingly with the thud of the rock striking it. The booming sound was loud, and Sissy was fearful that someone would approach from one of the surrounding adobe buildings. But she soon heard a voice speaking loudly from the other side of the gate. When she was certain that she heard footfalls approaching the gate, she dropped the stone and painfully hurried back along the path she had taken to reach the mission. Behind her, she heard the creaking sound of the mission gate being opened, and the quiet utterings of the person who had opened the gate. She hurried on. The infant boy was now in the caring hands of the friars of Mission Espada, where he would soon join his older brother. In due time, Sissy Amos returned from her absence, considerably thinner, but nevertheless no worse for wear, and Miss Lily welcomed her back into the fold of her fallen angels.

***

Brother William hobbled as fast as his gout-riddled feet would allow. He did not complain, of course, but he was not entirely happy that his duties on this still-dark morning included tending to the gate of the mission, looking out for any lost souls who might be calling. He carried a small oil lantern which he placed on the ground. He then shouted at the visitor who had been pounding on the gate. He thought it was odd that he received no reply. He pulled back the bar that held the gate closed and slowly pulled the gate open. No one was about. But then in the dim light, he saw the bundle on the ground. He was further surprised when the bundle made a small mewing sound and moved. This was not the first time he had witnessed such an occurrence, and he knew that another child had been entrusted to the Franciscan brothers.

He crossed himself and gathered up the bundle and his lantern and trudged back to the compound. He would need to tell the senior priest of his discovery, but first he made his way to the lighted kitchen, where two other friars were readying the sparse breakfast for the priests and friars.

One of the other friars called out to him, "So, William, what have you got there?"

Brother William was slowly removing the rags from around the baby. He read the note that was among the wrappings.

"I'm afraid, Brother Samuel, that we have another child, given by God, but ignored by its earthly family. And I am afraid that it is another Vogler." The friars looked at each other. They held their tongues, but each had his own thoughts. They knew what a hellion they had in the form of Thomas Vogler, the two year old who required so much of the brothers' time and attention. And it now appeared that he had a baby brother. The friars mumbled a low beseeching prayer of blessing, crossed themselves, and returned to their kitchen duties.

# Chapter Two

## Mission San Francisco de la Espada
## San Antonio, Texas - 1819

It was an unpleasant smell, but they took little heed of the odor. The two brothers sat on the ground behind the mission's communal outhouse, one of the very few places in the mission compound where the boys could hide for a short time without being seen by the priests. With deference to natural odors, the outhouse had been built in the most distant corner of the walls surrounding the mission compound. A few hardy rose bushes that sported small blossoms had been planted at the sides of the building in a mostly symbolic effort to counteract the smell of human waste that drifted through the open-air windows from inside the building.

Today, there was a competing aroma in the air at the back of the outhouse. In the hands of each boy was a corn husk, originally kept in the kitchen of the mission for use in making tamales. The husks had been purloined from the kitchen by the boys for their own use. The corn husks had been carefully wrapped around generous portions of tobacco; the same tobacco which only hours before had been in a tobacco tin in Brother James' room in the mission. Each boy had a grip on a home-made cigar, and they were eagerly puffing away; the tobacco smoke roiling upward in the still air. They whispered to each other and giggled softly. This was not the first time that the boys had met behind the outhouse for a taste of ill-gotten tobacco.

The boys were inseparable. They were truly brothers in every way. The younger brother, named Horace Vogler by the priests at the mission was now ten years old. Horace idolized his older brother, Thomas, who was now twelve. Unlike the majority of the other orphaned children taken in at the mission, the Vogler brothers were the antithesis of the laborious coaching and teachings of the good friars of Mission Espada. The two youngsters tried the holy patience of all who dealt with them. The clergymen were convinced that Satan had played a role in forming the two boys, as indeed, he probably had. No matter what tasking or learning assignment was patiently assigned to the two boys, twelve-year-old Thomas Vogler would find a way to evade the responsibility, with the younger Horace following diligently in his brother's footsteps.

While the two scoundrels were enjoying their home-made cigars, they were shirking their assigned work tasks. All of the orphans who attended school at the mission were assigned tasks to be completed following the day's classes. Thomas was supposed to be at the mission stables helping the friars clean the animal stalls and feed the livestock. Young Horace had been assigned to help clean the male orphans' sleeping quarters. The absence of the two boys was soon reported to the priest in charge of the after-class work assignments.

In deference to the older brother he idolized, and after he had taken another puff on his cigar, Horace asked, "Thomas, do you like smoking tobacco?"

Thomas was in the process of spitting out several pieces of tobacco that had made their way into his mouth.

"Yeah, I kinda like it," answered Thomas, as he gazed up at the drifting smoke. In truth, the only reason he said he liked it was that he was eluding the friars and avoiding the work tasks that he was supposed to be doing. This made the activity that much more pleasant.

As the boys reveled in their freedom from work and the knowledge that they were somehow outsmarting all of the other children and the friars at the mission, they were so engrossed that they did not hear the soft approach of sandal-clad feet. But they quickly became aware of the strong arms of Brothers William and James who had each grabbed a boy by the ear and commenced hauling them to the office of the priest in charge of the work assignments.

"Leggo of my ear," screeched Thomas. "You got no right to be yankin' on me like this, Brother William. You're just a big dumb jackass!" The twisting pressure on the struggling boy immediately got more painful as Brother William applied a bit more pressure.

"Lemme go, lemme go," Horace kept repeating as Brother James marched the younger boy along.

Father Marcus shook his head as he watched from the shade of the covered wooden porch which encircled the priests' quarters on one side of the mission compound. What he was watching was nothing new. The Vogler brothers were brought to him at least once every week. In addition, they made appearances before other priests at the mission for other infractions relative to those priests' areas of responsibility.

After a moment, with the boys held in check by a firm hand on each of their shirt collars, Marcus asked, "Where were they this time?"

"Behind the toilets, Father," answered William, "smoking away on their home-made cigars."

"Where did you get the tobacco, boys?" asked Father Marcus.

Thomas saw this question as an opportunity to implicate a nemesis. "It was Brother James's tobacco," he said, hoping that he could get the friar into trouble.

Father Marcus looked at Brother James and said, "Brother James, I have told you that smoking that pipe of yours is not a habit that the Lord smiles upon." But because James was not a priest and only a friar, Marcus allowed him to smoke his pipe when not in the presence of the priests.

Marcus turned back to the two boys. "Thomas and Horace, I would think that over the years you have been with us that we might have had a positive influence upon you. Yet, you are brought to see me nearly every week. And the punishment is nearly the same each time. I can only presume that you have grown fond of the pigs. You will both be cleaning the pig sty all of next week. Now open your mouths."

From a pocket in his robe, Marcus produced a large cake of home-made tallow soap. "Bite and chew," he said.

The priest and brothers watched as the two boys each took a bite of the soap and chewed it. The boys' faces were screwed up with their eyes squinting. Tears began readily flowing from the corners of their eyes. The boys were ordered to remain standing with the soap mixture in their mouths until Father Marcus finally told them to turn around and spit. The soapy liquid hit the bare dirt next to the porch and made dark markings in the dry soil. White soap pieces and iridescent bubbles sat on top of the wet marks.

"Tell me, Thomas, do you and your brother enjoy coming to see me?" asked Marcus.

Each boy shook his head from side to side. The tears caused by the strong soap they had had in their mouths were still flowing from the corners of their eyes.

"Tonight at vespers, I would like each of you to say a special prayer asking the Lord to watch over you and not let you stray from your duties here at the mission. Will you do that for me?" asked Marcus.

The boys nodded affirmatively.

But the contrite behavior of the two boys did not fool Father Marcus in the least. He knew that the boys would be back to see him soon. It was only a question of how many days before they would stand before him again.

"Brother William, please take the boys to the hogs' shed. They can work there until dark. They will have no supper this evening."

Father Marcus turned and went to the door, opened it, and entered his office without looking back. While his back was turned, Thomas stuck his tongue out at the priest's back, an action that was quickly followed by a reaction as Brother James's open hand smartly whacked the back of Thomas's head. The boys were quickly led away to the pig sty.

***

Much to the consternation and disappointment of the good priests and friars at Mission Espada, the recalcitrant Vogler brothers did not grow into responsibility, and their personalities did not change. While the calendar progressed, the actions of the Vogler brothers regressed. In fact, as they grew, so did the severity of their pranks. They showed a total lack of respect for the friars and many times ignored all well-meaning direction from authority. Needless to say, they spent a great deal of time engaged in the punishment chores assigned by the priests.

Sadly, as could probably be expected, the pranks of the boys evolved into petty crimes; mostly theft. A candlestick, or piece of pottery, or a few coins from the alms box would mysteriously disappear, in all likelihood subsequently traded outside of the mission walls. Where none of the other orphans had such treats, the Vogler brothers always seemed to have a stick of hard candy in their pockets, the fruit of selling the spoils of their petty thieving.

In addition to the thievery, and because of his age and size, Thomas had taken to bullying and fighting with the other boys in the mission, but he did not confine his actions to the boys. He was not above attacking the girls there too, if they had some item in their possession that Thomas thought should change ownership to him. These incidents were hard to deny, especially when they were witnessed by other orphans in the course of the act. But no matter what the nefarious deed was, when later questioned by the priests, all culpability was, of course, denied. Never-theless, suitable punishment was subsequently meted out.

The final act that overrode the kind generosity and fruitless attempts to properly teach the Voglers occurred when it was discovered that Thomas had removed a loose wooden knot in a board of the outer wall of the women's bathing shed. A small building at the edge of the mission grounds, the bathing shed was where the orphan girls and their female mentors would gather for their weekly baths. With Horace's help, Thomas had begun another misguided enterprise of ushering the male orphans to the peep hole. He and Horace were charging each boy a penny or another personal item to peek through the hole in the wall. Their enterprise was prospering and would have continued were it not for the fact that Mrs. Wilma Powell, the matron of the female orphans and a family relative of the senior priest, had finished her bath, dressed, and was assisting her young charges. As she leaned against the wall of the bath house to rest for a moment, she heard a sneeze that apparently had originated right next to her. But since none of the girls had made the noise, she became curious and had a suspicion. Quietly slipping out-doors, Mrs. Powell crept to the side of the building. As she did so, at some distance from the building, she saw a group of boys sitting quietly in a group talking amongst themselves. They seemed to be waiting for something. Wilma thought this was strange in itself, but even stranger, as she looked at the boys, they noticed her attention and slowly stood up and ambled away in different directions. Mrs. Powell then moved on and quietly peered around to the back of the building. What she saw confirmed her suspicions.

Sitting on the ground, leaning against the shed, and idly playing with the coins in his hand was Horace Vogler. Standing next to him, Thomas Vogler was watching another boy who was looking through the knot-hole. In six long strides Mrs. Powell, a hefty force not to be reckoned with, had the two Vogler brothers by their shaggy hair and was soon kicking the third boy on his backside as they made their way to the priests' office. After listening to Mrs. Powell, the priest thanked her and sent her back to her girls.

Turning to the boys, Father Marcus did not appear to be angry. Instead, he seemed to be resigned. He had been searching his soul for a course of action, and it seemed that now was the time to implement the plan. "Both of you report to Brother Bernard at the stables. Tell him you are to work through the supper hour."

Thomas could not believe his luck. He believed that the priest had simply given up and was letting him off with another work assignment cleaning the animal pens. Thomas grabbed Horace's arm and pulled him. "Let's go, Horace," he said.

***

Mission Espada was not a wealthy mission by any means. The enterprise was self-sufficient, to be sure, but contributed virtually nothing to the mother church's coffers. As a result, the number of orphans for which the mission could provide was limited. And at the present time, there were simply too many mouths to feed. Knowing this, the priests had set a time limit on when their charges would leave the mission. They had established a rule that when a boy reached fourteen years of age, everything would be done in an attempt to find the boy a means of employment; usually an apprenticeship with a tradesman in San Antonio. Aside from the fact that Thomas Vogler was awaiting the further punishment commensurate with his latest prank, he was now fourteen years of age. Father Marcus would now put his plan into action.

In addition to a regular Sunday mass, on most Saturday afternoons, Father Marcus and the other priests held early confession, followed by an abbreviated mass, both of which were usually completed no later than six p.m. Having experience with the ranch hands and cattle drovers, Father Marcus had worked out this system some years prior. He reasoned that it was easier to catch the vaqueros and cowboys when they came to town early on a Saturday and to cleanse their souls prior to the same souls being hopelessly drunk, fornicating, and generally being disorderly later in the evening. Of course, the fact that they had money in their pockets to place in the alms box before spending it all in the saloons and whorehouses also entered into his thinking.

***

It was not every Saturday night, but on many occasions, the owner of the Rocky Hill Ranch, Ryan McKenzie, would accompany his ranch hands to town. Ryan was an amiable, but stern boss, well respected by his vaqueros and ranch hands as a man who could do anything and who had previous years of experience doing the same work that he assigned to them. McKenzie was also a Catholic, with family beliefs that stretched back into Irish origins three generations ago. He made it a point to attend mass with his vaqueros on any Saturday night that he came into town. He would then have a few drinks with his ranch hands and return by himself to his wife and family back at the ranch.

Father Marcus had known Ryan McKenzie for many years. He knew Ryan to be a fair man, an honest man, and a fine example for his ranch hands to follow. On previous occasions, the priest and the ranch foreman had worked together. Father Marcus had a personal relationship with his church family. He kept track of which ranches were out on the trails, and which ones were at home. He knew that the Rocky Hill Ranch was due to push a herd to Campeche in the next few days, and he also knew that Ryan McKenzie would be attending mass that evening.

Sure enough, when confessions had been completed, Father Marcus began his processional. He was followed by two servers, one carrying a candle, and the other the incense. One of those altar boys was Thomas Vogler. While he walked, reciting the entrance chant, Father Marcus scanned the audience and confirmed that the Rocky Hill Ranch hands were in attendance along with their foreman, Ryan McKenzie.

The Latin Eucharist finally drew to a conclusion following communion. Father Marcus imparted his blessing on the congregation, and he made his recession. He waited outside the chapel doors, greeting the attendees as they departed. As Ryan McKenzie came outdoors he was pulled aside by Father Marcus and in a matter of a few moments, the details were discussed and the men parted. They would see each other again on Monday morning.

# Chapter Three

**Texas Hill Country**
**South of San Antonio – 1821**

Small spirals of dust puffed from beneath the wheels of the buckboard driven by Father Marcus. Fourteen-year-old Thomas Vogler sat beside the priest on the hard, wooden bench as the priest expertly drove the wagon.

They had left the mission at dawn with barely enough light to see their way. Thomas had been roused by Brother William and told to dress and follow the friar. Thomas was instantly suspicious of the friar's motives and could not help but wonder which of his latest nefarious escapades had been discovered by the friars. He was even more surprised to see the priests' buckboard hitched and pointed toward the mission's gate. His heart sank as he reached the wagon with Brother William and discovered that Father Marcus was sitting in the buckboard with reins in hand. In a moment, Father Marcus and Thomas Vogler rolled through the mission gate and headed south.

At some distance from the mission, when Thomas had concluded that they were not headed for the sheriff's office, he dared to ask the priest, "Where are we going, Father Marcus?"

"Have patience, my boy," said the priest. "You are about to embark on a new adventure in your life."

The buckboard finally came to a small creek to the south of the city that could easily have been forded as there was little water flowing in the creek bed. But the priest stopped the wagon near a live oak tree, hopped out, and brought out the tethering stone from the rear of the wagon. He walked to the side of the road into some scrub brush and dropped the stone. He then led the horse to the stone and tied the animal off so that it could graze on the scrub vegetation.

"Thomas, let's sit over here in the shade," said Marcus.

"What are we doing here, Father?" asked Thomas.

The priest was gazing to the southwest and saw what he was searching for. "Look over there, Thomas," said the priest. "God is bringing your future nigh."

Thomas looked toward where the priest was pointing, and in the distance, he noticed the dust cloud swirling high in the air. He continued watching it as the dull, monotonous drone of hundreds of cattle hooves pounding the hard ground reached his ears. He began to see the lead cattle, plodding slowly forward with their immense spans of horns, so typical of the longhorn breed. But then he saw something else. A lone horseman had broken away from the dust cloud and was making his way toward them. The rider was in no hurry and was obviously saving his horse. He made no unnecessary movement as the strong animal crossed the muddy stream and carried him to the priest and boy.

As a successful cattle rancher, Ryan McKenzie was a shrewd businessman in his cattle dealings, and he was not above taking a well-calculated risk to make money. A point in fact was that news had recently been received from some of the returning ranch hands who had relatives in the gulf community of Campeche. (Campeche was a name given to the settlement of Galveztown by privateer/pirate Jean Lafitte. Galveztown was the name of the settlement given to it by Spanish explorers. Later it would be renamed Galveston.) Word had spread that the pirate/privateer Jean Lafitte had been given an ultimatum by President Monroe to leave Campeche, as it was now under United States control as part of the 1803 Louisiana Purchase of over eight hundred thousand square miles acquired from France. This assertion was no doubt due to poor mapping procedures and the fact that the United States was still in disagreement with Spain regarding the boundaries of that purchase. Be that as it may, the returning ranch hands had also told McKenzie that the community of Campeche, with its temporary occupying army, and the crews of the naval vessels guarding the harbor, were desperate for fresh meat. Subsequently, some weeks back, Ryan McKenzie had sent a trusted runner to Campeche. The runner returned with a purchase order signed by the Captain of the schooner USS *Enterprise*, the senior U.S. military officer present in the city. As a bona fide representative of the United States Government, he was there to ensure the permanent departure of Lafitte. Ryan McKenzie was taking a rather large gamble, trusting that the Union forces would remain in the port city until his herd arrived. But if successful, the Rocky Hill Ranch would be paid handsomely for every head of beef they brought to the city. In less than two weeks following the signing of that contract, Rocky Hill longhorns were ambling eastward to cover the two hundred and fifty miles to the Gulf of Mexico.

Ryan McKenzie dismounted his horse, removed his hat, and shook hands with Father Marcus.

Turning to the boy, the priest said, "Thomas, I would like for you to meet Mr. McKenzie. He is the owner of the Rocky Hill cattle ranch, and he has agreed to put you to work helping on a cattle drive."

In dumbfound disbelief, Thomas shook the hand of the man who would now be his boss and mentor. He could not believe this was happening. He was being forcibly removed from the mission that had been his home for all of his short life. He had always known that he could not stay there forever, but this was so sudden, and he had not even been able to say good bye to his brother, Horace. Through the buzzing in his head, he barely heard the droning noise of Father Marcus blessing the cattle drive and asking God to look over the men while on the trail.

When the priest had concluded his prayer, Ryan McKenzie snugged the wide-brimmed hat back on his head and swung himself up into the saddle atop the horse. He extended his left arm down and said, "Swing up here behind me, Thomas, and we'll be on our way."

Thomas did as he was told, and the horse made its way in a fast walk toward the cattle herd. McKenzie turned slightly in his saddle and waved once more to the priest who continued to watch the departure of the boy.

"Vaya con Dios," said the priest quietly as he crossed himself.

***

Farley Reed sat on the rough wooden seat of the chuck wagon scratching at the growth of whiskers on his cheeks, and with reins in his other hand, he watched as his boss had ridden off to the side well ahead of the herd. As he drove the bumping wagon along, he could just make out the dismounted figure of Ryan McKenzie talking to what appeared to be a priest. It was not long before he turned in his seat and saw his remounted boss closing in on the wagon. He also saw the boy sitting behind McKenzie on the horse.

This scenario was not new to Farley Reed. He had been the cow-hands' cook at the Rocky Hill for a good ten years and had seen the young boys come and go. Most of them did not last long. They simply did not know what it meant to work in extreme conditions and only two of his previous helpers were now riding as full-fledged cowhands with the Rocky Hill herd. As a result, Farley did not relish training another young kid. Most of them that he had seen come out of the mission orphanage didn't know the front end from the ass end of a horse, and even less about hard work. He figured to himself that God would not appreciate the fact that he felt that the priests at the Mission Espada were too damn lenient with the boys. Therefore, getting the new boy to take up the work on a trail drive was like breaking a new horse. Some took to it and worked, and some didn't. And just like some lunkhead horses, they had to be made to see the light. But apparently, his boss felt that breaking in these green boys was a part of the trail cook's job.

Farley Reed was a good man. He had no personal life. In fact, his life had been similar to the orphans whom he periodically was asked to train. Farley had no family, but when he had been lucky enough to be hired by the Rocky Hill, he made the best of it and was reasonably happy with his lot. He was a hard man to work for. Some called him crusty, but he was fair. When he gave directions, he did not like having to repeat those directions to his helpers. And if the helper would not cooperate, he was likely to have a cast iron skillet whanged against the helper's body part closest to the cook's hand.

As McKenzie slowed his horse to a walk next to the seat of the rolling chuck wagon, Farley stopped the wagon and leaned toward his boss.

"Well, Farley, this here's your new helper. Thomas, this is Farley Reed, our outfit's cook. You're going to be staying with him and helping him for a while until we can teach you to sit a horse," said McKenzie.

Farley helped Thomas move from the back of McKenzie's horse to the wagon seat. Thomas sat stunned, saying nothing and staring straight ahead as the wagon began to roll with the herd as it moved ahead in a southeasterly direction, ever farther from San Antonio and the Mission Espada.

As long as there is vegetation for grazing and periodic water, a long-horn herd can comfortably travel eight miles per day without losing much fat, sometimes ten miles if conditions are ideal. At that rate the cattle drive to Campeche would take nearly thirty days. It would take all of those thirty days to "break" Thomas Vogler to work. But Thomas's malevolent spirit and resentment toward authority would never be broken. Even with the close supervision given by Farley Reed, Thomas carried out his tasking with resentment, and this attitude caused a great deal of friction between Thomas and anyone attempting to train or guide him. He was destined to a life bordering, and sometimes stepping beyond, the boundaries of civil law and the tenets of decency.

# Chapter Four

**Central Texas Feeder Trail**
**Six miles south of Brady, Texas – 1825**

He could not open his eyes, they burned so bad, and his bandana was caked with west Texas dirt. When he closed his teeth together they crunched. Sixteen year old Horace Vogler was riding drag behind two hundred and fifty Rocky Hill longhorns. They had been on the trail for nearly ten days, moving in a northwesterly direction to Abilene, Texas. He partially opened one dust-filled eye to confirm that his brother Thomas was up ahead of him on the right side of the herd. But as one of the two youngest hands in the outfit, Horace and another young man were relegated to the dirtiest job on a cattle drive; bringing up the rear of the plodding cattle. Only the wranglers and the remuda were further in the rear, and that was because they had the privilege of waiting until the dust settled or blew away from the cattle herd before they moved the horses to follow.

Thomas Vogler had been riding for four years for the Rocky Hill outfit. And for the entire four years he had trod a fine line between being a satisfactory hand and being fired. But eighteen year old Thomas was just biding his time. For the first two years, he had cooperated with Ryan McKenzie as the occasion dictated. But in truth, he was simply waiting until his younger brother Horace was sent on his way by the priests at Mission Espada. Thomas had tactfully asked McKenzie on several occasions to help his younger brother Horace join the Rocky Hill crew when he left Mission Espada. In a weak moment and against his better judgment, McKenzie had agreed. And so, Horace had also served his time on the chuck wagon working for Farley, but finally was given the opportunity to ride as a junior cow hand. For the past two years, the Vogler brothers had worked together for the Rocky Hill Ranch.

Ryan McKenzie kept an eye on the two brothers. He had finally come to the conclusion that, on his own and with guidance, Horace Vogler may have made a satisfactory hand. Instead, he was constantly under the influence of his older brother, Thomas, who, in the estimation of McKenzie, was a catastrophe waiting to happen. In the four years he had been working, Thomas was always in, or close by, when trouble occurred. Although he would never be caught red handed, there was always a suspicion directed toward Thomas when items went missing from the bunk house or from a cowboy's duffel. A fight would ensue, usually instigated by Thomas, and being younger and smaller than the other hands; Thomas would usually end up bloodied and lying on the bunk house floor.

On the occasion of his eighteenth birthday, Thomas had purchased a well-worn, used, cap lock, single-shot pistol, which he now wore strapped to his right side. The gun had seen better days and was probably more of a danger to its owner than anyone else. Most of the other vaqueros and cow hands did not own pistols; instead, they preferred their hand-loaded rifles, which rode in scabbards attached to their saddles. In addition to the purchase of the firearm, Thomas Vogler had taken up drinking. He had learned it, of course, from the other cowhands. At the end of a drive, the crew would let off a little steam and spend some of their wages in the town at the terminus of the drive. In the past four years, this had been mostly in the town of Abilene, Texas, where willing buyers would purchase the Rocky Hill herds and have them driven farther north by other hired drovers. Ryan McKenzie was firmly convinced that Thomas's ownership of a pistol and his over indulgence in whisky at the end of each drive had the makings of a stick of dynamite waiting for the fuse to be lit. McKenzie would be proven right.

***

The herd was bedded down for the night, the cook fire had diminished to glowing embers, and the pickets sat their horses at the edge of the herd. The Rocky Hill outfit was quiet under the star-studded west Texas sky. The remainder of the cow hands had ridden into Brady, two miles to the north, to play cards and have a drink or two. They would need to return in a few hours to catch some sleep before the herd was roused in the morning to resume their northern trek. Horace Vogler had picket duty and was cat-napping in his saddle as his horse stood stiff-legged with its head down fitfully sleeping.

Thomas Vogler was in Brady with a group of Rocky Hill hands. The ranch hands were sitting at a table nursing their beer and whisky. Thomas had already had too much to drink, and his bravado talk was becoming more pronounced, with his usual disregard for well-intentioned advice. He paid little attention to his acquaintances as they warned him to keep his voice down. Thomas's attention had locked onto something else. His eyes seldom left a well-dressed, slightly built, older gentleman at the bar who was passing the time drinking a beer and conversing with the bartender. The man had the look and smooth speech of a successful drummer. Thomas had watched with great interest as the man had reached in his pockets on two occasions and paid the bartender from a well-padded leather wallet.

Thomas nodded at his companions as they gathered their gear to leave the saloon and head back to the herd. They told Thomas that it was time to leave, but he insisted that he would just have one more drink and then catch up to them. He was left sitting alone at the table, surreptitiously watching the salesman. The opportunity for which he had been waiting soon arose, as the salesman once again paid the bartender, shook hands with the bar man, and walked out of the saloon. Thomas quickly rose and followed the man, but his action was seen by the bartender.

The drummer crossed the street and walked toward the hotel. But as he crossed an alley, he was suddenly tapped on the shoulder. Thomas Vogler faced the drummer and asked him for a match. As the drummer reached into his pocket, Thomas shoved him ahead into the darkened alley. Out of sight, Thomas drew his pistol from its holster, cocked the hammer, and shoved the barrel into the midsection of the drummer.

"I'll take that wallet from you mister," whispered Thomas.

"Sure, sure, mister, just don't let that damn gun go off," said the drummer.

Vogler backed up and watched as the salesman reached into his inside coat pocket. But instead of the wallet, the salesman's hand came back into view holding a small pistol of his own, with which he quickly drew aim. But Thomas had the quickness of youth on his side. He dodged to the side as the drummer's gun barked. The bullet grazed Thomas's upper arm. Thomas then pulled the trigger of his own pistol. The gun went off, and the ball flew from the gun barrel and entered the salesman's chest. The salesman would die in short order. At eighteen years of age, in cold blood, Thomas Vogler had murdered his first man.

But in the process of loading the old gun, Thomas had obviously over charged it, causing the barrel of the gun to fracture into several pieces as it fired, burning Thomas's hand. In pain, he dropped the old pistol. He then reached into the drummer's coat and withdrew the wallet. Remaining in the shadows as he walked, Thomas quickly made his way back to where his horse was tied. As he mounted his horse and trotted out of town, he saw several men running to the alleyway that he had just vacated.

In the early morning hours, while the other ranch hands ate a sparse breakfast in the semi-darkness, and away from the eyes of the other ranch hands, Horace helped his brother by tightly wrapping strips of the bloodied shirt around the wound on Thomas's arm. After changing shirts, Thomas and his brother joined the herd as it was being roused to begin moving.

\*\*\*

The sun was well above the horizon when the Rocky Hill herd and its attending cowboys left Brady behind them in the distance. Thomas was feeling better, relieved and believing that he had gotten away with the murder and robbery of the stranger in Brady. He unconsciously patted the salesman's wallet that was tucked into his waistband beneath his shirt and smiled slightly.

As they moved the herd, the sun became more intense, and the cow hands kept their eyes low in order for their wide-brimmed hats to shield their eyes from the glare. As a result, Thomas had not seen the lone rider approach the herd and speak to a cow hand on the other side of the mass of longhorns. When he did happen to look up and across the backs of the slow-moving cattle, he caught a glimpse of the silver metal star on the man's vest as the man reached down into a saddlebag and pulled out the remainder of the pistol with the exploded barrel and showed it to the cowhand. For a moment, Thomas was mesmerized as he saw the cowhand point over to him. It was then that Thomas spurred his horse and rode quickly back to Horace.

"I've got to get out of here, Horace," said Thomas. "That damn sheriff will hang me if he catches me. You need to stay with the outfit, and I will come back after you when things cool down."

Horace was left with his mouth hanging open as his older brother spurred his horse and took off at a gallop. It was no longer a child's game that Thomas was playing. He was being pursued by the law. He was soon out of sight, desperately running for his life, hidden in the draws between the surrounding hills and masked by groves of mesquite and post oak. Sheriff John Smallwood could only watch helplessly from his side of the herd until the long stretch of cattle with the dangerously sharp long horns had passed.

Smallwood would pursue Thomas Vogler for several days, only to lose the trail at the Red River. At that point, the sheriff had to turn back and return to his duties in Brady. A wanted poster, yellowed with age, and bearing the physical description of Thomas Vogler would subsequently hang on the wall outside Smallwood's Brady, Texas, office for years.

Thomas Vogler would continue northward, not stopping until he reached the upper Midwest frontier. He would be a wanted man for the rest of his life.

# Chapter Five

## Burlington
## Wisconsin Territory, Summer - 1834

The notice in the small newsletter being produced in the fledgling village of Burlington (which would later become part of the state of Iowa) on the banks of the Mississippi read as follows:

*Mr. Thomas Vogler, a settler in our village, was shot and mortally wounded yesterday in a shoot-out with a contingent of soldiers from nearby Fort Madison. It seems that Mr. Vogler, not very well regarded by our fair citizens, had been selling home-made whisky to an Indian encampment up north on the Des Moines River. In addition, it was established that the deceased was also involved in the sale of slave children, as a young Negro boy was found incarcerated in the cabin of the late Mr. Vogler. According to the Army in Ft. Madison, Mr. Vogler had been involved in these dastardly activities for a considerable length of time and had been pursued by the Army in the person of Captain Deke Monroe and his gallant troopers. The demise of the outlaw occurred within the confines of the Roush and Stroud trading post, an event of great terror for the Roush and Stroud womenfolk. Regretfully, Mr. Peter Stroud, co-proprietor of that establishment, received a wound in the gun battle between the Army and the late Mr. Vogler, inflicted by the same Mr. Vogler. I have been happily informed that Mr. Stroud is reported to be mending quite well. In the aforementioned shoot-out, Mr. Vogler received his mortal wounds from an Army trooper and Captain Monroe. Our community is certainly better off without the likes of Mr. Thomas Vogler.*

# Chapter Six

**September 1836 - Mission San Francisco de la Espada**
**San Antonio**

More out of habit and camaraderie than devotion, Horace Vogler attended an occasional Saturday evening mass with Ryan McKenzie and some of the other Rocky Hill hands at the same mission where he had been abandoned as a newborn and raised by the friars and priests. Although Father Marcus was now graying, slightly bent, and more weathered, he still led the services at the mission. And each time that Horace attended, Father Marcus made a point of seeking him out to greet him and shake his hand, a gesture that embarrassed, yet inwardly pleased the cowboy. On this particular occasion, Father Marcus again greeted McKenzie's crew and shook hands with the men of the Rocky Hill, spending a moment longer with Horace.

Turning to Ryan McKenzie, Marcus said, "Ryan, the good people who attend our mission are going to hold a special fiesta in the mission plaza next week following mass. Would it be possible for you and your men to attend?" He continued, "We are giving thanks for an abundant maize crop, and we are expecting many families to be here. There will be a great feast of fine food, and we would be honored to have you and your men attend."

Ryan McKenzie looked at his cow hands and could see that they seemed interested. This did not surprise him since he knew that the way to a cowboy's heart was through his stomach, and the chance to eat something other than Farley Reed's ranch grub was a deal maker.

"You can count on us being here, Father," said McKenzie. The two men shook hands again, and the cattlemen settled their hats on their heads and walked to the hitching racks to retrieve their mounts.

It was only a short ride down the street to the favorite watering hole of the Rocky Hill outfit, "The Riata," where the beer was nearly as warm as the women employed there. In only a few minutes the men were lined up at the bar with a mug of beer in front of each of them. With a little "jingle" in their pockets, a cowboy could nurse a few beers all evening, just passing time with his friends and having a grand time telling stories and poking fun at each other. Once in a while, a couple of the men would get into a card game, but none of them were gamblers of any skill. So they stayed away from any table that was inhabited by men who were known to make their living from playing poker.

The Riata was ordinarily host to many soldiers, primarily Mexican soldiers, so the cowhands were used to drinking with military men who loved to keep the cowboys entertained with their tales of bravado and battles. The cowboys believed very little of their inflated tales, but thought they were entertaining all the same. And because some of the senior soldiers made decent wages, they could also be counted on to put up a round or two during the evening if the cowboys acted like they were enjoying the soldiers' tales.

But this night was different. As the Rocky Hill gang looked around the bar area, there were, indeed, soldiers. But they wore a different uniform than the Mexican soldiers. Their uniforms were a dark blue with yellow stripes and brass buttons. They were U.S. Army soldiers.

There were two reasons that American soldiers were now in San Antonio. Three months ago, in June, and after many bloody battles, some occurring within the city limits of San Antonio itself, Mexico had surrendered San Antonio along with other disputed southwest territory to the Americans. U.S. Army soldiers now occupied the city. Secondly, the U.S. Government wanted American settlers to migrate into more of the Louisiana Purchase land area. For these reasons, Army contingents were being dispersed throughout the country to protect the settlements of American citizens.

It was not long before an older, somewhat grizzled Army Sergeant, along with two of his men stood at the Riata bar, between Horace Vogler and a few other cowboys. The conversation flowed and the soldiers began telling their tales to the cowboys who were only half listening. But when the sergeant bought a round for the cowboys, they began paying a bit more attention as the sergeant went on to say that he and his company of men had been reassigned to San Antonio from up north in the Wisconsin Territory. He told the ranch hands that their troop had taken over the old Presidio San Antonio de Bexar and made it into a barracks for the new resident American Army contingent.

The old sergeant cuffed Horace on the shoulder and stuck out his large hand.

"My name is Charlie Morgan, First Sergeant Charlie Morgan. What's your name, cowboy?"

Horace took the soldier's hand and shook it. "Horace Vogler, Sergeant. Nice to meet ya."

The sergeant held Horace's hand for a few seconds longer and looked intently at Horace.

"Vogler, Vogler. I've heard that name before somewhere. Vogler, hmm. Guess I'll think of it later," said Morgan.

Two more rounds of beer followed, accompanied by more stories, and the time was approaching when the ranch hands would be leaving to return to the Rocky Hill.

Suddenly the old sergeant slammed his beer mug on the bar.

"Vogler, now I remember where I heard that name." He turned again and looked directly at Horace. "Say, would you by chance have had any relatives living up the Mississippi River in a little village called Burlington? That's up in the Wisconsin Territory," said Morgan.

Morgan had Horace's attention now. "I don't rightly know," said Horace. "I didn't have no relatives except a brother, and he ran off years ago."

"Well, what was his name?" asked the sergeant.

"Thomas, Thomas Vogler," said Horace.

"Well damn my hide," said Morgan. "When I was a bit younger I was part of a company attached to Fort Madison up on the Mississippi. And there was this fellow that we had been chasing for many weeks; seems that he was selling bootleg whisky to the Indians. Well, we found him in Burlington, and when we found him, he shot at my captain, and this Vogler fellow was killed in the shootout that followed. You s'pose that could have been your brother?"

Horace was looking at the old sergeant, but then looked down at his beer. A cold, clamminess came over him. He knew it in his gut. His brother Thomas was dead.

Sergeant Morgan was staring at Horace's face. "Now that I study on you some, you sure do look a lot like that Thomas Vogler fellow," he said.

Without a comment, Horace turned and walked slowly out of the door of The Riata into the street, joining his friends who were mounting their horses for the ride back to the ranch. The rowdy cowhands, now considerably inebriated, talked and poked fun of each other all the way back to the ranch. Horace, however, did not say a word, and after reaching the ranch and tending to his horse, he went directly to his bunk for the night.

\*\*\*

Horace Vogler sat by himself on a large, rough, outcrop of limestone, away from the boisterous festivities. He was somewhat lost in his own thoughts, but relishing in the taste of the sweet sangria ponche as he swallowed another sip of the cool liquid saturated with fruit juices and a hint of sangria wine. It had been a week since he had heard the story told by the Army Sergeant who had been present when his brother Thomas was killed in the upper Mississippi River frontier. He was doing his best to push the memory to the back of his mind.

Although he could not quite forget the passing of his brother, Horace's appetite was not suffering. He set the metal cup down next to him and once again concentrated on the heaped pewter plate sitting on his knees. Two large chicken enchiladas covered with gravy sat next to a large, grilled chili rellenos stuffed with goat cheese. Horace attacked the food, savoring every bite of the spicy fare. To one side on the plate sat two peach enchiladas for dessert. They were drenched in fresh raisin sauce. The ranch cook did not make such delicious food, and the cow hands were truly enjoying the feast.

From the corner of his eye, Horace saw that Father Marcus was approaching. With him was a young woman carrying a water pitcher. She was a slim, attractive woman wearing a flowered dress with a broad-brimmed straw hat upon her head. But then Horace noticed an unusual physical feature. Pinned up under the woman's hat was the reddest hair that Horace had ever seen. In fact, he had rarely seen a redhead before and could not help but stare at the attractive young woman. They locked eyes for only a second or two, and he could not help but notice that her eyes were of a deep, tawny green color.

"Miss Beth Sanders, I would like for you to meet Mr. Horace Vogler," said Father Marcus as he looked at the young woman.

He then introduced Horace to her, and Miss Sanders said, "I'm pleased to meet you, sir."

Horace stood with his mouth open, holding the partially ravaged food plate in his hands. He finally managed to mumble a reply, but if he were asked later, he would never remember what he had said.

"Would you like a drink of water, Mr. Vogler?" asked Beth.

"Yes, ma'am, that would be fine," said Horace; yet he remained standing in the same spot, still holding the plate.

"Horace, you might want to get your drinking cup," said the priest.

Horace turned quickly, placed his plate on the rock, and hastily poured out the last of his sangria. His heart was pounding as he watched Beth pour the water into the cup he was holding.

"Miss Sanders is a seamstress, Horace," said Father Marcus. "She works in Miss Bonnard's shop on Center Street."

Horace had not even heard the priest. He was watching Beth Sanders with the same curiosity as a boy watching a new puppy. He was absolutely mesmerized by this pretty girl with the glorious red hair. He had not even noticed when the priest walked back to the fiesta revelers.

***

The lonely, twenty-seven year old cowboy and the equally lonely seventeen year-old seamstress were married a year later. Unlike the Vogler ancestry, there was no crime or thievery in her past, but Beth Sanders came from a similar situation. Her parents had come to the United States from Scotland, first settling in Missouri and later moving to San Antonio. Their life ambition had been to open a dry goods store, a goal that was achieved in both locations. Mr. Sanders' San Antonio store was a flourishing business, with favorable prospects for continued success. But Beth's father was accidentally crushed and killed under a wagon that collapsed upon him during a routine repair. And the following year, during a cold snap rain storm, Beth's mother contracted pneumonia and succumbed to the ravages of the disease. Due to the generosity of the dressmaker, Beth was then apprenticed to Miss Bonnard in her dressmaking establishment, a position in which she excelled. She was no longer an apprentice, but was now one of Miss Bonnard's most talented employees. At seventeen years of age, she had been on her own now for nearly four years.

# Chapter Seven

**Great Western Cattle Trail**
**Eight days south of Dodge City, Kansas - 1842**

Several years prior, Ryan McKenzie, as a smart, successful cattle rancher, had been ever mindful of the shifting market for beef cattle from Texas. The demand for beef had never been higher, but the real market was in the eastern portion of the United States. The problem, of course, was getting Texas beef to an ever-growing, demanding market in the east. Enterprising American industrialists would fill that need, with the burgeoning railroad companies seizing the opportunity. Rail lines were spreading across the country, sending tendrils of iron rails into the far-flung frontier. As a result, Dodge City, Kansas, had become a railhead hub for shipping cattle to the east. Using the Great Western Cattle Trail, Ryan McKenzie's Rocky Hill Ranch had begun yearly cattle drives to Dodge City, a distance of nearly seven hundred miles to reach the rail hub. The prices paid for his cattle in Dodge City by competing cattle buyers far outweighed the extreme adversity associated with such a long, hazardous drive. On this cattle drive, on this particular day, the Rocky Hill herd was nearing its destination of Dodge City.

A considerable amount of time and physical maturing had taken place before Ryan McKenzie was convinced that Horace Vogler could ride with the best of the seasoned hands of the Rocky Hill. Ryan had had no real problems with Horace Vogler since Horace's brother Thomas had high-tailed it from the law some years back. Horace had gone through a period of melancholy following his brother's departure, but got along well with the other hands and pulled his share of the work on the ranch and during the drives. Horace's marriage to Beth Sanders had settled him even more. Having hired and fired a good number of cow hands in his time, Ryan McKenzie was a fair judge of the nature of men whom he encountered. He had never said it to Horace when Thomas had high-tailed it away from the ranch, but McKenzie was certain that Horace would never see his brother again in his lifetime.

*** 

It is a great disservice to a man who makes his living riding a cantankerous horse, herding a foul-tempered herd of longhorn cattle in the midst of every hardship that Mother Nature can throw at him, to simply say that the life of a cowboy is hard. It is back breaking, soul searching work with little reward. By the very nature of the work, there is a constant danger of injury or even death in the form of scrapes, wounds, falls, goring, rattlesnake bite, and broken bones at the whim of unruly animals, rustlers, or Indians. As a result, there were few cowboys past the age of thirty-five. By that age, the hard work had taken its toll on a young man, and he was either dead or "stove up" so bad with poorly mended broken bones or other ailments from sleeping on hard cold ground for many years that he could no longer do the work. But the hard-spined men riding herd on vast cattle ranches, if offered other employment, would accept no other life. Such was the sentiment of the men of the Rocky Hill outfit.

Horace Vogler rode in the typical posture of his fellow Rocky Hill hands. He was relaxed with his back absorbing the plodding, slightly swaying gait of his cow pony. A lariat was held loosely in his right hand, while his left hand held the reins in a split fingered fashion, allowing him quick control of the horse when needed. His wide-brimmed hat was pulled a bit lower in the front, shielding his eyes from the sun's glare. But his roving eyes never left the cattle, watching for strays, or a rebellious steer that simply decided he had had enough walking and would wander away from the herd to find wild fodder. At each such instance, Horace would give a gentle nudge with his spurs to alert and draw his horse's attention to the errant steer. A well-seasoned cow pony knows exactly what to do when urged, and Horace's horse would begin the process of out-maneuvering the steer, dodging back and forth, never looking away from the head of the steer until the rebellious steer was finally convinced that it should rejoin the herd. This same process went on dozens of times each day as the herd moved toward its final destination.

Sitting upon a well-worn saddle atop one of the two horses of the remuda assigned to him, Horace was at home. He had grown to love the rough outdoor work and the camaraderie of his fellow trail riders. The Rocky Hill bunkhouse cowboys were a team, and Horace Vogler was proud to be a contributing member of the team. He was happy with his life on the open range.

As the sun became warmer over the Kansas prairie, the warmth soothed the cattle, eliminating some of the rowdiness of the more troublesome steers of the herd. As a result, the herd settled into its monotonous walk, ever north, following in the tracks made by dozens of herds prior to them.

Horace had been up several hours during the night, stationed as a picket at the edge of the dozing herd. He was tired. The breakfast biscuits, smothered in a greasy flour gravy, and warm coffee had satiated his appetite and coupled with his lack of sleep, he was becoming drowsy in the swaying saddle. His mind wandered, producing mental pictures of the woman he loved. He pictured a laughing, red-haired beauty. In his mind, Beth was looking at him and smiling. In her arms she was holding the sandy-haired toddler whom they had named Henry. Henry had been born two years after they were married. Horace chuckled to himself and imagined holding the squirming toddler in his arms. Henry Vogler was a handful for his mother. The baby was fussy and raised a vocal fit when he did not get his way. Although she never mentioned it to Horace, Beth was concerned that little Henry seemed abnormally quarrelsome. But Horace loved his little boy, as he loved Beth. It was always sad when he left home for another long cattle drive, and he missed them greatly. As the thoughts of home faded from his mind, Horace slowly closed his eyes to rest as the horse continued onward.

Horace Vogler occupied one of the most dangerous jobs of the time. Grave injury and death were common on the cattle trails. When medical treatment was needed, it was usually administered by ranch hands more familiar with administering to the needs of four-legged patients. Hence, recovery from serious injury was far from being a sure bet for a trail-driving ranch hand. Only due diligence and concern for one's own well-being kept cowboys from harm. And failure to remain alert in a dangerous job can lead to dire consequences.

With no input from a dozing rider, Horace's horse was also plodding along in what might be described as a walking sleep. The horse was simply following the sounds made by the cattle as they walked northward. Horse and rider were nearly oblivious to their surroundings.

\*\*\*

Most of the reptile's body was exposed to the warm morning sun, absorbing the sun's rays to warm the animal's inner body temperature. Its flattened, triangular head and a portion of the body were in the shade of the half-buried rock under which the three foot long animal was coiled. The female prairie rattlesnake was light brown in color, with a distinctive black-bordered, geometric pattern down its back. Only an hour earlier, the snake had emerged from a close-by burrow where she had joined other female rattlers giving birth to their live young. The burrow, once home to prairie dogs, was now a communal nest and occupied by several large female rattlers and many newly-born young snakes, which were also capable of inflicting poisonous bites. After giving birth, she had left the burrow and was now ready to hunt.

The rattler's forked tongue passed through the snake's rostral groove, a small notch in the lip of the snake, to briefly collect airborne chemicals. Upon return of the tongue to the snake's mouth, the tips of the tongue lay next to two openings in the roof of the mouth, called the Jacobson's organ. The chemicals on the tips of the tongue were quickly analyzed by the snake's brain to determine the action to be taken by the snake. Combined with the snake's analysis of ground vibration, the snake was aware of the passing of animals far larger than her usual prey. Her instinct was to remain partially hidden until the danger had passed her by.

But in a few moments, the snake's extraordinary senses detected that a large animal was advancing toward her. She slowly brought her head back into her coil to ready herself. The larger animal was moving closer. At this instant, she sounded a warning by shaking her tail. The rattling noise could now be heard.

Horace's horse was now less than three feet from the prairie rattler when it finally heard the rattler's warning. No stranger to the sound, the horse became instantly fully alert. Instinct drove the horse to bring its front legs away from the snake by rearing up onto its hind legs. The movement of the horse was so swift that Horace, in his drowsy condition, was not ready to prepare and brace himself. As a result, the cowboy rolled backwards off of the horse. As he neared the ground in his fall, his arms flew behind his back to catch his fall. Horace landed roughly on his back with his arms behind him. His head then struck the ground, dizzying him. In his dizzy state, he did not know that one of his arms was buried up to the elbow in the same snake burrow that the female rattler had emerged from minutes earlier.

Although he was wearing leather gloves, Horace was wearing only a light cotton long-sleeved shirt, which was worn by the cowboys primarily as protection from the sun and light brush. The shirt was not heavy enough to be impervious to a rattler's fangs. As he lay stunned, at least three adult female rattlers sent their fangs through the light shirt and into the skin of his arm.

The toxicity of the prairie rattler, although deadly potent, when compared to certain other serpents is not nearly as lethal, and a man stands a good chance of surviving a single prairie rattler bite. But those survival chances diminish greatly if there are multiple bites, which thereby greatly increases the amount of toxic poison in the man's system.

For three days, as the herd continued moving northward, Horace Vogler rode in the chuck wagon, lying behind the driver's seat. The afflicted arm was now swollen to the point of being even larger around than his legs. Red striations crisscrossed his chest. The simple act of breathing was taxing him, and he rasped with each labored breath. His eyes had taken on a yellow hue. He was dying.

On the sixth day following the accident, and two day's south of Dodge City, Horace Vogler died, leaving behind his wife Beth and his son Henry in San Antonio. After a brief tribute by Ryan McKenzie, Horace was buried in the shade of a clump of scrub oak. Two small oak branches were laced together to form a cross, which was placed on top of the grave of the cowboy. The Rocky Hill herd and cow hands continued northward.

# Chapter Eight

**San Antonio, Texas - 1845**

Beth Vogler had mourned the death of Horace for over a year. She had loved her cowboy husband deeply and was not sure she could continue her life without him. But she was stronger than she believed. Her employer, Emily Bonnard, was good to her and watched over her in her grief. Beth also put great faith in her belief that God would look after her and continued attending mass to hear the consoling words of Father Marcus.

Without a husband, Beth had moved into a boarding house. Unfortunately, it was very difficult to find a lessor who would allow a widow with a child. As a result, she was living in a "harder" neighborhood than what she would have preferred, especially for Henry's sake. Henry, who was now five years old, required constant monitoring; he was an incessant worry to Beth. Beth's landlady had promised to keep an eye on Henry while Beth was at work, but Beth knew that the sometimes bawdry behavior of the landlady, coupled with her liberal consumption of spirits, was not an ideal situation in which to leave Henry all day.

Henry was getting an education, but it was a street education. Without adult supervision during the day, he became the mascot of a group of older boys in the neighborhood who took great pleasure in causing mischief along with petty thievery. One of their favorite schemes was to leave little Henry on a busy street corner in a better neighborhood while the gang waited in the wings. When a concerned stranger came along and found forlorn-appearing Henry without an attending adult, the stranger would naturally stop and talk to Henry to try to rejoin him with an apparently missing parent. But while the stranger talked to Henry, the gang would then approach and begin talking to the stranger, telling him or her that Henry was their brother. But while the boys talked, one or two of them would relieve the stranger of a wallet or another valuable. If that didn't work, they would resort to begging the stranger for a few coins to get something to eat. They were so relentless, that in most cases the stranger would give them a few coins just to be able to escape. For his part in the charade, Henry would be given a piece of candy. Oh, yes; Henry was getting an education. As time passed, Beth Vogler was watching the transformation of her son from a mischievous, yet loving, small child to a conscienceless boy, and she was distraught about the situation. She desperately hoped for a means to move from the rough and tumble San Antonio environment that was negatively malforming her son.

***

Beth Vogler was not completely without family. When her parents had emigrated from Scotland years ago, they had first made their home near Independence, Missouri. Beth's father, Quentin Sanders, was a savvy retail businessman. He had heard of Independence from fellow immigrants who had told him that it was the hub city for trails going further westward into the American frontier. The Independence area was, indeed, the starting point for the California Trail, the Oregon Trail, and the Santa Fe Trail. Quentin Sanders saw the potential for a retail operation that would serve these westward travelers. So, along with Quentin's sister, Henrietta (called "Hattie"), who had emigrated to America with him, his wife and daughter, the Sanders had settled near the confluence of the Missouri and the Kansas rivers. The location was ideal for commerce. Travelers by water and those by land who ventured westward, as well as those who were returning to the east, passed by this very location. Quentin Sanders became a relatively wealthy man. But Mother Nature makes no proviso for wealth, and Quentin Sanders, while quick with numbers, was not a studious man. He was a fine and somewhat greedy merchant, but not well versed in the wiles of nature. Back in Scotland, where he had spent many pleasant days sipping coffee near the River Clyde, he had no way of knowing that the Missouri and the Kansas rivers were very much unlike the rather tame Clyde. Indeed, the Missouri and the Kansas were prone to catastrophic flooding in years of heavy rain. Hence, on a late spring day, in late afternoon, the Sanders family stood on high ground and watched the flood-gorged Missouri River sweep their means of livelihood down the river. A large part of Quentin's wealth was invested in inventory lining the shelves in that wooden structure store that tragically bobbed down the river. It was at this point in his life that Quentin Sanders went seeking a new, warmer and dryer location, subsequently moving his family to San Antonio. His sister, Henrietta, and her husband, Bill Shaw, a career Army sergeant whom she had married, were left behind in Independence.

***

Sergeant Bill Shaw was inherently a good man with a Scottish lineage, a tie that he shared with Hattie's family. He was a gentle man who had fallen in love with Hattie Sanders immediately after he had spied her in the Sanders' store while shopping for a tobacco plug. They had married soon after. Bill was a career soldier, assigned by the Army to nearby Fort Osage. When he was not working, he and Hattie shared a small, sparsely furnished room at a modest Independence hotel. But Bill had a common problem associated with many of the career soldiers of the time. He loved old "John Barleycorn" to the extent that a goodly portion of his monthly pay found its way into the coffers of a favorite local spirits emporium. Unfortunately, this condition generally meant that Bill and Hattie Shaw were scraping by to pay their bills. When her brother Quentin, his wife, and daughter moved away, Hattie worked in a dry goods store to help make ends meet. But no matter how hard it was to keep the wolf from the door, Hattie still loved her "little Scottish soldier boy."

Life became more complicated for Bill and Hattie when the Army closed Fort Osage. Bill was then assigned to Fort Charette, much further away, but still on the Missouri River. This meant that Bill was not always able to come home on his days off because of the longer travel, and when that happened, he would unwisely join his troopers at a tavern close to Fort Charette. Less money coming home made things more difficult for Hattie. She was forced to move from Independence into a rather unkempt boarding house in Town of Kansas, a boarding house that was mostly occupied by a class of people with whom she had not heretofore associated. She was extremely unhappy.

As if things could not get worse, the store where she was working had seen a reduction in its revenue, and Hattie was reduced in the number of hours that she was able to work. But the final blow came in 1843, when the Missouri river charged over its banks in a monstrous flood which carried Fort Charette away. Sergeant Bill Shaw had drowned in the flood.

During her bereavement, Hattie received a bit of luck in that the Army had made a decision some time ago that it would pay a small stipend to the widows of soldiers killed in the Indian wars. While Bill had not necessarily fought any Indians, Forts Osage and Charette were considered bulwarks against a possible threat from the Shawnees. Therefore, Hattie received a small monetary payment each month. That, combined with her part time wages was just enough to allow her to survive. But she was still forced to remain in the squalid boarding house, and she was heart-achingly lonely. She knew from a distant, past letter that Horace Vogler had died. Hattie's loneliness is what drove her to the postal service office to mail a letter.

# Chapter Nine

## San Antonio, Texas - 1846

Hattie's letter moved ever so slowly in the inefficient postal service of the time. The letter, along with other mail, left Town of Kansas (later to be called Kansas City) by packet boat, and sailed on the Missouri River to Saint Louis. From Saint Louis the mail was consolidated and laded on a river boat going south to New Orleans. From New Orleans the letter rode on overland coaches until it reached San Antonio.

Beth Vogler had received very few letters in her lifetime. This was the reason that she simply stared at the man's hand as the mail messenger tried to deliver the letter. She finally took the envelope and closed the door to her room at the boarding house. She walked to the small table, sat on one of the two chairs, and placed the envelope on the table. She stared at the envelope, somewhat afraid of its contents, but finally lifted it and gently tore the envelope to open it. She read:

> *Dear Niece,*
>
> *When I received your letter last year with the news of your dear husband Horace's death, my heart grieved for you. And I wish to inform you that my Bill has died too. I grieve for him sorely. As you and I have no other relatives, and I miss you greatly, I am asking if you would like to come live with me. I have no fancy home, only a rented room, but I manage. With the two of us and little Henry, maybe our lives would be better. I hope you will respond favorably. Love and kindest regards,*
> *Hattie*

Having no relatives in San Antonio, and thinking that she could take Henry away from the bad influence of his nefarious friends, Beth responded affirmatively to her aunt in Town of Kansas.

# Chapter Ten

**Just South of Fort Smith Arkansas - 1846**

Many years ago, when Beth Vogler had travelled in the opposite direction with her parents to settle in San Antonio, her memory categorized that trip as a pleasant adventure. But now, as an adult with a child of her own, she was not finding the trip north to be anything close to pleasant. Butterfield stagecoaches were built for speed, not for comfort. Her back ached from the days of jouncing along rutted paths. Dust roiled from the iron rimmed wheels and found its way into every nook and corner of the coach. The three lady passengers each held a handkerchief to her nose and mouth in an attempt to thwart the choking dust. The two men in the coach rested their hats on their laps and stared stoically out the ever-open windows. Six year old Henry rode on top of the coach along with two other male passengers, where he was not subject to nearly the amount of dust as the interior riders.

Beth sat on the rear row of the three row coach, along with the other two women. The two rear rows faced forward, while the front row faced to the rear. The middle row was empty at this time and the two gentlemen sat facing the rear of the coach on the front row. Two leather straps hung from the ceiling of the coach and were attached to the middle row bench. The straps served as back rests for anyone unlucky enough to be sitting in the middle row.

The coaches travelled non-stop, day and night by changing horse teams and drivers at way stations on the route. Passengers were expected to sleep sitting in their seats and "comfort" stops were made for fifteen minutes every three hours. The coach had made only one overnight stop thus far on this journey, but they were scheduled for an overnight stop at Fort Smith, where passengers could purchase a hot meal and a warm bath. While the coach wheels were repacked with grease and all the rigging serviced during the night, passengers could sleep on a blanket on the floor of the station, or take their blanket outdoors and sleep on the ground under the stars. The stagecoach would continue its journey at first light the next morning.

The passengers who had purchased a hot meal were treated to a greasy bowl of stew, consisting of gravy with a bit of unknown meat, fat clumps, and a few rare bits of potato. A dry, but warm biscuit completed the evening's fare. Gentlemen were offered the opportunity to purchase a dram of watered-down home-brewed whisky served in a side room of the station, an obvious attempt by the station keeper to augment his modest wages. Passengers could purchase extra biscuits and dried jerky for eating on the stagecoach as it continued its journey the next day.

After supper, in a back room of the way station, Beth sat on a low stool placed next to a communal bath tub. She was exhausted, and after his bath, she seemed to be drying Henry with a large cloth by memory. She helped him back into his clothes and told him to return to the main room of the station and play. After he was gone, she slipped out of her clothes and stepped into the metal wash basin. The same bath water would be used by several bathers, but the women and children were allowed to use it first. She sat back and let the warm water soothe her tired muscles. She would have gladly fallen asleep in the tub, but she knew others were waiting, so she washed her hair with the course soap and then the rest of her body. She was about to get out of the wash basin when the room door opened again. She quickly sank back into the brackish water.

"You need to hop on out of there missus. Others are waiting." It was the station manager's wife and as she spoke, she unceremoniously dumped a half bucket of clean hot water into the tub, the hot water nearly burning Beth's legs. The older woman turned and left. Beth quickly wiped down with the same cloth she had used to dry Henry, and put on her dusty clothing.

Later that evening, Beth and Henry lay curled up next to each other on a dirty blanket on the floor of the stagecoach station. They rose the next morning and shared two eggs and two biscuits and watched as the other passengers ate and then left the rough-hewn table to answer nature's call before reboarding the stagecoach. As the morning sun sat calmly on the eastern horizon, Mother and son attended to their toilet discreetly behind a clump of bushes and walked to the coach. In a few moments, with all passengers on board, the driver yelled to his team of horses, and the stagecoach continued northeast on its journey.

# Chapter Eleven

**Town of Kansas - 1846**

Her disappointment undoubtedly had shown on her face when Beth, along with Henry, had first seen Hattie's room. It was located on the second floor of a boarding house that was in the area known as "the bottoms," an area where no one lived by choice. The large house itself was in considerably poorer condition than the San Antonio accommodations that Beth had left days ago. The clapboard siding, which had once been white, was now grey with bare boards showing here and there. Where once the old home had had a full set of window shutters, now there were only a handful of unkempt vestiges. The proud, wide front porch of the house sagged in several places, and the brick steps leading up to the porch were cracked with several bricks askew. What had served as a front yard was now a patch of weeds, with two scrawny bushes tenaciously hugging the edge of the front porch.

More disappointing was the neighborhood in which the boarding house was located. A mixture of seedy bars, flop houses, and retail establishments catering to blue collar workers, the poor, and the down-and-out lined the streets in the immediate neighborhood. Red lights glowed in several second story windows each evening. Scalawag, truant, dirty, and unkempt street urchins roamed the streets in small gangs, begging for hand-outs, or opportunistically stealing from the unsuspecting. Instead of bringing her son to a more favorable place in which to grow and mature, Beth had brought Henry into a much courser environment. It was a decision she would regret for the rest of her life.

With the passing of only three days in the shabby rented room, Beth would have quickly boarded a southbound stagecoach to return to Texas.

But with limited ready funds available, she was forced to make the best of a miserable situation. Her aunt, whom she had barely known prior to the move, was the only favorable facet of the relocation. In Hattie Shaw, Beth found a kindred spirit; someone with whom she could share her thoughts and concerns. Hattie was a good listener, a kind soul, and she grew fond of her determined niece who had been placed into a life situation similar to her own.

Hattie Shaw did not have a mean bone in her body. She was a plain woman who always wore a light colored, long sleeved blouse with a dark ankle length skirt and a small silver brooch at her neckline. She had a frowsy look to her, a ruddy complexion, probably due to·her Scottish ancestry. Hattie was a good number of years older than Beth, but Beth never knew, nor did she ask Hattie her age. Although somewhat plump, Hattie's health was good, though she always became a bit winded when climbing the stairs of the boarding house. But she was cheerful, and genuinely happy that her niece had come to live with her. And she doted on Henry, playing with him, and reading excerpts from a well-worn Bible to him, all the while with a smile on her face. She had grown very fond of her grand-nephew.

Hattie's hours at the mercantile had increased to the point that she was working full time again and earning a bit more money; but not enough to even initiate an idea to move from their poor abode. But Beth was determined to make their lives better. She had formed a plan to move from the shabby boarding house as soon as they were able, but this meant that Beth would need to quickly find a job in a more suitable neighborhood. For three weeks, Beth trudged a mile to the north and east into Independence and the more affluent neighborhoods looking for dress shops catering to wealthier clientele. During her search, she would stop for a ten cent bowl of weak soup, her lunch for the day. And each evening she would wearily walk home exhausted to discuss her day with Hattie, disheartened by her lack of success.

Perseverance generally pays off in the long run, and Beth, at last, secured a position in an upscale dress shop, with duties as a sales clerk and seamstress. Her hours were long, as she was expected to wait on trade and continue sewing after the store closed. At last, with the combined income of the two women, they were able to set aside a bit of money each week, pay their bills, and purchase a few more necessities.

With both Hattie and Beth working, it meant that Henry was alone all day. The care of Henry fell to the daughter of a fellow rooming house boarder, who was happy to earn a few cents per day to look after the boy. The young woman, named Constance, who tended to Henry, was of the age that she had taken a keen interest in the roguish, worthless young men who roamed the neighborhood. This resulted in her callers, at times, assembling on the broken front steps of the boarding house telling stories to the young woman of their feigned love and bravado, truly for one primary purpose. If only one caller came round and happened to have a nickel in his pocket, it was a common practice for the promiscuous Miss Constance to shoo Henry into the front yard to play while she and the young man would lie on the floor of Hattie and Beth's room to conduct their lascivious behavior.

And so, young Henry's informal education continued. Unbeknownst to Miss Constance and her short-term beau(s), on numerous occasions Henry had availed himself of the keyhole in the door of his mother's room and watched the carnal gyrations of his babysitter. And if he became bored with that activity, he would remain in the front yard of the boarding house and mingle with the unsupervised urchins of the neighborhood. Many times he would wander away with them and get into mischief. Stealing treats from the shelves and outdoor displays of a nearby grocer was nearly a daily occurrence, as was beggary and picking pockets. He was continuing his "street education."

When Constance the baby sitter would finish her bouts of lustful activities she would return to the front steps of the boarding house knowing that she would probably not see Henry. She was well aware that Henry wandered away when she turned her back. Each time, she thought nothing of it, made no attempt to search for the child, and simply waited until he finally returned. Babysitter and her charge were content with the arrangement; and Beth and Hattie had nothing more than occasional suspicions of these activities.

## Chapter Twelve

### Independence - 1850

Months passed with both women working diligently and managing to put aside as much as they could before they felt confident enough to begin looking for improved lodging. A bone-chilling winter had set in on the northern plains, but once again, in her free time, Beth walked neighborhoods looking for a better home for herself, Henry, and Hattie. Her determination resulted in finding a boarding house in a much better neighborhood in Independence. It was an unremarkable dwelling that was run by a kindly, Christian couple, Mr. and Mrs. Gordon Schiller. She was able to rent a small three room apartment. With a sitting room/kitchen and two small bedrooms, the women would sleep in one room, with Henry in the smaller second bedroom. While there was a kitchen sink in their apartment, with a well pump at the sink for drawing water, a small wooden shack at the rear of the house, and next to the communal outhouse facility, served as a bath house for all tenants. The small heating fire in the bath house was lit only on Saturdays, and tenants took turns pumping the small well pump next to the shed, taking the water into the shack, placing the bucket over the grill of the fire, then bathing in the warm water that was poured into a round metal tub. Each tenant then had to dump the bath water out of a chute located at the rear of the shed so the next bather had an empty tub. As primitive as it was, it was superior to the accommodations they had lived in at the Bottoms.

In the midst of a gently falling snow, the women packed their meager belongings, and with Henry, they soon moved to Schiller's Boarding House in Independence. Beth and Hattie both believed that a more wholesome neighborhood would help to mold Henry in a more favorable manner.

Perhaps not surprisingly, a melancholy Henry, at ten years old, was not happy to be leaving his street-wise friends in the Bottoms. Even at his tender age, he had grown accustomed to the free life with no supervision and the thrill of petty thievery. He determined to himself that he would not let a move to a different neighborhood put a halt to his petty criminal activities; and it did not.

The formal education of Henry had previously not been a priority for his mother, who was simply trying to get by from day to day. In addition, the school located in "the bottoms" was a building that had all the appearances of a rundown barn. One look at the school and the students who reluctantly trudged to the building each day had convinced Beth that her son would not benefit from attending. Therefore, Beth had foregone enrolling Henry under such despicable conditions. But after moving, Beth was determined that the boy would get an education. The Schiller's boarding house was in a neighborhood that had a fine public school, and Henry had unwillingly accompanied his mother to be registered and begin his education shortly after moving. Because of his age, and lack of prior formal education, Henry was behind his classmates of the same age and was forced to attend classes with children younger than he. Although Henry was not stupid, and rather quickly grasped the rudiments of reading and writing, he wanted no part of the rigid daily classroom schedule and the repetitive studies. While there was no such thing as a part time student, Henry became just that. On many days, he would arrive at school, sit in the classroom half-heartedly listening to the teacher, and then disappear after lunch break to join his street buddies in his old neighborhood, which was located a considerable number of city blocks away.

Naturally, his mother and great aunt knew nothing of his quite common truancy. That is, they knew nothing about it until report cards were issued to the students. Henry's report card reflected a lack of learning, but also showed that he was absent from school a great deal of the time. Under the tutelage of his street-wise friends, Henry did not let that bother him. He simply forged his mother's signature and handed the report card back to his teacher the day after the cards had been issued, thereby ensuring that his mother never saw the report card. But in passing conversations with other mothers in the neighborhood, Beth learned about the quarterly report cards given to the school attendees. She also learned when the next cards would be distributed, and she confronted Henry on the day the students brought them home. But the motherly tongue-lashing by Beth appeared to make no impression on Henry. Over time he had become immune to the scoldings of his mother. No matter how many times she cajoled and implored her son, Beth resigned herself to the fact that Henry would never be a scholar. As it was, each year that passed held an unknown outcome as to Henry's retention in school and whether or not he would pass on to the next grade. It was probably due to the fact that no teacher wanted the young thug in their class for two years in succession that Henry was passed on to the next higher grade to be some other teacher's headache. Henry would then continue his pattern of showing up for school on sporadic days for a few hours or less, followed by skipping the remainder of the school day so that he could join his gang of nefarious friends in mischief contrary to the law.

The fruits of the gang's endeavors led to the boys splitting up their daily loot, which came in the form of food items, which the hungry boys dispatched immediately, cash, jewelry, and other trinkets of unknown value. Like every boy in the gang, Henry needed a place to hide his proceeds of the loot.

Unbeknownst to both his mother and his great aunt, Henry kept an old sock squirreled away from their vision and knowledge. The sock contained currency of various denominations, along with jewelry and trinkets, none of which had been honorably obtained, and which Henry had acquired with the help of his friends. His small cache had all come from stealing and begging. Henry found this borderline behavior to be exciting, and the fact that he had his own stash of money, known only to him, made the schemes of he and his boyhood cohorts that much more tantalizing.

Beth Vogler and Hattie Shaw knew nothing specific of Henry's criminal behavior. They believed that the now ten-year-old Henry was in school each day, well, most days anyway, and was being watched after by their neighbor, Maude, in the after school hours. Such was not the case, of course. The new babysitter's name was Maude Greer; a kindly, elderly woman who happened to live in the same boarding house. Maude loved children, but her own children, raised many years ago, had not blessed her with grandchildren. While saying she loved children, she had long ago forgotten the rudiments of taking care of the same, specifically the fine art of instilling discipline and responsibility. In fact, she had forgotten a multitude of things in her life and was, quite frankly, a bit "daft." But each evening when Beth and Hattie returned home, they found Henry in their rented room, with nothing but a good report from Maude.

In truth, Maude had tended to her tatting all day without so much as a thought of the boy she was supposed to be watching. Every now and then, after a few hours would pass, Maude's thought processes would click, and she would remember Henry. She would become concerned, walk down the hall to Beth and Hattie's room, rap quietly on the door, return to her own room, and peer out her window, where she watched trees swaying in the breeze in the back yard of the boarding house. After standing for a few moments watching the hypnotic motion of the trees, she would completely forget her previous concern for Henry, forget why she was looking out the window, and return to her sewing. She only really spoke to Henry late each afternoon when he came back to the boarding house and poked his head in Maude's door to say hello. Maude would look at him, smile and greet him, then look at a small clock on her wall and say, "Your mother ought to be home soon." Henry would then walk to his room, smiling as he walked, with his hands in his pockets, playing with the newly acquired coins and baubles to be added to his collection.

***

Three years passed, and in 1853, at the age of thirteen, Henry had assumed the persona of a small time neighborhood hoodlum, the same as the friends with whom he associated. He dressed like them, he talked the same street jargon as they did, and he nurtured a mutual growing dislike for the ideals of honesty and working for rewards. He relished in his ability to blend in with his older hoodlum friends and prey on unsuspecting victims. As a result of his actions and demeanor, he had no friends in the neighborhood, the neighborhood that his mother, Beth, had selected to enrich her son's life and help to set him on the correct path in life. Beth's concern for her son continued to grow. All of Henry's friends were the hoodlums of the old neighborhood. But to him, his life was complete, and it all seemed so easy. A heartbroken Beth now knew that her son was destined for a life of wrong-doing.

Sometime before, Henry had shifted his hidden booty, which he had been keeping in a sock, into two, empty, brightly embossed cigar boxes; cash was placed in one box and jewelry and trinkets in the other. The cigar boxes were remnants of the gang's periodic pilfering at a local drug store. The original box contents had been split up and enjoyed by the gang. Henry's cigar boxes were hidden beneath the bottom drawer of the small four drawer chest of drawers in his sleeping room. The only legitimate son of a Vogler was following in the outlaw trail of his grandfather and uncle. Such a path, followed through a lifetime at Henry's own volition, could surely come to no good.

# Chapter Thirteen

## Independence - 1857

Two years prior, when Henry Vogler had reached fifteen years of age, there was no longer any demonstrated pretense regarding his attendance at school. He simply stopped the sham and quit going. His mother and his great aunt knew of this and tearfully pled to ears that refused to listen. Henry would have none of it. Life was far too tantalizing with its never ending harvest of treasure from those less skilled and unsuspecting. He had money to spend and the small criminal world in the Bottoms was the oyster's pearl for him and his gang of disreputable friends. School was a world apart from the lives of the gang, a world in which they did not fit and of which they wanted no part. The situation caused great sadness to Beth. After all, there is no mother alive who doesn't want the best for her children. Finally admitting that it was a lost cause, Beth and Hattie gave up their attempts to encourage Henry to attend to his classroom education.

In 1857, when Henry reached seventeen years of age, his mother and his great aunt had finally lost all control of the young man. And even yet, Beth held out hope that Henry would leave his friends and make an effort to lead an honorable life. Neither Beth nor Hattie knew exactly what it was that predominantly occupied Henry's time. What they did know was that the young man had grown physically to nearly six feet tall, was surprisingly well-muscled, and could no longer be physically restrained by either of the smaller women. They also knew that when they came home from work each evening, they would find Henry either in bed or sitting in a chair at the end of the front porch of the boarding house smoking. A considerable number of cigarette butts lay on the lawn at the side of the porch where he had tossed them over the course of months.

But there were other clues to Henry's activities in the absence of his mother and great aunt. On more than one occasion, Beth and Hattie returned home to find Henry slumped over in his chair at the end of the porch, peacefully snoring as he slept. An empty wine bottle lay among the cigarette butts in the grass next to the end of the porch. Beth would pick up the empty bottle, throw it in the trash bin behind the boarding house, and return with Hattie to their room, leaving Henry to sleep off the effects of the fermented red. Wine and cigarettes were not the only items appearing at the boarding house. There were times when strange food items appeared in their room. These were items that were far too costly for Beth or Hattie to purchase at the local grocer's shop. They could only surmise that Henry had brought home yet more ill-gotten items.

In addition, Henry always had money, yet had no job known to Beth or Hattie. Without a job, there was only one explanation for the young man having a seemingly unending supply of cash. Both Beth and Hattie were forced to regretfully conclude that Henry was involved in some form of criminal activity.

Yet another indication of Henry's sphere of endeavors was the occasional visit by one of his ne'r-do-well, crony friends. On more than one occasion in the evening, either Beth or Hattie had answered a sharp rap on their door to find a dirty, unkempt-appearing character on the other side of the door leering at them, and who then mumbled in a scurrilous manner that he wanted to see Henry. Each time this happened, the women would be horrifically taken aback. Henry would then leave the boarding house with this character without saying a word to his mother or great aunt. The sight of these young thugs with whom Henry associated gave chills to Beth and Hattie.

There was yet another reason for Beth and Hattie to begin to have grave concerns for Henry, but even more so, for their own well-being. On several occasions in the recent past, when his mother or great aunt would attempt to reprimand the boy for minor issues, such as helping to clean up after himself and keep a tidy room, or take out the refuse, tasks that all children learn in a cooperative family environment, Henry would refuse to help. When pressed on the issue, Henry would return a hateful, disturbing look at the two women, who were desperately trying to instill a sense of responsibility in the young man. The look was withering, and the fact that Henry balled his hands into fists, flexing his forearms as he glared at them, indeed frightened the women.

***

On a pleasant, breezy and warm Saturday afternoon in early April 1857, Beth and Hattie had thrown open their windows to let the fresh spring air move into and displace the musty air in their rooms. In the absence of Henry, who had left the house early the night before and had not yet returned, they had carried bed linens and their small rugs down the stairs to air on a clothesline at the back of the house. They laughed as they worked together thwacking the rugs that hung on the line to remove dirt and dust. They left the bedding and rugs on the line to air and climbed the stairs back to the second floor. They were now deter-mined to give the small apartment a thorough cleaning with strong tallow soap and water. They spent the morning on their hands and knees, scrubbing the wooden floors until they were satisfied that they had removed the winter grime. At nearly midday, they had only one room left to scrub. They had saved the worst job for last; Henry's room.

A considerable amount of time was spent picking up articles of clothing and soiled dishes in Henry's bedroom before they could begin cleaning. They then pulled the soiled sheets from the unkempt bed and returned to their hands and knees to begin scrubbing. They started at the back of the room, each working on opposite sides of the bed, and progressed toward the bedroom door. On the same wall as the door, stood the worn, oaken, four-drawer dresser that held Henry's clothes and personal items. A grainy mirror was attached to the top of the dresser. Hattie had scrubbed the floor up to the side of the dresser. Beth soon reached the other side of the dresser as Hattie sat on the floor resting.

"Beth, help me push the dresser to the side so that we can reach behind it," said a visibly, very tired Hattie. She unconsciously pushed a few strands of her graying hair to the side and tucked it up under the scarf that was covering her hair.

The two women pushed at the side of the dresser, but the dresser moved only slightly. It was simply too heavy.

"Perhaps if we removed a drawer or two it would make it easier to move," said Beth. "I'll take out the top drawer," she said.

"While you do that, I will take out the bottom drawer," said Hattie, and she stood to the side while Beth removed and placed the top drawer on Henry's bed. Hattie then got down on her knees and pulled the bottom drawer out. But the drawer stuck before she could get it fully out of the dresser. Beth got down on her knees then, and with both women pulling, the drawer finally was pulled free with a jerk, and both women plopped backwards onto their backs, the drawer lying between them on the floor.

The women were so tired that they both lay on their backs laughing for a moment. But Beth slowly rose to a sitting position and gazed at the dresser. Her mouth opened slightly as if to speak, but she said nothing, until finally she quietly spoke, "Hattie, what do you make of this?"

Hattie rolled over onto her hands and knees and looked into the space which had been under the bottom drawer of the dresser. She continued to look into the space for a moment and did not speak.

Initially, the women did not realize that they had stumbled upon Henry's cache, which held his ill-gotten criminal loot. Slowly the women began to examine the objects in the assortment. They opened several cigar boxes, discovering that they were nearly full of bills and coins, amounting to a small fortune. In a cloth sack, they found several pocket watches and ladies' jewelry. The value of the entire collection was beyond the women's comprehension. They realized that there was only one explanation for the stash of goods. Since he had no working income, Henry had obtained these items dishonestly. As they looked at each other for a few seconds, Beth bent her head down. Her body began shaking as she silently cried.

"I tried, Hattie. I tried to watch over him and do my best as a mother. Yet look at what he has done." Beth began a heart wrenching wail that only a mother could utter or understand.

Hattie pushed the drawer from between them, sat next to Beth, and hugged her. Sympathetic tears fell from Hattie's eyes as she held and rocked her niece.

"It's not your fault, Beth. You are a good mother, and you always looked out for the boy. Sometimes you just can't understand what goes through a boy's head. There must be something in the make-up of the boy that makes him this way. Maybe there's some bad blood in the Voglers from long ago," said Hattie. Little did she know of the truth in that statement.

As the women continued to cry and console each other, they had not heard the outer door of the apartment open and close. Henry had planned his entrance accordingly. He had stood listening in the hallway outside the apartment for a moment, and when he had heard nothing, he was under the impression that his mother and aunt were not at home. In his hand, he carried a pair of silver candle sticks carelessly wrapped in rags, his share of loot divided by the gang after breaking in and robbing an upscale shop in a neighborhood two miles away the previous evening. He wanted to stash the candlesticks away before his mother and great aunt returned.

But as Henry stepped inside the door of the apartment, he heard faint talking and the sound of crying. He stood still for a few seconds, suddenly realizing that the sounds were coming from his bedroom. His mother and great aunt never went into his room. He had often told them to stay out of his space. An alarm went off in Henry's head. He panicked and quickly moved to his bedroom door which was standing ajar. As he looked into the bedroom, he saw his mother and Hattie sitting on the floor in front of his dresser. The bottom dresser drawer lay to the side of them. Two of his cigar boxes with their lids open on the floor in front of the two women revealed stacks of gold and silver coins.

Like steam escaping an over-pressured pipe, Henry's wrath exploded and was, unfortunately, aimed at the only two people in his life who cared for him and actually loved him. His mother and his great aunt had invaded his treasure cache; something that in his immature mind took precedence over everything else in his life. His cache was his persona. It made him feel as if he was in charge of his life, and that he had succeeded in being better than all the fancy rich people who had far more than he did. His life of crime allowed him to imagine that he was better than all of those people; and by extending those internal opinions, he felt somehow that he was much better than even his mother and aunt. He was enraged that they had the audacity to intrude on his life.

He angrily shouted at the two women. "What the hell are you doing? Those are my things. You have no right to be snooping around in my room. I've told you before to stay out of here. Now get the hell out."

Henry's face was bright red. Veins stood out on his forehead and neck. His arms flailed, until one of his hands held the wrapped candle sticks over his head.

Hattie looked up at Henry and simply said, "Where did this money come from, Henry?"

"It's none of your goddamn business, old woman. Now get out of here before I throw you out."

Beth slowly stood up and faced her son.

"Henry, you must make this right. You must turn yourself in to the police. They will know what to do," she said.

He continued shouting. "Like hell, I will. Those cops are all on the take. They would just grab my stuff and throw me in jail. And I ain't going to jail!"

Beth put her hand gently on Henry's arm. "Henry, please. What you have done is wrong. You can't live your life as a wanted criminal."

Henry shook her hand away and simply became angrier. "I can live my life any way I want to," said Henry. "And there's nothing you can do about it."

"No, Henry. No," said Beth, and she attempted to put both her arms around her son.

Henry would have none of it. His free hand went across the throat of his mother, and he forcibly shoved her backwards. Beth stepped back but tripped on the dresser drawer behind her. She fell to the floor, landing first on her bottom, followed by the sharp sound of the back of her head striking the floor. She lay stunned on the floor, not moving.

Hattie screamed and bent over her niece. She stared up at Henry with fire in her eyes. "Now look what you've done. Your own mother who loves you, and you may have killed her. Can't you see that your mother only wants what's best for you?"

Henry stared at his great aunt's eyes, but only for a few seconds. In that short time, Henry knew that his mother and his great aunt were right. But he loved his life of crime even more that he loved his mother and great aunt. And his warped feelings of superiority led to his next actions. He once again felt that an individual was trying to be superior to him, and that feeling was directed at Hattie. In those few seconds, wrath and hate bubbled to the surface of his psyche, and he dealt with it in the manner that had been taught to him by his gang of criminals. He lashed out with one of the candle sticks that he had been holding in his hand and struck Hattie on the side of her head. The blow caught Hattie completely off guard, and her eyes remained open as her body slumped to a prone position. She lay beside Beth, both women now unconscious.

Beth wore a small gold locket on a gold chain around her neck. She never removed it. It was one of the few things that she still held dear. The locket had been her mother's, and her mother had given it to her just before she died of pneumonia many years ago. Henry knew this and could see the gold chain peeking from beneath the collar of his mother's dress. His wrath still filling his body with hate, he reached down, and with a quick jerk of his hand, he broke the clasp of the chain. He looked for a few seconds at the gold locket, then shoved the locket and chain in his pocket.

Those few moments had sealed the fate of Henry Vogler. He was sure that he had killed his great aunt Hattie and probably his mother as well. He knew that he must flee or be arrested. He hastily gathered up a blanket from his bed and scooped up all of his loot from the floor and threw it in the middle of the blanket. He then threw a few articles of clothing, including his coat, onto the pile and tied up the corners of the blanket. He rushed out the door of the apartment, just as he heard footsteps hastily coming up the stairs from the first floor. As he started down the stairs, Henry met Gordon Schiller running up the stairs.

"What in tarnation is going on up there, Henry?" asked Mr. Schiller.

Henry paid no attention to the old man and shoved him to the side as he rushed down the stairs.

Physically shaken by Henry's roughly bumping into him, Gordon raised his voice and said, "Come back here, Henry. You need to tell me what is going on. Mrs. Schiller and I won't have this kind of behavior in our house. Come back here, I said." But by this time the front door of the boarding house had slammed closed following Henry's escape.

Henry had fled to parts unknown, unknown to his mother, great aunt, and the authorities, that is. In fact, Henry was holed up in a dirty, run-down shack in the Bottoms that he and his gang used for their own purposes. He told other members of the gang the details of the past couple of hours, and that he would be leaving City of Kansas before the police came looking for him. He did not intend to be around when that happened.

Henry had befriended one of the gang members more so than the others. "Gospel Billy" Rollins was two years older than Henry, but he had taken Henry under his wing when the gang had first accepted Henry into the group. Even though he was older than Henry, Billy was shorter and scrawnier. At nineteen, he appeared to be fourteen or fifteen years of age. He was not known in the gang as a fighter. Instead he relied on guile and shrewdness to carry out his nefarious deeds. Billy Rollins had earned his name because of his innocent look, and his habit while fleecing the unsuspecting public. While he was picking a pocket or selling a worthless trinket to another gullible rube, he would use the phrase, "I'm telling you, it's the gospel truth." And most of the time, his victims would believe him.

Billy Rollins had no family. He had been roaming the streets since he was thirteen years old, after his only relative, an elderly uncle, had died.

After Henry had told the gang of his intentions, Billy Rollins spoke up. "I'm going with you Henry. I think I've worn out my time here in the neighborhood. Hell, I've got every cop on the beat looking for me. Too many little old ladies have told them about me. So, it's probably a good time to get out of town." Henry nodded in agreement. He would certainly welcome the company of his friend. Within an hour, the two young men were riding in an empty box car attached to a train making its way from the rail yard in the City of Kansas Bottoms and crawling westward.

# Chapter Fourteen

**Monday morning - April 1857**
**Leavenworth, Kansas**

The exterior of the worn wooden siding of the boxcar was painted with the words, "Missouri Pacific." Henry lay on the rough wooden floor of the empty box car as it sat idle in the rail yard at Leavenworth. Henry's stash was still wrapped and tied into the old blanket and was under his head as he lay gazing out the door. Billy was lying close by. His coat showed signs of bulges at various places, as his stash was stuffed into the pockets of the coat. An orange-colored sun was rising, and it promised to be a warm spring day.

It had been a miserable night, both boys trying to get some sleep and wishing that the freight train would move faster. As it was, the train had crept slowly along, alternately stopping and restarting as it moved west and north. Yet in total, the train had only moved roughly thirty miles during the night, with the few empty box cars shunted off to a rail siding in Leavenworth. And that is where Henry had awakened to find himself looking out the half-open door of the boxcar as it sat motionless. His view encompassed nothing of interest to him; simply more rail stock, with an occasional yard steam engine shuttling a few cars here and there in the yard. Henry didn't even know where he was. He had never ridden a train before, but he had heard plenty of stories about how easy it was to move about the country by hitching a ride on a passing train. To him, it did not seem like a very efficient way to get anywhere very fast.

During the night as the train moved slowly from the outer edge of City of Kansas, two other men had jumped aboard the same car as Henry and Billy. But they had picked opposite corners of the car in which to sleep and did not bother the boys. In the increasing morning light, Henry turned his gaze to those other two men who were older than he and Billy. One was sitting up rubbing the sleep from his eyes. The other man was standing up, urinating out of the partially open door on the other side of the boxcar. Glancing over at Billy, Henry could see that he, too, was watching the two strangers.

The man who was standing turned to face them, his frame outlined in the light of the door opening while he buttoned the front of his trousers. As he finished, he looked over at his friend who was getting to his feet. He, too, moved to the partially open door, unbuttoning his trousers as he walked. He looked at Henry and Billy and said, "My name's Calvin Smith. They just call me Smitty. That there's my friend Bob Wells," he said, nodding his head toward his companion as he took a position to relieve himself through the open door. When he was done, he turned back to the boys. Smith was the shorter of the two men and had a ruddy complexion. The small amount of hair remaining on his head was sandy colored. He wore a scruffy light brown beard. Wells, on the other hand, was taller and swarthier appearing. He wore a slouch hat on top of his black hair and had a full black mustache, with at least a week-old beard. His chin was stained with the spittle of tobacco.

"Now then," said Smith. "Don't believe I've ever seen you two around here before. Who are you?" he asked. As Smith asked the question, Wells had taken a knife from his pocket and was idly scraping dirt from beneath his rather long fingernails. He continued to eye the two boys suspiciously as the knife worked on his nails.

Henry was wary. He did not like the looks of the two men and glanced at the knife as he answered. "My name is Henry, and this here is my friend Billy." Billy nodded at the two men.

Smith seemed to think for a moment and then asked, "Where you boys headed?"

Henry did not know how to answer. He and Billy hadn't given much thought to where they were going to end up; they had simply known they had to get away from Independence. Therefore, Henry was surprised when Billy spoke up. "We heard tell of a place called Topeka. We thought we might go and see if we could find a job there." Henry suddenly caught himself, realizing that his mouth was agape. Where in the world had Billy come up with that story? He closed his mouth and simply nodded.

"Topeka, huh," said Smith, as he continued to look at the boys. "Ever been there?"

"No sir," said Billy.

"Hmm, well it ain't much," said Smith. "Do you even know where it is? Hell, do you even know where you are?" Wells looked up and grinned at the boys.

"No sir, we don't know exactly where we are, but we were told that if we rode a train west we would come to Topeka." Both Smith and Wells laughed.

"Turn around and look out that door," said Smith. "Can you see that big building up there on the hill?"

Henry and Billy looked up to where Smith was pointing. "Yes sir, we see it."

"Well that there is the Army's Fort Leavenworth. Place is full of soldier boys. And you boys are in the rail yard of Leavenworth, Kansas. Topeka is another day west of here, but you would need to catch another train going there. This here's the end of the line for this old boxcar."

Henry and Billy just looked at each other, each hoping their ignorance wasn't obvious to the two older men.

Wells had taken a step closer to the boys. A glob of dark colored brown tobacco spit shot from Wells' mouth and landed at Henry's feet.

"What you got in that bag, boy?" said Wells, as he pointed his knife at Henry's pack.

Henry was instantly alert. Some time ago he had also taken to carrying a knife in his trousers pocket, but he had only used it once against a man who had gotten wise to the gang attempting to separate him from his wallet. Unconsciously Henry moved his hand toward that pocket. He eyed Wells warily. "Got my clothes in there," he said.

Wells stood still, but waggled the knife to and fro in his fingers. "You boys got any money?" he asked.

Again, Billy spoke up. "Yeah, we got about two dollars between us," he said.

Just as Wells was about to speak again, Smith said, "Now, now, Bob. We don't need their money. Let the boys keep their two dollars. Boys, a hobo doesn't need money, but it never hurts to have a couple coins in your pocket. That's why Bob and me are here in Leavenworth. Are you boys sure you want some work?" he asked.

Work was probably the farthest thing from Henry's mind, considering that neither he nor Billy had ever held a real job in their lives. His mind clicked, and he was now wondering how Billy would talk his way along in this conversation.

"Yes sir," said Billy. "You see, me and my friend ain't got but a couple dollars, and we figured we better find a little work so we can continue our trip."

Calvin Smith had not reached age forty-five by being anybody's fool. He had been riding the rails and relying on handouts for years. He had been to every hobo camp from Massachusetts to Kansas and had met every sort of man possible. He could surmise simply from the looks of the two young men that they were grifters. Their clothes were not those of a working man, and the hands of the young men showed no signs of wear or callous. But among hoboes with whom Smith had associated throughout his life, there was a set of unwritten rules. One of those rules was that you did not question the background or motives of other travelling men as long as they left you alone. He had learned that each man had his own secrets, and those secrets were no damn business of others. He knew Henry and Billy were holding something to themselves, but it was not his place to try to dig this out of them.

Bob Wells, however, did not always hold to the hoboes' creed. Although he too had ridden the rails for several years, he was known to sometimes walk the edge of the travelling men's code. As a result, he was not always well received in the camps, but had never done anything to cause his banishment. He also knew that the boys were hiding something, but he would bide his time.

The momentary pause in their conversation was suddenly pierced by the high-pitched sound of a steel whistle. In a few seconds, it was followed by another loud whistle which came from the opposite direction of the first. Smith and Wells looked at each other, and Wells quickly folded and put his knife in his pocket. "Time to go, boys," said Smitty. "The train coppers are coming."

Henry and Billy just looked at each other. They had no idea what Smith was talking about.

More gruffly, Smitty said, "C'mon you two. No time to lose. Come with us or you'll end up in the pokey," and he spryly jumped out the door of the boxcar.

Henry and Billy quickly scrambled after the two older men.

Warily watching the rail yard police signaling each other with their whistles while they searched boxcars, the four men made their way across multiple sets of rails, eluding the police. In moments, they were safely away from the rail yard.

As they trudged slowly up a long hill, Smitty said, "If you boys were serious about needing some work, you are welcome to tag along with me and Bob. We're going on up the hill here to the fort and sign up for work."

Henry and Billy stopped. They had not counted on this. When they had told the older men that they were looking for work, it had been a lie, a cover story. Yet now, there didn't seem to be a way to back away from the predicament they had concocted. Smitty and Bob Wells kept walking until they noticed that the boys had dropped back and stopped. They turned and looked back at the boys. "Well, are you coming or not?" asked Smitty.

"Uh, yes sir. I just need to talk to Billy here for a minute," said Henry. "We'll catch up." They watched as the two older men walked away.

"OK, big mouth, what are we going to do now?" asked Henry. "I'm not sure I trust these guys, and I'm really not sure I want to be inside a fort with a bunch of soldiers. What kind of work do you suppose it is?"

Billy was also unsure of their next move. He fidgeted a bit, and then said, "I don't know, Henry. I'm not exactly thrilled about any old job. Then again, I'm curious. What do you say we just tag along and find out what is going on? Then maybe if we don't like the sound of it, we just disappear." Henry spat to the side, shrugged his shoulders and followed Billy.

The boys continued walking and caught up to Smith and Wells. They trudged up the hill and were nearing the fort.

"Say, what kind of work did you say this was going to be?" asked Billy.

"I didn't say," said Smitty. "But since you're wondering, it's railroad work. You see, the Army went and built themselves another fort on west of here. They call it Fort Riley. Least that's what I hear. But they need to extend the railroad from here to Fort Riley to bring supplies to the fort. And there ain't but a few railroads in Kansas except up by Saint Joe, Missouri. Anyway, the Army's going to need men to build this new line. They are hiring as many men as they can. Wells and me plan to work for a while to get a little grubstake and then head back east. You best make up your minds real quick if you want to work, 'cause we're almost there."

Indeed, the dark, foreboding shape of the fort was just ahead. Henry looked at Billy and watched as Billy stood looking at the fort for a moment, and then continued walking.

\*\*\*

Fort Riley Kansas had been established in 1853, just four years ago. It was the primary protection for settlers in the territory who were travelling westward on the Oregon, Santa Fe, and California trails. The fort continued to grow and was now also being used as a training facility for the Army's cavalry units. Camp followers and merchants were drawn to the Army forts, and a settlement soon sprang up next to the facility and became the thriving community of Pawnee. The rail line was desperately needed.

# Chapter Fifteen

**Thursday evening - April 1857**
**Independence, Missouri**

The sun had set some minutes before, and the room was rapidly darkening. The two small oil lamps in the room cast dancing shadows on the walls. Beth watched in stoic silence as the distinguished looking gentleman with the white mustache and his assistant in the nun's habit slowly began to pull the crisp white sheet up to cover the face of the old woman lying in the pauper's hospital bed.

Beth struggled with a meaningless question in her head. Had Hattie died fifteen minutes ago when Beth noticed that she was no longer breathing, or had she really died six days ago when she had lain on the floor of the apartment and never said another word? After the blow to the head inflicted by Henry, Hattie had remained in what the doctor had called a coma, and she did not respond to speech or touch, yet continued to breathe.

At the hands of Henry, Beth Vogler had lain unconscious on the apartment floor until Gordon Schiller discovered both women. With his wife's help, Mr. Schiller was able to revive Beth with cold compresses to her forehead and temples. Beth had been knocked out by the blow to the back of her head when she fell and hit the floor, but she quickly recovered, suffering only a nasty headache for the next three days. Beth's aunt, Hattie Shaw, was not so lucky and never regained consciousness. She had taken her last breath only thirty minutes ago.

Before the sheet fully covered Hattie, Beth leaned down and kissed her aunt's ashen face. She stood up straight and pushed a strand of red hair back under her hat. Tears streamed from her eyes, but she made no sound. She watched as the doctor and nurse fully covered Hattie's face. Beth turned and walked from the hospital to the Schiller's boarding house.

With Gordon Schiller's help, burial arrangements were made in a potter's field cemetery. Beth was able to purchase a very small metal urn for the top of the grave. It was inscribed with Hattie's name and dates of birth and death.

Beth would physically recover, but would forever be heartsick over the circumstances of the death of her aunt. Hattie Shaw was the kindest, most gentle person that Beth had ever known. Not only was she a relative, but she had been Beth's much-needed source of console following Horace's death, as well as a fount of wisdom and comfort regarding the raising of Henry. And finally, above all else, she had been Beth's best friend. Of paramount concern in the entire issue was the fact that her own son had killed Hattie; the son she had given birth to and loved for the past seventeen years. She simply could not grasp that she had raised a killer, someone who could, without conscience, take the life of another human being. There were moments throughout the rest of her life when she wished that she could have also died.

After several more days had passed, attired in customary black, Beth boarded a stagecoach for the long, arduous trip back to San Antonio. She was not sure that returning to Texas was the right and proper thing to do, but her memories of life in Texas were much sweeter than those in Independence.

Beth Vogler resumed her seamstress profession and subsequently started her own business in San Antonio, which flourished with the great demand by wealthy patrons for the beautiful, artistic, and hand-crafted clothing that she created. She was content. She worked hard, attended mass twice each week, and gained many friends, among whom she was well respected. But each night, she would pray to her God to look over, protect, and change the heart of the son whom she had loved but lost. Though her faith was strong, she held little hope that her prayers would be answered.

# Chapter Sixteen

### June 1857 - Leavenworth, Kansas

In 1855, the legislature of the territory of Kansas approved the incorporation of a railroad to be called "The Leavenworth, Pawnee, and Western Railroad Company." The new railroad was to be built from Leavenworth to or near Fort Riley, and from there it would continue to the western boundary of Kansas, which was the eastern boundary of Colorado. Later amendments to the legislation included building another line to the southern boundary of Kansas, which would link up with a line extending to the Gulf of Mexico. The steel rail tendrils were crisscrossing the nation as fast as they could be built.

Labor to build the nation's rail lines was a problem. There simply were not enough men in the outlying territories to do the tough, physical labor of laying all of those steel rails. As a result, railroads were forced to hire any available local men of reasonable fitness, including those who wandered in from hobo camps along the rail lines. This would still not fill the quota for laborers, and the railroads resorted to bringing immigrant labor to the far flung construction locations. Laborers from as far away as Ireland and China found themselves at railroad construction locations across the nation. The railroad construction camps were indeed a melting pot of working men.

The speed at which the railroads insisted on working meant that the most prudent safety measures were not always followed. Shortcuts were made at the expense of the safety of the construction crews. To the south of the Leavenworth construction, the Pacific was building a line to be the first railroad from St. Louis to Jefferson City. As the rail line attempted to cross the Gasconade River on a hastily built wooden trestle, the bridge collapsed, killing over thirty people. The news of this disaster reached the crews on the Leavenworth line and served to enforce the men's opinion of an employer who placed the lives of men secondary to speed and success.

***

For the past two months, Henry and Billy, along with the others in the train work gang had not moved out of Leavenworth. Instead, the railroad was amassing a huge quantity of supplies that would be necessary to begin the actual laying of rails to the west. Wagons, animals, food, rail sections, ties, tools, a portable kitchen; everything that could possibly be needed to build a rail line was being staged next to the Leavenworth rail yard. Construction would not begin until every item arrived and was accounted for. None of the men could understand this until one day when their foreman explained that it was all about money. Banks lent the railroad the money to build the rail lines, and the lines could not be built until the banks were satisfied that their money was protected and the rail line would not fail in the construction process. So, for the time being, the rail crew was being used to unload the incoming supply trains, sort, stack, and stage all the materials in preparation for the beginning of construction.

It was a curious community, the rail builders, comprised of men who had been selected from nearly four hundred men who had come to Leavenworth to obtain a job working on the rails. They came from all over the country. In addition there were men who spoke no English, many coming from European nations and from as far away as China. A large portion of the men came from Ireland and the eastern United States, where they had gained experience working on other rail lines.

Henry stood on the ground by the open door of the boxcar as another wooden keg was muscled down to him. He rolled the keg and lifted it on top of another keg already on his two-wheeled cart. He then started rolling the cart to the designated staging area. As he walked, his mind drifted back two months when he and Billy had stood in a long double line watching a man who would ultimately be their foreman walk down the line tapping men on the chest. Those who had been tapped on the chest would remain and become the rail crew. The others were told to leave. Henry grinned when he remembered the foreman facing him and Billy.

"How old are you boys," the gruff man had asked.

Henry answered that he was eighteen, and Billy answered that he was twenty. Each had added a year to their correct age.

When those not chosen had gone, the foreman gathered the remaining seventy-five men and spoke to them. Henry glanced around him and saw that Calvin Smith and Bob Wells were among the remaining group.

"My name is Morgan; Bull Morgan. And from now on, you call me Mr. Morgan. I am your foreman. And you men are going to be my rail builders. Some of you have experience and some of you don't. But to me, you are all the same. You're just here because you need the money. Well, let me tell you something. You are going to work for that money. And this ain't no candy shop job. This is work that can break a man in two. Some of you won't last a week. Some of you will be lucky to make it for two weeks. Your pay is two dollars per day, and you will get a fifty cent bonus each week if you make it through the week."

Morgan had continued. "We've got some rules in this outfit. First, you do as you're told, and you will keep your job. If you don't do your fair share of the work, you're fired. Next, there will be no fighting. If you get in a fight that you started, you're fired. You're going to be living in a bunk car or sleeping on the ground in a group. You need to get along with each other. If anybody steals from another man, you're fired. It's as simple as that. Now that we've got that out of the way, for the next few weeks we are going to be right here unloading freight cars. My two assistant foremen will tell you what to do. Oh, and one more thing. By the looks of some of you, you don't know the handle from the head of a pick axe. I suggest that before tomorrow when that first freighter comes in, you wander over to town and get some work clothes, a bedroll, and pack sack to carry your gear." Morgan had coincidentally been looking at Henry and Billy when he said this.

Henry chuckled again as he rolled the cart to the staging area. If you had asked the two young men when they started their work whether they would have stayed with the rail workers for more than the first two weeks, they would have laughed out loud. But that attitude changed only two weeks after they had started work. In the middle of the afternoon that day, the men were busy offloading wooden rail ties that had been shipped on flat bed rail cars from eastern forest sawmills. Kansas was flat, with no substantial growth of usable trees on the endless prairie. As a result, rail ties were shipped from forest mills in the eastern part of the nation. When those shipments arrived, the ties had to be unloaded from the railroad flat cars. The work was heavy, with six men grabbing a tie from the flat bed car, walking to the edge of the car, and transferring the tie to the upstretched hands of six more men standing on the ground. These men then carried the tie to a waiting horse-drawn wagon that would move the ties to the construction area, where they would be arranged on the ground in a long line extending westward.

Henry and Billy were standing in line with several other six man crews, waiting their turn to receive a tie from the flatcar, when Henry felt a hand on his shoulder. It was Calvin Smith. "You two come with me right now! C'mon," said Smitty. The young men quickly followed Smitty, who led them behind a nearby pile of supplies.

"What's going on?" asked Billy.

"Lookee over yonder," said Smitty.

Henry and Billy looked where Smitty was pointing. Two men, who each wore a silver star on their shirts, sat astride their horses while talking to one of the assistant foremen.

"I was over there getting a drink of water and overheard those two lawmen. Seems they are looking for two young punks who may have killed an old lady over in Independence and damn near killed another younger woman. They said that the younger woman lived and later left Independence to head back to Texas where she had lived some years back. They also want to question them about some robberies in that area. As I recall, one of you may have mentioned Independence in our jawing. I figure those boys are looking for you two. Am I right?" asked Smitty.

"I don't think so," said Billy. "Don't think we've done anything that would bring a lawman looking for us." Lies came easily from the mouth of Gospel Billy Rollins.

"Well then," said Smitty. "We might just as well go on back to work. Are you coming?"

Henry and Billy didn't move. "Yea, that's what I thought," said Smitty. "You best keep watching those fellas and stay out of sight until they leave." Smitty then walked away and returned to join a line of men waiting to receive ties from the flat car.

The two lawmen rode their horses slowly around the groups of working men, pausing frequently to watch. It was apparent that they were looking for someone, as they moved from group to group. Henry and Billy moved among the supply stacks, keeping out of sight. They were not seen by the mounted horsemen.

Sometime later that day, after the horsemen had departed and while the men paused in their work for lunch, Henry and Billy approached

Smitty and Bob Wells. "I just wanted to thank you for what you did," said Billy. Henry nodded his agreement.

Calvin Smith continued chewing on a stale biscuit and finally looked up from where he was sitting. "Listen, kid; I don't care who you are and what you did, 'cause I don't ask any questions. I just don't like lawmen, and I would have done the same for anybody. But I'll give you a little advice. Since those lawmen have looked here, they probably won't be back. I would advise you to keep your heads low and stay here working for a while until the dust settles. And one more thing, you better watch out for that assistant foreman, Fred Dawson. He's the one that talked to them lawmen." Smitty then went back to stabbing the beans on his plate. Henry and Billy looked at each other and slowly walked away. They couldn't have seen Bob Wells continuing to watch them as they returned to where they had been eating their lunch.

# Chapter Seventeen

**November 1857 - Just east of Fort Riley, Kansas**

They were becoming more restless with each passing week. The young men were now lean and hard muscled. The physical labor had been good for building their bodies, but not necessarily their minds. With colder weather coming, they wanted to move on, leave the railroad crew, and return to their less physical and less than honest livelihood in which they could rely on their wits instead of their brawn. But each time they began to make plans for leaving, thoughts of the two mounted lawmen who had been looking for them at the rail camp some months prior defused their fervor for leaving.

But on this unusually cold, drizzly morning, as he walked back from the privy, Billy Rollins had made up his mind. Lawmen or no lawmen, he was leaving and heading someplace warmer. The wind blowing from the north over the Kansas prairie was more than he could stand, and it would only get colder with each passing day. It chilled a man "to the bone," and slightly-built Billy was suffering from the cold. Henry was faring better, but he also disliked the intense prairie wind. And since the rail line to the fort was nearly completed, it seemed that the timing was about right to leave.

The cold day continued to be gray, with a drizzle falling all day. As the day wore on, the drizzle turned to a sharp sleet, and the entire work crew suffered. The men had no clothing that would stand up to the rain and sleet. Most wore simple cotton or wool outer coats. As a result, the crew was soaked, with their wet outer clothing having lost its ability to keep the men warm. The men went through the motions of completing their work tasks, but even Bull Morgan could see that the men were shaking with the cold, and the ground was too wet to work on the all-important task of setting the rail ties properly. As dusk set in at four p.m., he called it a day. Cheers were heard up and down the line of working men, and they ran to get out of the inclement weather. The men hurriedly stowed their tools out of the rain and sleet, and ran to the bunk cars.

Crude wooden shacks built atop two flat cars served as the rolling bunk cars, which sat on temporary, hastily built sidings next to the main line under construction. Three-tiered wooden bunks were built into the two sides of the shacks. A small wood burning stove provided some heat in the drafty bunk cars. Small shuttered openings which served as a means for ventilation in hot weather were closed. To one side of the bunk cars, a common trench privy with a make-shift lean-to north wall and roof served all the men. All of these items would be moved as the rail line progressed westward. Water for washing and cooking was carried from nearby creeks or rivers, which the rail lines tended to follow so that steam engines would have sources of water. Later, water wells would be dug near the tracks after the rails were laid, to provide a more permanent and cleaner source of water for the huge, thirsty steam engines.

As the men entered the bunk cars, they stripped off their outer cloth-ing, then their shoes, shirts, and trousers and draped the wet clothing on ropes which were strung from side to side inside the car. The smell of wet, dirty clothing permeated the rail car. Standing in their union suits, they formed a ring around the warm stove. As the men warmed slightly, they drifted back to their bunks. With the sleet dancing on the roof of the car, some of the men slept, and a small group of men began playing cards at a table in the corner of the car. One man softly played a mouth organ generating a quiet, soulful tune.

Henry lay in his bunk, knowing that there would be no supper to-night. It was too wet and cold for the cooks to keep cooking fires going outside the dining tent. Billy lay on the bunk below Henry's. As they lay resting, the quiet was suddenly pierced by a train whistle. The sound was at first from far away toward the east, but then grew louder as the train approached. Before long the men could hear the screech of the train braking, followed by the chuffing sound as the engine sat idle.

Henry was lying next to one of the shuttered windows. He opened it slightly to peer outside, but not so far as to allow the cold air to gust inside. In the icy, deepening-gray, late afternoon light, he saw the train that had rumbled to a stop near them. As he continued to watch, a four-horse team pulling a wagon through the muddy ground drew up next to a freight car of the train. The wagon contained eight armed Army troopers, all clad in oilskin ponchos. A sergeant and a young lieutenant sat upon the seat of the wagon.

"Billy," said Henry, keeping his voice low so others would not hear.

"What do you want?" answered Billy.

"Climb up here and look out this window with me," said Henry.

Billy did as he was asked and was soon kneeling on Henry's bunk, looking out the window with him.

They watched as four of the troopers climbed down from the wagon, slogged through the mud, went to the door of the boxcar next to them, and banged on the door. The door of the boxcar opened, and more Army troopers could be seen in the dim light of an oil lamp hanging from the ceiling of the boxcar. They continued to watch as each of the four troopers was handed a metal strongbox that he carried back to the waiting wagon.

The lieutenant had climbed down from the seat of the wagon. He walked over to the open door of the boxcar and was handed a sheaf of papers by a man dressed in civilian attire. The lieutenant hurriedly signed several of the sheets of paper, took one of the papers and stuffed it in the pocket of his overcoat, walked back to the wagon, and regained his seat.

The civilian in the rail car waved at the wagon as it began to roll away. "See you next month boys," he said.

As the wagon rolled away, Bull Morgan, Fred Dawson, and the other assistant foreman then walked up to the open boxcar door. Henry could see that Morgan wore a gun belt with a holstered pistol on the outside of his coat where it could be easily seen. Each of the assistant foremen threw an empty metal strongbox up into the rail car. The metal boxes clattered as they hit the floor of the boxcar. The men were soon handed a replacement, heavy metal strongbox. Bull Morgan signed papers given to him by the civilian, and he put one of the papers in his coat pocket. The three men then turned and walked away, presumably to go to the foremen's shack with Morgan's two assistants carrying the strongbox.

Both Henry and Billy knew the significance of what they had just seen. They had watched this same scene play out every month like clockwork. The train, which only a few moments prior had rumbled to a stop next to their rail car, was the monthly payroll train which had originated in the east. The metal strongboxes off-loaded from the train were to pay the Army soldiers at the fort and the rail construction crew. From what they had overheard, the payroll train originated at the U.S. Mint in Philadelphia, Pennsylvania. Neither Henry nor Billy had any idea where Pennsylvania was. All they knew was that a shipment of gold and silver coins left the mint each month under heavy guard and made its way west, stopping at Army forts and depots all along the rail lines. At each location, strongboxes were transferred to the facilities to pay the Army troops stationed at the forts. The soldiers were paid from two dollars to fifteen dollars per week, depending upon their rank and military longevity. The rail construction workers were each paid their usual two dollars per week with bonuses for working the full week. With Fort Riley presently being at the terminus of the westward rail line, it was the last stop of the payroll train. Pay day for the Fort Riley troopers, and the civilian railroad workers would be the next day.

Henry leaned in next to Billy so he would not be overheard. "There's got to be a way to grab some of that payroll money," he said.

"You're loco, Henry," whispered Billy. You want to get into the armed robbery business? Those damn troopers would shoot anybody trying to steal their money."

Henry closed the wooden shutter. "Still, I'll bet I could figure out a way," he said. Neither Henry nor Billy would let the images of that payroll train be lost to their memories, where they would resurface on occasion.

# Chapter Eighteen

**U.S. Mint**
**The corner of Chestnut and Jupiter**
**Philadelphia, Pennsylvania - 1857**

The United States in 1857 did not yet have universal paper currency. A small number of "trust notes" floated around the country, but they were used primarily by financial institutions and their wealthy patrons. They were simply a more sophisticated form of IOUs, but were legal tender for the bearer of the note. "Greenback" paper currency would not become widely used until later during the course of the Civil War. Hence, everyday commerce was done in coins, which were laboriously stamped out at the U.S. Mint in Philadelphia, Pennsylvania.

The white marble building stood sedately as pedestrians walked by each day. Greek style columns graced both the front and the rear of the building. One hundred fifty feet wide and two hundred four feet deep, the building had replaced a building one fifth its size. This was the second Philadelphia mint, where the legal tender coinage in use by the United States was pounded out daily for distribution to the nation's banks and government offices. Armed trains and wagons left Philadelphia daily with shipments of coins destined for the far corners of the growing nation. Nearly as often, gold and silver bars and ingots arrived at the mint under armed guard from the off-site smelting house. The precious metal was moved to the basement of the building where it would be melted and poured into molds of blank coins. The metal blanks would then be pounded into coins by steam driven machinery to produce the coins needed by the nation.

It was from this marble building in Philadelphia that payroll trains rolled westward to pay the military men at forts across the frontier, including the men at Fort Riley, Kansas.

# Chapter Nineteen

**January 1860 - Pawnee, Kansas**

With final completion of the rail line from Leavenworth to Fort Riley, there was a lull in the construction until the men began working on the line to the south. The numbing, cold, snowy and drizzly winter weather had set in on the plains. This made the surveying work and road-bed building slower, interspersed with days when construction simply could not proceed. On these days, the wage-sucking businesses in Pawnee did their best to separate soldiers and railroad laborers from their hard earned money.

Pawnee wasn't much of a town; it never had been. Its life was shortened in an odd manner. In May 1855, Pawnee was made the Kansas territorial capital and represented itself as a capital of a "free state." It served as capital for five days, until the territorial legislature, unhappy with the choice of Pawnee as its capital, quickly chose a different location. Jefferson Davis, Secretary of War and later to be President of the Confederate States, developed a nefarious plan to ensure that the Free State status of Kansas could be changed. He ordered the expansion of Fort Riley to encompass the settlement of Pawnee; thereby effectively eliminating the touted "free state" settlement capital.

On this cold January day in 1860, the remnants of the settlement remained, serving a colorful, base purpose for the soldiers and workers who toiled in and around the fort. A series of decrepit gaming joints, bars, and houses of prostitution were all that remained of the town, and they lined the frost-crusted mud street which served as the main avenue of commerce for the town. Card sharps, lawless scoundrels, and conniving whores preyed on the young soldiers and railroad workers encamped at Fort Riley.

Three dark brown, winter-coated Army horses, their breaths plainly evident as it roiled from their noses, were hitched to the posts outside; while inside, Henry Vogler and Billy Rollins stood at one such bar with their winter coats still buttoned against the cold in the nondescript ramshackle building. A paint-faded sign hanging on the outside of the building gave evidence that the bar was named the *Rusty Spike*. A steady wind made a two-note whistling sound as it blew freely around the ill-fitting door of the hastily constructed bar. Cigar and pipe smoke swirled above the gaming tables and bar, but was soon dispersed in the drafty surroundings. The inside walls of the bar were unfinished, and the wind wafted through the rough planking no matter what the seasonal conditions. Aside from the heat emitted by the wall oil lamps and the body heat of the patrons, the indoor temperature was closely akin to that of the outdoors. Billy's body trembled with the cold as the two men nursed their beers.

"I don't give a good goddam about any lawmen, Henry. I've got to get out of here and head to some place warmer. I've had it with this railroad work. Only a sucker would stick with this place," said Billy.

Henry did not respond. For months he had put up with his friend's near constant complaining. Billy was now singing just another verse of the same song. But in truth, Henry was unhappy with his lot also. He, too, was extremely dissatisfied with having to do physical labor and hide out from lawmen. He was ready to move on, but he had no plan on where or what he was going to do. This would soon change.

\*\*\*

Fred Dawson had exhausted his mental capacity to ascertain the whereabouts of a certain pack sack. For months, he had been obsessed with a burning yen; he had been searching for the pack sack that had been carried by Henry Vogler for several days when he had first been hired. Dawson had seen how Vogler had guarded the canvas pack to the extent that it was never out of his sight. Dawson was certain that there was something very unlawful in the background of Vogler and Rollins. After all, he still remembered the day that lawmen had come into the railroad camp. In his gut, he knew the two men were running from the law, and he was still fuming that the incompetent territorial sheriff and deputy had not more diligently searched out the men when they had come to the rail camp months ago. But at the time, Dawson had not helped the lawmen for fear of forever being branded a "snitch" by the close-knit rail crew laborers. In addition, he reasoned that he would never be able to get his hands on the elusive pack sack if Vogler and Rollins were apprehended by the law.

Having seen the manner in which Henry Vogler had protected the pack sack, Dawson was convinced that robbery had been involved in the secretive background of Vogler and Rollins. But after the men had settled into the daily routine of working, Vogler's pack sack was nowhere to be seen. Dawson was sure that Vogler had hidden it somewhere to be readily available, if necessary. Therefore, with every free moment, like a snake searching for a vole, Dawson had furtively searched the camp, probing into every location that might hold the hidden belongings of the two men. While the other railroad men worked, Dawson had stolen away from work and searched every corner of the bunk car. In numerous search locations around the camp, he had even probed the ground with a long knife blade whenever he suspicioned that the object of his search might be buried. His frenzied efforts had yielded nothing.

Cleverness was not one of the attributes of the assistant foreman. In addition, Dawson was downright lazy. Out of desperation and laziness, he had enlisted a partner in his quest to find Vogler's stash. Many times he had witnessed the manner in which Bob Wells interacted with Vogler and Rollins and was convinced that Wells strongly disliked Vogler. In casual conversation with Wells, it was revealed that Wells was also convinced that both men had been carrying something of value when he had first met them on the boxcar months ago. Wells wanted to get his hands on whatever it was that Vogler had been protecting, so he relished searching out Vogler's stash. With a rogue's agreement to split whatever was found, it took no convincing to bring Wells in on the action. And on this particular cold, raw, day, Dawson and Wells intended to carry out their plan.

The rail crew worked every day but Sunday, and depending upon the amount of daylight, they might work as many as twelve or thirteen hours per day. On this Saturday, the crew had begun their work as normal at six a.m., but the weather had turned cold enough that work ceased in the afternoon. Later that evening, many of the men could be found drinking their wages in Pawnee; and at that time, Dawson and Wells knew exactly where Henry Vogler and Billy Rollins were. Vogler and Rollins were in the *Rusty Spike*. Dawson and Wells each sat nursing a beer in a ramshackle tavern across the street from the *Rusty Spike*. They would bide their time until darkness fully settled in on Pawnee.

As usual, Henry and Billy had stayed at the bar a bit longer than they should have, but since the following day was Sunday, they would not have to rise early the next morning. They stumbled out the door of the *Rusty Spike* and began ambling toward the rail workers' camp. They would take the short cut used by all of the rail workers as they returned to camp. The path passed through a heavy stand of scrub bushes and red cedar, and because it was about half way to the camp from Pawnee, it was a conveniently private place for the returning workers to rid themselves of some of their excess liquid refreshment.

As they made their way along the path in the heavy darkness, Henry and Billy had not seen two other men in the distance trotting on a course somewhat parallel to their own. They were now in the cedar thicket and had stopped to relieve themselves. Their urine splattered on the hard-packed half-frozen dirt next to the path, and the two men did not hear their attackers silently break from the cover of the shrubbery. In seconds, Henry and Billy each felt a knife placed against his throat and a strong arm across his chest.

A voice said, "Make a fast move, and it will be your last."

Caught in a compromised position, both Henry and Billy slowly re-buttoned their trousers.

"On your knees," said the voice, from behind Billy.

Henry now recognized that voice as he slowly bent his legs and settled on his knees. It was the same voice he had heard daily since he had begun working for the railroad. His captor now roughly held Henry's hair in his fist and kept the knife to Henry's throat.

"What do you want, Dawson?" growled Henry.

"Why, we don't want nothin', boy," replied Dawson. "We just want to jaw with you for a while. Ain't that right, Bob?"

There was a low grunting laugh from the knife wielder behind Henry. Henry now knew it could only be one man; Bob Wells. Henry did not fear Dawson; he knew he was a coward at heart. But he respected the size and strength of Wells.

"Now you listen, and you listen good, Vogler," said Dawson. "You and your fellow jackass came into this rail camp carrying a stash. You know it, and I know it. And I know the law is looking for you for your shenanigans in City of Kansas. Therefore, I want two things. I want your stash and the stash of Rollins, here. And then I never want to see you two again, ever. And if you don't want to take care of that, then the morning sunshine will light up two dead men, and nobody will even care. It's that simple. Now, where is that stash?"

"You're crazy, Dawson. I don't know what the hell you are talking about," replied Henry.

"Well, we'll see about that," said Dawson. "Persuade him, Bob."

Henry felt the knife increase its pressure on his neck to the point that the pain was quick and intense as his skin was cut. A rivulet of blood dripped down on his shirt and onto the ground in front of him. Henry was desperate. He knew now that the sadistic Wells would just as soon kill him as find Henry's stash.

"What do you say, Vogler. Ready to tell me where you hid your pack?" asked Dawson. Henry did not answer. His brain was mulling through his options. In seconds, he acted.

Twisting just slightly, Henry judged Wells' position. Mustering all of his strength, he sharply threw his elbow backwards, thrusting into Wells' groin. As Wells felt the pain of the blow to his groin, he fell back, drawing the knife to the side, further cutting Henry's neck. But Wells was now bent over at the waist, moaning. The knife was still in his hand. Henry leaped to his feet, turned, and smashed Wells on the side of his jaw with his fist. Wells fell back, stunned. Henry hit Wells again, and followed Wells as the bigger man hit the ground. Henry then jumped and landed with both feet on Well's knife wielding arm, breaking a lower arm bone in the process. Wells howled in rage, but the pain rendered him immobile. In another twenty seconds the fight was over. Henry had wrestled the knife from Wells' hand, stabbed the man three times, and deftly slashed Wells' throat. Wells would die in a very short time.

While Henry had wrestled with Wells, Billy Rollins had performed much the same maneuver on Fred Dawson. Foolishly, Dawson had turned his head to look when Henry had elbowed Wells. At that instant, Billy had hooked an arm behind Dawson's knee and yanked Dawson off of his feet. But Billy was outweighed by Dawson, and the two men were still wrestling on the ground with Billy desperately holding Dawson's wrist of the hand holding the knife. The two men rolled and crashed into the underbrush. Billy was not sure he could hold out much longer. He did not have to. A heavy boot crashed into the side of Dawson's head, stunning him unconscious. Henry stood above Billy and the unmoving Dawson. Henry then took the knife from Dawson's limp hand and thrust the blade into the hollow of Dawson's neck, just above his chest, plunging the knife to the handle. He left the knife there and withdrew his hand. Dawson's body convulsed with his muscles twitching. Bloody bubbles frothed from the knife's entrance wound. In seconds, Dawson, too, was dead.

Billy Rollins' eyes were open wide. He sat next to Dawson's body. He had never been this close to a dead person and was on the verge of vomiting. He then looked up at Henry, then back to Dawson's face. Blood trickled across the top of Billy's hand.

"Are you all right?" asked Henry as he looked down at his friend.

Billy swallowed, pushing down the bile he felt in his throat. His face was a pasty white. "I think so, but I think Dawson stabbed me. My arm hurts."

The small cut on Henry's neck had clotted and stopped bleeding. "Take off your coat, Billy."

Billy did as he was told, and as he did so, in the dim moonlight they could see that his shirt sleeve was saturated with blood. Billy removed his shirt and almost immediately started shivering in the cold night air.

Henry bent over the two dead men. After cleaning out their pockets, he removed Dawson's coat and then his shirt. Cutting strips from the tail of Billy's shirt, he tightly tied multiple strips of cloth over the wound in Billy's arm to stop the bleeding. He gave Dawson's shirt and coat to Billy, who quickly put them on.

Very quietly, Billy said, "You killed them, Henry." Billy was again looking at the dead men lying on the ground. "What are we going to do now?"

Henry's stomach was doing summersaults. He was not sure that he wasn't going to be sick. His hands were shaking with the gravity of the situation. "Shut up, Billy. You know damn well that if they weren't dead, then you and I would be. Did you ever think of that?" asked Henry. As he spoke, he was still shaking uncontrollably. "Now help me here," he said as he lifted one foot of Bob Wells' body.

The two men dragged Wells and Dawson into a thick growth of bushes.

"Here, Billy. You got yourself a new watch. Straight from the pocket of the man who was going to kill you," said Henry as he handed him Dawson's pocket watch. Billy just looked at it, and then handed it back to Henry.

"I don't want it," said Billy.

"Suit yourself," said Henry as he stuffed the watch into his coat pocket.

"So now what do we do?" asked Billy. "They'll be looking for all of us come morning."

"Don't be so sure," said Henry. "Remember, nobody is working to-morrow. They'll just figure we spent the night with a couple whores. I need you to just stay here off the trail. I'm going into camp and retrieve our stash. I should be back in no more than an hour."

Billy just looked at Henry and watched as his friend turned and began walking to the rail camp.

The only safe place to hide the two men's belongings, now consolidated into Henry's pack sack, turned out to be the one place no one wanted to be around unless necessary. The odor struck and bit the inside of Henry's nose as he neared the outdoor privy. At the rear of the privy, behind the wind screen, Henry began quietly digging with a small shovel he had taken from the carelessly stowed tool bin.

He had been digging for less than a minute, when a voice cried out, "Hey, who's back there? Is anybody there?" A late night reveler had returned to camp and had come to the privy.

Henry froze. He made no further noise.

By the natural sound of things, the man had settled himself at the privy. "Goddam rats," he mumbled. In a few minutes, Henry heard the sound of the man's footfalls moving away from the privy. To be certain, he waited another minute and then resumed his quiet digging. It didn't take more than a few minutes longer until he lifted the pack sack out of its trench and left the shovel on the ground. Listening carefully, he quietly moved back through the camp and made his way to the trail back toward Pawnee.

Billy heard him before he saw him. Henry was walking quickly, and the two men soon joined up.

"C'mon, Billy. We need to move," said Henry.

"Where we going?" asked Billy.

"Don't know yet. Just come with me and stop asking questions."

The two men walked the path back to the ramshackle buildings. Henry knew what they were going to do. He knew that they had to put as much distance as possible between themselves and Pawnee. They stayed in the shadows against the buildings, only emerging from the dim light as they approached the *Rusty Spike*. They saw that a fourth Army horse had now been tied to the hitch rail alongside the three they had seen earlier.

Neither Henry nor Billy had ever spent much time on the back of a horse. While they knew the rudiments of horsemanship, in the rail camps they had only ridden a mule or two as it pulled a cart of supplies to another work location.

"Let's go," Henry said to Billy as he quickly unwrapped the reins of one of the horses from the hitch rail. The animal, which had been peacefully dozing, did not protest. Billy was quick to follow, mounting a second horse. With gentle coaxing, the two animals, carrying their horse-thief riders, were soon walking out of town. As they drew out of sight of the Pawnee buildings, they kicked the horses' sides and quickened the pace, moving in a southeasterly direction.

Sunup found the two exhausted men on tired mounts. The horses drank their fill and chomped the grass next to a small stream where the men had stopped to rest. They slept fitfully for nearly two hours, and then remounted the horses and continued south.

Back at the rail camp, it was just as Henry had predicted. Most of the crew were sleeping off hangovers from nasty, cheap whiskey, and some had remained in town, waking in the amorous embraces of their favorite sporting women. The bodies of Wells and Dawson would not be found until the natural scavengers had begun their work, and they were discovered by a passerby on Monday afternoon. Henry and Billy would have nearly a two day head start on any pursuers.

Pursuit did not come from anyone at the rail camp. The business of building a rail line took precedence over any less than diligent rail worker who chose to appear late, or not at all when work recommenced on Monday morning. Workers who were late to work or did not show up at all simply did not get paid, while other workers took up the additional workload. Nor did pursuit take place by any territorial lawmen; at least not immediately. The territory was far too large, and the deputy marshals too few and far flung for news to reach them in a timely manner. Any trail for them to follow would be very cold by the time they arrived. No, the only pursuers who began a search were the Army soldiers at Fort Riley. On Monday, after summarily court-martialing the two soldiers who had carelessly allowed their horses to be stolen while carousing in a Pawnee tavern, a small patrol was ordered and subsequently sent out to follow any trail leading away from Pawnee. But an unexpected gulley washer on Monday afternoon had put finality on that pursuit. The trail of the scofflaws was obliterated by the rain storm. Henry and Billy would not be held accountable for their crimes.

# Chapter Twenty

**Late March 1860 - Summer Prairie Ranch**
**Two Miles Outside of Tioga, Kansas Territory**

It was a beautiful piece of property. Gently rolling hills, ample water in shallow creeks, several groves of old-stand oak and mesquite, all ensured that the range cattle were easily able to forage on the nearly five thousand eight hundred acres in the nine sections which now formed the Summer Prairie Ranch. The nearly square tract of land, roughly three miles on each side, had been claimed and plotted by Robert Summers nearly a decade ago. As a gentrified, young man, Robert had broken from his wealthy eastern family, eloped with his intended bride who was sixteen years old at the time, and moved to the Kansas Territory to become a cattle man, a vocation of which he knew nearly nothing. The call of the frontier had snared Robert Summers. Against all formidable odds, and with a great deal of luck and hard work, Summer Prairie Ranch had become a success story. The Hereford cross-bred cattle flourished on the prairie grass, could tolerate the bitter prairie winter wind, and drew a fine price when driven to market in Wichita. Robert Summers, and his wife, Virginia, were now one of the wealthiest cattle families in the Kansas Territory. Virginia was a hands-on ranch wife. She took a very serious interest in learning all facets of the ranch while working alongside of the man she loved. The couple was admired by their ranch hands, who knew them to be courteous, fair, and hard working.

\*\*\*

From a wind-swept rise, in a grove of scrub brush and trees, Henry and Billy had been watching the ranch house for half of a day. Their interest was focused on the corral located not far from the house. It held a dozen horses. Their Army horses were beyond the capability for further hasty travel. The two horses hung their heads with weariness. The animals needed a good feed and rub down, but they wouldn't get that from their two outlaw riders.

Hours later, leaving the Army horses tied in the grove, and at the risk of being shot outright for trespassing and theft, the two men crept toward the Summer Prairie Ranch corral under the cover of a moonless night. They each carried the bridle from their Army mount. Stealthily entering the corral in the pitch black darkness, they had little trouble bridling two of the horses that were nearly asleep. The horses made no noise as the men led them through the gate of the corral. They continued to lead the horses at a slow walk in order to make as little noise as possible.

As they walked, they passed a low shed, where Henry stopped suddenly. He handed the reins of his horse to Billy and whispered that he should not talk. Henry then turned the wooden closure latch on the shed and entered it. In seconds, the coop occupants began a low clucking chorus, not yet at an alarm level. Henry soon reappeared, holding his coat closed in the front. He quickly took the reins from Billy with a free hand, and the men continued walking.

As they walked, Billy quietly asked, "What did you get back there, Henry?"

"Breakfast," said Henry. "Now shut up."

When they had returned to the Army horses, Henry handed the now fully-awake chicken to Billy and rummaged through the saddlebags. Finding a length of twine, he trussed the legs of the chicken. Then the men quickly unsaddled the Army mounts and saddled the two horses they had stolen from the Summers' ranch. They continued riding in a southerly direction. As the sun rose, they had not seen any other riders and felt that they were safely clear of the ranch land. They rode into a small ravine formed by a slow moving creek. Taking matches from the Army saddlebags, they started a small fire, butchered the chicken and roasted the meat over the fire. They ate ravenously, until only chicken bones and viscera lay on the ground around the fire. After drinking from the creek, Henry and Billy lay down to rest.

***

Five hours earlier, Robert and Virginia Summers were sitting on the covered front porch of the ranch house. As they sat drinking their second cup of coffee, they watched two mounted ranch hands approach the house. Each man was rope-leading another horse.

"Morning, Mr. Robert," said one of the cowhands as he removed his sweat-stained hat. "We found these two worn out cayuses out yonder. They appear to be Army horses, what with those brands on 'em."

Robert rose from his chair on the porch and walked around the horses looking at the brands. Sure enough, on the left shoulder of each horse was the "US" brand, and a number was branded on the left hip of each horse to signify the regiment to which the horse belonged.

Virginia, who had been watching, said, "Well, I reckon we will have a visit soon from some Army boys looking for their stock. Put 'em in the corral, boys and make sure they get fed."

No sooner had he turned to walk back to the porch when one of the cowhands came walking quickly to him. "Mister Summers. Sir, someone's been messing with the corral stock. I count two horses missing this morning," he said. As he was speaking, other ranch hands had walked up to Robert's side, listening to the conversation.

It did not take Robert Summers more than thirty seconds to fit the pieces of the puzzle together. "Well, boys, it looks like somebody wanted to drop off a couple of Army nags and take a couple of our horses." He turned to a senior hand. "Go get four or five more riders and let's go find our horses. I'll go change clothes while you saddle my horse. The rustlers can't be very far. Make sure the boys bring their bedrolls and a few biscuits. We may be out overnight."

In less than fifteen minutes, Robert Summers stood on the porch holding his bedroll and a rifle as he watched his horse being brought up to the porch. Four other ranch hands were walking their horses to the porch. Among that group was a wizened old hand whom everyone simply called Gus. In addition to being the best hand, Gus was also the best tracker on the ranch. He would be able to follow the trail of the two horse thieves easily. Each person, including Robert, wore a pistol rig and had a rifle stowed in the scabbard attached to his saddle. As soon as Robert had tied his bedroll to the cantle of his saddle, he mounted his horse, and the six riders spurred their mounts into a trot. With Gus coursing ahead of them and riding well-cared-for stock, they could keep this pace up for hours.

It didn't take long. With only one stop for stretching their legs and ridding themselves of their morning coffee, they rode over a slight rise and saw the faint wisps of smoke from a fire. The Summer Prairie group spread out to surround the source of the smoke. When the other men were in position, Robert and Gus walked their horses near the edge of the small ravine. Quietly dismounting and dropping their reins, they each retrieved their rifles, walked to the edge of the ravine, and peered down on Henry and Billy, who were still napping. The stolen horses were hobbled and contentedly grazing nearby. Their saddles and bridles lay on the ground next to the sleeping men. Robert waved his rifle in the air, signaling the rest of the group to approach the ravine. He then fired his rifle into the air.

The noise roused Henry, who shook Billy awake. They both stood up and immediately saw Robert, Gus, and another ranch hand staring down at them from the top of the ravine, with three rifles pointed at them. Feeling their presence, Henry turned to see three other ranch hands on the other lip of the ravine with rifles in their hands. As Billy looked at the dead-pan expressions of the owners of those six rifles, he felt sure that he was about to die. He spoke first. His voice wavered as he said, "Don't shoot. Don't shoot. We ain't got no guns, and that's the gospel truth." Henry did not speak. He was trying to figure out how he and Billy would get out of this mess.

"Why don't you two no-accounts come on up here where we can take a good look at you? C'mon, climb on out of there," said Robert. He told one of the hands to rope the horses, remove their hobbles, and bring them out of the ravine. The cowboy did as he was told, ignoring the saddles, bridles, and Henry's pack sack on the ground.

In a moment, Henry and Billy stood in front of Robert, Gus, and the ranch hands. "Don't believe I know you two boys, but it's pretty obvious you ain't any too bright. Around here, we hang horse thieves. You got anything to say for yourselves?" asked Robert.

Henry and Billy were silent.

"I thought as much. So, I believe that we will just go ahead and hang your sorry carcasses from that cottonwood over there. Slip on out of your coats, your shirts and pants," said Robert.

"What?" protested Billy. "Why do we need to do that?"

Robert Summers pointed his rifle toward Billy and fired. The bullet missed Billy's foot by inches, causing Billy to jump sideways; his eyes looking wildly at Robert Summers. "I don't like to repeat myself, boys. Now strip on down unless you want to die right now."

Henry and Billy did as they were told. But as Henry stripped off his trousers, he palmed the gold locket that he always carried in his pocket. Unseen, he dropped it into his boot. In another moment, Henry and Billy stood shivering in their union suits, their boots still on their feet. Their hands were tied behind their backs. The cowhands shoved the two men toward the tree and tied ropes around their necks, looping the end of each rope over a tree limb. The ropes were then tightened and tied off. Henry and Billy stood on their toes as the rope chafed their necks.

Robert Summers had no intention of killing Henry and Billy. It just wasn't in his nature. In fact, he had walked over and slightly loosened the leather thongs which held their wrists. It might take a while, but he felt certain that the two men could ultimately escape their bindings. He walked back and sat upon his horse. "Let this be a lesson to you two hombres. If you step foot back on my ranch, you will be shot on sight. Let's go boys," he said as he wheeled his horse and trotted off toward the ranch. His ranch hands followed, leading the two previously stolen horses with them.

*** 

As it was, it took more than two hours for Billy Rollins to finally slip out of the bindings on his wrists, painfully slip the rope from around his neck, and free Henry.

Henry was seething mad. He had been embarrassed and humiliated. The thought that he could have been legally hanged for equine thievery did not even enter his head. Rage was blinding him from seeing the insanity in his thoughts. He was so enraged that he swore to get even with the ranch owner. Even in the face of superior numbers and against all odds at the Summer Prairie Ranch, he went back into the ravine, picked up one of the horse bridles, and with his pack sack on his shoulder, he began walking in a northerly direction, all the while shivering in his union suit.

"Where you going, Henry?" asked Billy.

"I'm going to get some clothes. I ain't about to stand around here and freeze my ass," Henry answered.

Billy, who had grabbed up the other bridle and had begun following Henry, stopped in his tracks. "Now I know you're crazy, Henry. Remember what that fellow said. 'Shot on sight!' I don't relish tangling with any of them cowboys. We're just damn lucky to be alive. Let's turn around and go the other direction."

Henry ignored Billy and kept walking. Billy was soon by his side. As they walked, the men kept a sharp eye for any of the Summer Prairie crew.

After nearly four hours of walking, the two men were exhausted. They sat down in the prairie grass to rest. They idly watched a small dust cloud which swayed in the air to the rear of their path. But in a moment, the vision of the dust cloud became clearer and gave way to the sight of four mounted horsemen riding toward them. Billy began to rise to run, but Henry pulled him back down.

"Lay down," hissed Henry. "Maybe they haven't seen us."

They had been seen all right; the Kiowa hunting party was soon upon them. The four mounted Indians formed a square around the now-standing men. The Indians talked among themselves and apparently made jokes concerning the appearance and lack of proper clothing of the two white men they had come upon, because they laughed among themselves. One of the Indians reached out with a spear and touched Henry with the end of it. He then let out a whoop, which was answered by his companions. Two of the natives then slid from their horses, and each drew a knife from a sheath tied to their waists. Henry dropped the bridle and his pack sack and put up his fists. Billy followed suit. But the fighting prowess, or lack thereof, of Henry and Billy was no match to the lightning speed of the Indians. The two men soon found themselves lying face down with an Indian astride each of them and a knife held next to their necks. The other two Indians were now going through Henry's pack sack. Ignoring the money that was in the bag, the Indians took the pocket watches and jewelry from the bag and were gleefully jabbering and showing their find to each other. Once again in a single day both Henry and Billy were sure they were going to die. But within a few minutes, the Kiowa braves selected the jewelry pieces and watches that they wanted and released Henry and Billy. The two men tried to rise to stand, but they were kicked and punched back to the ground where they remained until the Indians had remounted their horses and ridden some distance away.

Again, bitterness and hatred rose in Henry's throat. He was irate, and if able, he would have killed the Indians with his own hands. He and Billy picked up the remainder of their loot, stuffed it back into the pack sack, and continued their walk to the north. After another six hours of walking, they had a stroke of luck. Their clothing, worn and filthy, was of no use to the Summer Prairie ranch hands and had been simply discarded along the trail back to the ranch. As poor as the garments were, they would at least keep the men warm. Henry retrieved the gold locket from his boot and put it safely in his trouser pocket, pausing to pass his thumb slowly back and forth across the body of the locket.

A full day and a half of walking passed until Henry and Billy finally took up a well-concealed place among tangled bushes to observe the Summer Prairie ranch house. And once again, in the pitch black of a cloudy night, the two men entered the ranch corral. But this time, they bridled the two Army horses and quietly led them from the corral. Henry reasoned that the ranch hands were not likely to come after them again since they were not taking ranch stock. As they led the two horses past the chicken coop, Henry was tempted to take another chicken, but wanted to get away from the ranch as fast as possible. When they were safely away from the house, they mounted the horses, retracing their previous steps. After four hours of riding, they paused only long enough at the ravine to pick up the Army saddles and put them on the horses. When finished, they rode on.

After riding until noon the next day, both the men and the horses were too tired to continue. Fortunately, it was at this point that they found the outriders' cabin. It wasn't much. Just a soddie hut with buffalo skins tied and stretched to make a roof. It had a small door with no windows and sat next to a small stream, amidst scrub bushes and mesquite trees. A small, low corral was next to the hut. Using lariats from the hut, they staked out the horses next to the stream to let them graze. Inside the soddie, they found a crude shelf structure that held some cans of beans, matches, and candles. Lacking a fireplace, a circle of ashes attested to the fact that the center dirt floor of the cabin served as a fire pit to provide warmth, a cooking fire, and to keep wandering animals from entering the hut. Using a sharp rock from the creek bed, Henry was able to crudely break through the top of a can of beans for each of them. They would not go hungry. That night, using dead fall from the mesquite trees, they built a small fire and slept through the night.

The following morning, fearing that Summers' ranch hands might venture upon them at the outriders' cabin, they sat astride their horses to move onward. Earlier, they had split up the stash they had carried in Henry's pack sack, and Billy's coat pockets were again full of coins and jewelry.

"I'm heading east, Henry. I'm going as far as the Mississippi River, and I aim to light somewhere around Saint Louis. I've been thinking that the saloon business might be something I could work at. Anyhow, if you ever get over that direction, look me up," said Billy.

"I'm not sure where I'm going, but I know I'm goin' farther south. I've had enough of this damn wind and cold," said Henry. "You've been a good friend, Billy. And I sure will look you up if I ever get to Saint Louis." An unexpected lump rose in Henry's throat as he reached across and shook Billy's hand. He would miss his friend. The same was true for Billy. Billy wheeled his horse and headed toward the rising sun. Unconsciously, Henry reached in his pocket and ran his thumb across the smooth gold of the locket he still carried with him. He then turned to go his separate way.

***

At nearly the same time that Henry and Billy had parted company, an Army patrol consisting of a shave-tail lieutenant, a sergeant, and six troopers arrived at the Summer Prairie Ranch. One of the men was obviously an Indian scout, attired in native clothing aside from an Army coat he was wearing. The patrol had been riding for two days and was weary and hungry. The men dismounted and watched as the lieutenant and the sergeant moved toward the porch of the ranch house as Robert Summers and his son, Will, emerged from the front door of the house.

The Lieutenant removed his hat, as did the sergeant. "Howdy mister."

Robert nodded his head at the Army men.

The lieutenant continued. "We're mighty tuckered out from riding. Would you mind terribly if we bedded down here tonight in that yonder grove of trees so we can get out of the wind?" he asked.

"Reckon it'd be OK," said Robert. "Where are you boys headed?"

The lieutenant replaced his hat and continued. "We've been trailing a couple horse thieves, and we think they may have come by your place. Would you happen to have seen a couple men riding Army horses?"

Robert smiled ever so slightly. "Yep, we saw them," he responded. He then told the lieutenant the story of the two rustlers who had stolen two of their horses and left the Army horses at the ranch several days ago. Then, he told them how he had recovered the ranch stock and left the rustlers several miles south, and that the rustlers had apparently returned and stolen the Army horses out of their corral. And since he had gotten his horses back and didn't have a stake in Army horses, he had not wasted effort in trying to track down the two men again. He described the two rustlers to the lieutenant.

The young lieutenant conferred a moment with his sergeant and then commented further. "There's some speculation that those two varmints may have somehow been involved with the murder of two men on a railroad crew working up near our Fort Riley. Would you know anything about that?"

"Heavens no," said Robert. "Those two couldn't be more than twenty years old or so. Are you sure about that, Lieutenant?"

"Not sure about much of anything, sir, except that my colonel told us to see if we could track down the thieves who stole a couple of Army horses."

"Hmm. Well, anyway, you're welcome to camp over in the grove there, and I'll have my cook rustle up some hot ham and biscuits and bring them out to you after a bit," said Robert. The Army troopers would at least eat well that night.

The next day, the patrol resumed their trailing, but by afternoon it became apparent that the two men they were trailing had split up, with one heading south and the other one moving east. Both directions led to areas outside the Kansas Territory and into territory in which the Army from Fort Riley had no providence. The patrol reluctantly gave up the chase and turned back to the north to return to the fort.

Henry Vogler and Billy Rollins had made good their escape.

\*\*\*

The horse was a problem. Henry had been traveling several days, using the cover of night to steal from darkened ranch houses, cabins, and village trading posts. He avoided civilization during the daytime, primarily because of the horse with its distinctive Army brands. He had not had an opportunity to "trade" horses at any of the settlements he had encountered. In addition, the horse was not built for long distance traveling. It was fast for short runs, but was just not sturdy enough for the long haul, and it was now favoring one of its front legs and could only walk very slowly.

He did not know it, but Henry was now in Oklahoma Territory. Being in the heart of land set aside for several different tribes of not-always-friendly Indians should have been a concern to Henry, but he was not aware of his danger.

The horse had stopped and refused to go farther, but as Henry sat wondering what he should do, he saw smoke on the horizon. He sat watching it for a moment and decided that it surely must be a camp. He slid down from the saddle, loosened the girth and dropped the saddle, then unbridled the horse and let it free. He watched as the Army horse slowly limped away. He would have to get another horse. He sat on the ground and opened his pack sack. He withdrew two shirts, a pair of trousers, a union suit and a pair of socks; all of which had been stolen as he travelled. He then drew all of his coins from a pouch and distributed them in all of his coat and trouser pockets. He did the same with the jewelry, but kept a silver pocket watch in his trouser pocket. He re-stowed his clothing, picked up the horse bridle and his pack sack, and began walking toward the smoke he had seen.

Smoke was rising from the chimney of the small wooden cabin. Horses were tied up in front of the cabin, and a small corral was off to the side of the building. Other crude shacks sat nearby, as well as huts and tepees covered with animal skins. Henry stood a distance from the scene. He was afraid to approach the settlement, especially since he saw numerous Indians walking about. He wondered if he had wandered into an Indian village. But when he saw several white people among the group, he decided to approach. Standing in front of the cabin, he saw people entering and leaving the structure. As he looked up, he noticed a sign with most of the printed words faded to gray by the seldom-relenting sandy dust that blew from the west. He was still able to read "Perryman Trading Post" on the sign. Two rough-appearing men came out of the cabin with brown paper-wrapped packages which they shoved into the saddlebags of two horses hitched in front of the cabin. Without so much as a glance at Henry, the two men mounted the horses and rode away. Henry's curiosity got the best of him, and he timidly opened the door of the cabin. As his eyes adjusted to the dim interior, he could see a counter, a display case under the counter, a man standing behind the counter, and shelves of dry goods from floor to ceiling.

"Hello stranger. Welcome to my store," said the man behind the counter. "What can I get you?"

Henry was momentarily at a loss for words. "I could use some food, I guess," was all he could think to say.

Lewis Perryman had seen every kind of man come through the door of his trading post, and he was quickly sizing up Henry. He saw a young man, no more than eighteen or twenty, who did not have the look of a ranch hand. He had the calluses of a working man, but grit and determination of a working man did not show in the young man's eyes. He pegged him as a drifter, and probably penniless. He could also not help but see the small round brass disk on the side of the bridle the young man was carrying. The brass had turned black from oxidation, but the letters "US" were still faintly visible. He could not help but wonder where the young man had gotten an Army bridle. But he had learned long ago not to pry into other folks' business, knowing a man could suffer some nasty consequences if he didn't follow that rule.

"My name's Perryman," said the merchant as he stuck out his hand. Henry shook his hand, but did not offer his own name. "Are you living on your own, son?"

"Yes sir," answered Henry. An awkward silence followed, while Henry decided that he had better start spinning a story. "Say, what is this place, mister?"

Perryman chuckled. "Probably near the end of the earth, young man, but the native Lochapokas call it Tulasi. When they say it, it sounds like Tulsa, so that's what the white folks call it; Oklahoma Territory."

"How come there are so many Indians?" asked Henry.

"Well, for several years now, the government has pushed a whole bunch of Indian tribes to this area to live. So there are mostly Indians here. But we get along with them just fine as long as we respect each other. I don't cheat them and they know it," said Perryman. "Are you going to need a grub stake?"

"I guess so. I probably better have a bedroll and poncho, too. I'm on my way to Texas, and my horse went lame so I turned him loose. Guess I would like to buy a horse, too, if you got one."

"I'll see what I can do," said Perryman, still thinking that the young man in front of him would be highly unlikely to have any money.

As the trader gathered the food stuffs, bedroll, and poncho, Henry's eyes wandered around the store, finally resting on the display case, where he studied an unusual jack knife. The blade of the knife was nearly five inches long. Next to it was a pistol rig with pistol and belt. A box of foil cartridges sat next to them.

Perryman had placed flour, dry bacon, beans, beef jerky, and hard tack biscuits on the counter. "Let's go out back, and I'll show you my livestock," he said to Henry.

They reached the corral and Perryman pointed out several horses and two mules that he could sell. The two men stood at the corral rail looking at the horses. Perryman could tell by watching Henry that the young man did not know the first thing about judging a horse. But rather than cheat the young man, Perryman made a suggestion. "Did you ever ride a mule, sir?" he asked.

Perryman's assessment was correct. Henry had no idea what he should be looking for when buying a horse. He was afraid that Perryman's question was a test, but he had no other answer than to say, "No sir."

"Come with me," said Perryman. He slid through the rails of the corral. Henry followed. Perryman walked very slowly among the horses until he was standing next to a rather large, fifteen-hands-tall mule. "This here is Zeke," said Perryman. "He's about three or four years old, the smartest, most easy going, and easy riding animal in this corral. Unlike the horses, he can stand the heat much better, can carry more weight, and eats less than a horse, and is a hell of a lot smarter than a horse. He is exactly what you need for the long trail to Texas. And that's the gospel truth," said Perryman.

The phrase shocked Henry, and he snapped his eyes on those of Perryman. Thoughts of Billy Rollins came to his mind as he studied Perryman's face. In seconds, he knew the merchant was telling the truth and was honest. An extremely rare smile crept onto Henry's face.

"I've got a used saddle and saddle bags that were traded to me, and I can give those to you with Zeke. They ain't pretty, but they're well-worn and the leather is soft."

Henry ran his hand down the neck of the big mule. Zeke turned his head slightly, but went on grinding a few old corn kernels that he had lipped up from the dirt. Henry had never had a true companion animal pet of his own, and he was strangely taken with this powerful animal that docilely stood before him. Somehow, he knew that he would buy Zeke. But he wasn't quite ready to give in to Mr. Perryman.

"I don't know, mister. I guess it depends on how much this is all going to cost," said Henry.

"Let's go back in the cabin, and I'll figure it up," said Perryman.

Henry stood in front of the counter, watching Perryman jotting on a scrap of paper. His eyes strayed again to the jack knife and pistol in the glass case under the counter. "Looks like it comes to right at twenty dollars for the grub and Zeke," said Perryman.

Henry didn't say anything for a moment, but then asked, "How much if you throw in that jack knife and pistol?"

Lewis Perryman never turned down money if it was offered, but he also had a healthy respect for firearms and knew very well how to use them. He had seen several young men meet their untimely, foolish end by carelessly boosting their self-esteem with a sidearm. "It's none of my business, young man, but do you know anything about properly taking care of a firearm?"

"I guess I aim to learn," answered Henry.

"Hmm." Perryman scratched his beard. "Well I guess for forty dollars, that gun and knife are yours too. That pistol is a Colt Navy Revolver. Just loading it is a bit dangerous, so I think I better give you a couple lessons in how to operate that gun." Perryman scratched his beard again. "Have you got the forty dollars?"

Henry reached into his pocket and laid the silver pocket watch on the counter. "How much will you give me for this watch?"

Perryman picked up the watch, opened the case, wound it, and held it up to his ear. Satisfied that it seemed to be working, he closed the case and put it back on the counter. "I guess I could give you three dollars for it," he said.

Henry's hands went back into his pockets and he then placed a ring on the counter. "How much can you give me for the ring, mister?"

Perryman now knew that he was dealing with a young man with a larcenous nature. Anybody who carried jewelry in his pockets probably acquired it in a less than honest manner. He picked up the ring and examined it. It was a pretty ring, yellow gold with a small stone inset. "Well, I'm not a jeweler, sir, so I don't even know what that rock is in the middle of the ring. But I guess I could give you three dollars for it, too. So that's six dollars off your bill, but I don't want any more trinkets. The remaining thirty-four dollars needs to be in cash." Perryman seemed certain that Henry did not have that kind of money. But to his astonishment, Henry counted out the coins from his pockets equaling thirty-four dollars.

"Can you show me how to work that pistol now, Mister?" asked Henry.

# Chapter Twenty-One

**January 1862 - Circle S Ranch**
**East of Perryville, Capital of the Choctaw Nation**
**Oklahoma/Indian Territory**

The gentle night breeze felt good on his cheeks as he tipped his hat back and faced the cool air. The temperature had dropped a few degrees since the unusually warm January day, which was expiring, and he thought it might frost or even snow before the night was over. In another hour or two, a new day would start. Henry had the night watch at the eastern edge of the herd. A great part of the herd was lying down, either asleep or gently chewing their regurgitated stomach contents. Zeke's head hung down as he tried to nap. But for some reason, Henry was not sleepy. As he looked up at the barely visible moon playing tag with the moving dark clouds, he was thinking about his life. He had become more bitter in the past two years. None of his daydreams had reached reality, and he had little to show for nearly two years of living off of the land, stealing everything that he needed and answering to no one but himself. Finally, at twenty-two years of age, with nothing to show for his scattered efforts in thievery, he had been forced to resume working for someone; something he had sworn he would never do again. He was a ranch hand for the Circle S ranch. He didn't much like ranch work, but he had mistakenly blundered into the job. He had been caught one late night sneaking into one of the corrals on the ranch, intending to make off with a horse or two to sell. But he had been seen by a night watch ranch hand, and Henry had been forced to tell him a story that he was looking for work. To the surprise of Henry, he was put to work the following morning. That had been nearly a year ago; and in that year of 1861, a great deal happened in the United States, not the least of which was the admittance of the state of Kansas, which had declared itself a free state, into the union and the firing on Fort Sumter by Union gunboats in the harbor of Charleston, South Carolina. It would be quite some time before this news reached the ears of men working the ranches on the prairies of Middle America. And frankly, if these events had been told to Henry Vogler, he would have merely shrugged them off. They meant nothing to him.

Henry had to admit that he found the work to be easy. He was tall and strong, easily able to complete any task assigned to him by the foreman. And he had grown to enjoy the company of several of the cowboys and vaqueros with whom he shared the ranch bunkhouse. His needs were simple. Three meals a day (most days), a roof over his head, and a place to stable Zeke were pretty much all he needed. On paydays when the hands went to town, Henry would go with them. He usually drank a couple beers and returned to the ranch. With such light spending, he had saved a bit of his wages to add to his stash.

Under thickening clouds, a slight, cold mist had begun and Henry thought of unlashing his poncho, but decided he would take care of some personal business before he donned the rain gear. He rode further from the herd and into a stand of oaks, where he slipped off of Zeke's back. He walked a few feet away and dropped his trousers and squatted. After completing his business, he rebuttoned his union suit flap and pulled up his trousers. As he clasped the belt buckle to rehook it to the belt, he saw them coming. A group of horsemen were rapidly riding toward him. He quickly strode to Zeke and remounted. But before he could spur the mule, the group of horsemen surrounded him. In the dark mist, which was falling heavier now, he could not make out their faces.

One of the men spoke out. "Who are you, boy, and what are you doing here?" Henry had a feeling that this chance meeting was not going to bode well for him.

Lately, the talk in the bunkhouse at night had been of a war that had started between states. The Oklahoma Territory was a land set aside for the Indians, but the Confederacy saw the territory as a source for feeding the Confederate Army with food, material, and men. The various Indian tribes in the territory were split in their alliances with either the Confederacy or the Union. The prosperous ranchers in the territory were finding it difficult to simply remain neutral and continue ranching. The other bunkhouse topic centered on the roving bands of conscription enforcers. These were roving patrols set up by the Confederate military to physically conscript men by force to feed the Confederacy's desperate need for soldiers. The ranch hands had been warned to run for the protection of other ranch hands if any of these patrols were sighted, or face being forcefully recruited to serve in the Confederate Army. A knot rose in Henry's throat as he answered.

"My name is Vogler, and I'm a hand on the Circle S, sir; and you are on our ranch land."

His accosters were unimpressed as Henry heard a few of them chuckling. "That's all I wanted to hear," said the same voice. "You're going with us."

One of the men in the group roughly grabbed Zeke's reigns while another one slapped the mule on the rump. They allowed him to keep his pistol, as it would be futile on Henry's part to attempt to shoot his way to freedom with the number of men surrounding him. One of the men loudly said, "You're a Confederate soldier now, boy. Welcome to the Army."

# Chapter Twenty-Two

**March 4, 1862 - Late evening**
**North of Fayetteville, Arkansas**

Throughout the day and into the night, stragglers drifted into the encampment. They were the remnants of skirmishes that had been fought all around Fayetteville in the past few days. The entire contingent under the command of Brigadier General McCulloch ranged across a ridge far to the north of the city. They were watching the flames leap into the night as Fayetteville was torched and burned to the ground by McCulloch's men to prevent the pursuing Union forces from obtaining any of the town's resources.

McCulloch's Army was made up primarily of men from Texas, Arkansas, and Louisiana. A sullen Henry Vogler sat with his platoon watching the flames into the night. He gnawed on a piece of hardtack. He was sick of the fare of the soldiers. His whole body ached from days of marching, and he seethed inwardly as he watched his company's captain riding Zeke in a slow walk throughout the campsite. He had been as mad as he had ever been in his life in February when he was told that his beloved mule now belonged to the Confederate States of America and that only officers rode horses and mules. Henry had yelled at the men who forcefully took him from the saddle. He had watched as the pompous, belittling captain had mounted Zeke. He had yelled at the captain then that if he ever hurt his mule, he would kill the captain. For a week after that incident, Henry had been kept under armed guard as the Army had marched eastward.

In the early morning of the day following the burning of Fayetteville, the Confederates began marching northward. On the afternoon of March sixth, the Army assumed a temporary position to rest for the night. It proved to be a cold, uncomfortable night for the Confederates. The morning of March 7 dawned, crisply cold, with a blue sky foretelling a beautiful day. Birds chattered in the nearby trees and bushes as they foraged for food. The Confederates rose and began marching east on Ford Road. Cavalry units led the column, and among that cavalry were Indians who had allied themselves with the Confederacy. Henry had been told that several different tribes including the Cherokees had joined the Confederate cavalry.

Henry plodded along with the rest of his company. He wore no uniform, nor did the majority of the men in his company. Like him, many of the men were conscripts, hastily gathered by conscript patrols that carried no uniforms for their detainees. He carried an Army issued rifle, powder and ball, his pistol rig, and his worn pack sack was strapped to his back. Every step brought an ache from his feet. His anger bubbled just beneath the surface. His mind was occupied with only one thought, as it had been for the past two months. He must find a way to escape. But he was not going to leave on foot. He knew that if he walked, he would be recaptured before he could get away from the camp, and he would not leave without his mule, Zeke.

At noon, when the Army was to take a short rest, they were attacked. Union cannons began shelling the Confederate troops that were strung out along the road, and well-hidden Union skirmishers were systematically picking off the Confederate soldiers. Smoke rose from the firing as the Confederate infantry took cover in trees and bushes and began firing at random. The company captain rode across the infantry's line brandishing a saber and shouting pompous encouragement, which fell on deaf ears. He had no effect on the panicked soldiers under his command. In fact, even the captain had no idea exactly where the Union forces were. In a short time, the smoke was so thick that visibility was down to twenty-five yards or less. Henry saw his chance.

He was hunkered down behind a stout tree stump. He had not fired his rifle as there was no visible target. Soldiers were spread out to his sides, and they were firing haphazardly and reloading to fire yet more futile shots. Henry cradled his rifle on his arm, waiting patiently. His target approached. The rifle kicked as the trigger was pulled, and Henry watched as the company captain slumped in the saddle. Henry held on to his rifle, sprang up, ran to Zeke's side, and pulled the dying captain from the saddle with his free hand. He then jumped up onto the saddle, grabbed Zeke's reins, and kicked the mule. Zeke bolted and began running to the rear of the Confederate line in smoke so thick that no one could see the identity of the rider galloping past them. Henry did not slow the mule until the sound of firing guns could be only faintly heard above Zeke's heavy breathing.

On the following day, Henry continued to distance himself from the Confederate Army. And on that same day, back at the location where he had deserted, near a place the soldiers called Pea Ridge, along a stream they called Little Sugar Creek, Union forces drove the defeated Confederate Army from the field of battle. Thousands of the Confederate soldiers deserted and began long journeys on foot to return to their homes. Many would be forcefully conscripted again to return to other battlefields; but not Henry Vogler.

Henry gave no thought to his having murdered his Confederate Captain. He looked on the incident as simple payback for having been forcibly conscripted into the Army. And besides, he reasoned, he greatly disliked the pompous captain who had taken Zeke for his own use.

*\*\**

For several days following his desertion, Henry had been travelling generally in a southwesterly direction. He had now surmised that travelling during daylight was extremely risky. He searched for cover in which to hide during the day, and he travelled at night. He slept lightly, and from his hiding places, he had observed bands of men roaming about during the day. Many were walking deserters from both sides of the war; but others were mounted, armed, and dangerous. He had also seen Indian hunting parties, many of them dressed in discarded Confederate Army clothing. He reverted to his prior means of subsistence; when the opportunity arose, he stole what he needed. But after travelling for only two weeks, Henry once again found himself at the mercy of another group of men.

Like all travelers on the frontier, water was a necessity. Neither man nor animal could survive very long without it. This led to the common practice of travelers camping at or near water; be it lake, river, or stream. Unfortunately, Henry followed this practice so that Zeke could forage, and they could both have water. It was in such a place that he had camped in a grove of trees and bushes, giving him cover from anyone passing. He was dozing on a soft grass clump when he heard the sound of metal ringing on harness and the soft thud of horses walking. Henry bolted upright, looked all around him, but still did not see the riders. He ran to Zeke, removed a rope with which he had tied the mule to a sapling, and led the animal into a thicker growth of bushes. He held Zeke's nose to keep him from whinnying.

Now he could see them. There was a group of riders, all well-armed, moving to the north. Three of them were riding close to the stream. Where Henry had been lying, two of the men stopped their horses. They were talking quietly and looking at Zeke's fresh droppings on the ground. When the third man joined his companions, all three of the men began peering intently into the surrounding vegetation. One of them was looking directly toward Henry.

"C'mon out of there, mister. Else we'll blast you out," said the man. The other two had raised their rifles to aim in Henry's direction. It was no use to think otherwise. They had seen him. Henry slowly led Zeke back to the stream edge. Other riders now joined the group. Henry studied the men, each of whom had a firearm pointed in his direction. No one in the group wore a uniform, so he reasoned that they were not a conscript patrol. Neither did he see anyone wearing a badge, so they were not law men. Henry figured that they must be outlaws of some sort.

"Well now. What do we have here," the apparent leader of the men said. "Where you from, boy?"

Henry's mind was working. "Texas," he answered. He did not even know why he picked Texas.

"Where from in Texas," asked the outlaw.

"San Antonio," Henry answered, "and I'm headed back home."

"Well, then. Where've you been?"

Henry was unsure how to answer, but he figured that he could tell part of the story. "I'm coming from Arkansas; a place called Pea Ridge. I was in the Confederate Army."

"Hmm. What was the name of your General?"

"I'm not sure, sir. But I heard someone say McCulloch. I think that was him," said Henry. He noticed that most of the men were now holstering their pistols. His interrogator still held his in a ready position. "The Yankees sort of routed my company and regiment, and the Army broke up and scattered. I thought maybe it was a good time to head for home."

One of the men laughed and said, "A deserter!"

Henry bristled. "I ain't no deserter. There wasn't any Army left to go back to," he said. In his mind he knew this was untrue, and in fact, he had deserted.

"Where'd you get that mule, boy?"

Henry stared straight at the man. "He's mine. I bought him before I went to the war. I even let my company captain ride him in the fighting. And when the captain got shot, I took my mule back and headed for home."

Several of the men now laughed.

"What have you been living on, boy?" asked the man.

Henry was getting madder. "None of your damn business, but I get by," said Henry.

The group again laughed. The leader had drawn the same conclusion that the other men had. He knew that Henry was an outlaw. It was unlikely that anyone would have given that answer unless he was stealing from others to get by.

Henry's bravado had come to the surface. "Who are you guys, anyhow," he asked.

The men murmured among themselves and chuckled. The leader spat to the ground. "I don't reckon we have any name. Some folks call us 'bushwhackers,' but I don't cotton much to that handle. Don't hurt me any though," he said. "You see, we prefer to think of ourselves as an extension of the Confederate Army. The Army likes to fight on a battlefield, but we prefer to fight among the people, where the poison is easier to neutralize."

The outlaw continued. "Now, boy, do you still believe in the cause of the Confederacy?"

In truth, Henry didn't give a whit for either the Confederacy or the Union, but he was smart enough to know that if he did not answer this question correctly that he could face more trouble. "Yes, I guess so. It's as good as any other, I suppose."

"Not a very strong answer, boy. But I'm going to give you a choice." He lowered his pistol to point at Henry. "If you truly believe in the Confederate cause, you either come along and ride with us, or I put a bullet in your head right now." The pistol in the man's hand did not waver, and he stared straight into Henry's eyes.

For a few seconds, Henry just stared at the outlaw leader. Then he turned and climbed up on Zeke.

"Let's go men. Quantrill is waiting for us," said the leader.

# Chapter Twenty-Three

**September 4, 1862**
**Ten miles southwest of Olathe, Kansas**

The evil that manifested itself in Henry Vogler's soul was now displayed openly. He was a murderous, thieving outlaw who had been riding with William Quantrill's bushwhacking raiders for nearly six months. They were wanted by every law enforcement agency in the area. That is, all law enforcement agencies that were abolitionist. And at times, it was extremely difficult to tell which parts of Missouri and Kansas were abolitionist, and which were pro-slavery. These opposing views often varied from county to county, city to city, and neighbor to neighbor, resulting in scores of murders and mayhem.

Quantrill's Raiders, a fluidic army of men who joined the group, often left the group, and rejoined again when it was convenient in their personal lives, could sometimes count as many as three hundred men in the group at any given time. Generally the group was much smaller. Presently, the raiders were camped on a rise from which they could see anyone or any group approaching.

William Quantrill held a high opinion of himself, even calling himself General. In truth, Quantrill and his men had been officially mustered into the Confederate Army only a month prior. The Army had responded to Quantrill's successful decimation of the Union Army camp at Independence, Missouri, and rewarded him and his men by making Quantrill a captain in the Confederate Army. Quantrill and his men operated as a guerilla band, using hit-and-run tactics against their targets. Their usual modus operandi was to swoop down on a known abolitionist farm, settlement, or town, killing the men in the group, robbing the people, and burning down said farm, settlement, or town after stealing the provisions they needed. They had little fear of apprehension. No area law enforcement agency was large enough to take them on, and the bands of abolitionist Jayhawkers were too few, and not large enough for anything but minor skirmishes with the raiders.

Henry Vogler had found a home in the raiders. Although he was apolitical, he had no qualms against robbing and killing. Just like the rest of his fellow raiders, he wore his evil on display and with pride.

***

The scouts had watched the town of Olathe for three days. The community was known for its established stance of being part of a free state and embracing abolition. Unfortunately, this drew the attention of William Quantrill and his raiders. They meant to teach the town a lesson.

Like most small towns in the area, Olathe was protected only by a small-town sheriff and no Army troops. On the night of September 6-7, Quantrill and the roughly one hundred and forty men with him descended upon Olathe. For the next several hours the town was terrorized. Houses and businesses were broken into, with anything of value taken by the raiders, who used deadly force as necessary. Money, jewelry, and food were prime targets, and oddly enough, pictures of young women. Quantrill was fond of these pictures and added them to his collection. Horses and mules were stolen, and pack horses were loaded with stolen goods. Finally, nearly every building in the town had been burned to the ground. Six people were murdered in cold blood. Three of them were civilians protecting their families and belongings, and the other three were young men who had recently enlisted in the Union Army. The spoils of the murderous raid were later divided among the men who had participated, including Henry Vogler.

# Chapter Twenty-Four

**August 1863 - Mount Oread**
**Outside Lawrence, Kansas**

The bushwhackers' group, with William Quantrill in command, had grown on this day to nearly four hundred men. Quantrill was making ready to exact his own form of misguided revenge once again.

As a result of a Union Army general order issued in May 1863, anyone in the Missouri and Kansas area who was guilty of aiding Quantrill's guerrilla band was to be imprisoned. Consequently, many of Quantrill's men had relatives locked in a jail in Kansas City. Among them was the sister of Bloody Bill Anderson, one of Quantrill's lieutenants, two cousins of Cole Younger, the wife of another member of the raiders, and several other relatives and friends. They were housed in a jail that was unsafe to such a degree that it collapsed, killing the aforementioned sympathizers. Quantrill meant to take retribution.

Early in the morning on August 21, the murderous force of four hundred men descended on the sleeping town of Lawrence, Kansas. Henry had aligned himself with four other men. As they moved into Lawrence, they streaked past the groups of men who were already breaking into houses, ransacking those homes, looting, and beating the residents. Henry's group stopped at a house, and the four men dismounted and entered the building. A shot rang out as Henry crossed the threshold of the home. The lead ball entered Henry's right leg just below the knee. It ripped through the muscle and tendons, fractured the tibia, nearly breaking it into two pieces, and exited the rear of his lower leg. Henry stumbled and fell. He looked up to see a young boy, only twelve years old, holding a smoking pistol in his hand. Henry's own pistol rang out, filling the room with the horrible loud report. The young boy fell, dead in seconds after the lead ball struck him in the face. Henry's companions soon found the parents of the boy and killed both of them.

In four terrible hours, the raiders turned the town into a blazing inferno, looting and burning everything in their path. One hundred and eighty men and boys were killed. One of those murders was committed by Henry Vogler.

Henry's companions tore strips of clothing from the dead occupants in the house they had ransacked. They wrapped Henry's wound tightly with the strips of cloth and hoisted him onto Zeke. Immediately, they strode back to the house, doused the living area with coal oil, and torched it. The house was ablaze as they walked their horses from Lawrence. Henry's leg wound caused him excruciating pain as he determinedly kept up with the raiders making their way west, deeper into Kansas.

The Union Army lost no time in pursuing Quantrill and his sympathizers. Their relentless pursuit kept the raiders on the run, pushing them farther to the west, away from the Kansas/Missouri border. With no respite from the Union Army pursuit, Quantrill decided to double back and rest his forces behind Confederate lines. The plan was for the raiders to pass through Oklahoma and head into Texas. Enroute, they entered Baxter Springs, Kansas, in the southeast corner of the state. The Union Army had built a fort at that location, and Quantrill and Bloody Bill Anderson decided to try their hand at attacking the fort. Their attack was thwarted by the Union Army within the fort. But an unfortunate Army patrol that was in the process of returning to the fort was swarmed upon by the raiders. One hundred three soldiers were killed before the raiders resumed their trek south. Henry sat astride Zeke and stoically watched his cohorts kill the Union soldiers. His injury prevented him from more actively participating.

In the winter of 1863, the raiders crossed the Red River into Texas. They entered Mineral Springs, Texas, where they would spend the cold months of winter.

\*\*\*

Most of the men had been camped along the Sulphur River for nearly a month. Quantrill and his lieutenants stayed in town where Quantrill had befriended a family and their thirteen-year-old daughter. There were rumors circulating in the camp that Quantrill meant to marry the girl.

One of Henry's comrades had helped him construct a crude set of crutches, enabling Henry to hobble to meals and to a community latrine. His leg was healing, but painfully and slowly. As the bone knitted, small pieces of the leg bone were missing, causing the leg to have a slight abnormal curve. As a result, Henry walked with his weight on the outside of his foot on that leg and would always walk with a noticeable limp. A skilled surgeon could have repaired Henry's wound at the time of its incurrence, but because the wound was never attended to by a physician, bone chips remained in the leg. The combination of misaligned bone and bone fragments in the leg would cause him pain for the rest of his life.

With more time on his hands while in the recuperative process, Henry spent hours reliving memories. He slowly began to recognize that he was a failure, and that very fact disgusted him. Yet he continued to cling to the hope that someday he would become rich by carrying out some sort of nefarious plan.

When he was finally able, Henry began to distance himself from his comrades. Some of his acquaintances good naturedly began teasing him and calling him a hermit. Next to a creek feeder to the river, he built himself a small crawl-in shelter made from mesquite branches and leaves, and used discarded ponchos as a roof from the rain. Zeke was tethered nearby. His thoughts became more introspective, and he thought more and more that his life had become meaningless. He had grown weary of the company of outlaws, with little to show for his crimes but a pair of worn-out boots and a tired mule. In another ten days, he felt that his leg was strong enough. Early one morning when the sun had just lit the eastern sky, he bade farewell to a couple of the men whom he had befriended, pointed Zeke in a southwesterly direction, and rode away from the Quantrill raiders.

# Chapter Twenty-Five

**April 1864 - San Francisco de la Espada**
**San Antonio, Texas**

Every day, Henry sat on the same rickety chair at the rough-hewn table where he could look out the door of the cantina. He was facing the old mission and could casually watch the faithful enter through the large wooden door to attend morning mass within the mission walls. The mission itself had not changed in the past forty years, but Henry did not know that. He had no idea that he was looking at the institution that had played a large role in the life of his father and uncle. In fact, he barely remembered his father, and he did not know that he had once had an uncle. All he knew was that this was an old church, and the woman came here every day. His hand was stroking his sore knee and lower leg as he rested the leg on an adjacent chair. He took another sip of the strong, hot coffee. His hand then unconsciously moved into his pocket, where his thumb gently rubbed the face of the gold locket.

His mother had not been hard to find. Her name was on a painted sign hanging above the door of a dress shop that she owned. Unseen, he had watched Beth Vogler for several days. He knew where she lived, he knew the hours she kept at her shop, he knew where she took her meals, and he knew that she went to mass each morning at Mission Espada.

Every night he spent time in a saloon, slowly drinking until he was inebriated, then allowing one of the prostitutes to lead him by the arm to her room. He had lost track of the number of women with whom he had consorted in the last several days. But each morning he slowly regained his sobriety and sat in the restaurant.

He had occupied the same chair and table for four consecutive days and had watched his mother as she entered the mission. She was smaller than he remembered, and she had a short, purposeful walk. Her red hair still shown from beneath her hat, but the hair now had some lighter streaks mixed in with the red. This morning, he waited, drinking another mug of coffee until he saw her retrace her steps as she left the mission and turned to go to her shop. Each time he saw her exit the mission and walk from his view, his stomach turned, and it was all he could do to check himself from shedding a tear. In three more days, without ever meeting with his mother, he left San Antonio and headed north.

***

In the evening of the day that Henry left town, Beth Vogler turned the key in the lock of the front door of her dress shop. She bid good night to one of her seamstresses as they both departed the shop at the end of the day. She began the walk to her small casita that she rented from a grocer friend and her husband. On the way, she turned in at their store, greeted the couple, and picked out her dinner to take home. She had seen the oranges the grocer had received yesterday from the southern valley, and she picked one of them and asked the grocer to cut a small slice of ham for her. She then selected two, freshly baked hard rolls. One would be her supper with the ham, and she planned to have the orange for dessert. The other roll she would save for her breakfast. Beth paid for the items, chatted for a moment with her friend, and left the store. She walked several blocks down a side street, finally reaching her house.

It had been a busy day, and she was tired. She entered the front door, closed and locked the door behind her, and took her food to the kitchen. She then walked to the rear of the house to her bedroom, where the curtain moved ever so slightly in the breeze from the partially open window she had left open for ventilation during the day. She removed her hat and jacket and laid them on the bed. She would hang them up when she returned from the kitchen later. As she turned to make her way to the kitchen, her eyes glanced to her dresser and caught sight of an item that was out of place. She was not able to see it clearly and lit a small oil lamp. Then, looking more closely, she picked up the item. It was the gold locket that she had been wearing over seven years ago; the locket she had been wearing the last time she had seen her son, Henry; the locket that had been forcefully taken from her neck by Henry. She drew a quick breath, and nearly involuntarily, she quickly looked behind her and then slowly peered into the parlor. There was no one there, of course. Her eyes returned to the locket. A cascade of thoughts crossed her mind as her thumb idly rubbed across the smooth gold front of the locket. A tear grew and dropped upon her hand that held the hitherto nearly forgotten piece of jewelry.

# Chapter Twenty-Six

## December 1865 - Mission San Francisco de la Espada
## San Antonio, Texas

Beth Vogler voluntarily helped out on Sunday afternoons at the nursery in the Espada Mission; a pastime that she thoroughly enjoyed. On this particular Sunday, there was great joy in her heart as she watched the toddler fall once again on his rump as he attempted to walk unsteadily across the floor in the nursery of the Espada Mission. The little toddler had taken his first steps only a few days before, and Beth watched him in adoration. The baby she was watching was very special to Beth. Although it could not be proven, it was her grandson; she was sure of it. She had known it the first time she had seen the child eleven months ago, and she had wept when she saw the baby. With his wispy red hair and blue eyes, she could see her late husband and her son in the face of the baby.

As a newborn, the baby had been voluntarily submitted to the care of the mission by a woman known to work in a sporting house, and who was unable to keep a child born to her out of wedlock. The father of the child was unknown. But from the time that had passed from when she had discovered the gold locket on her dresser, Beth knew. Over the following weeks after first seeing the baby, she had quietly made arrangements with the senior priest to adopt the child. Only she and the priest shared Beth's secret belief that the baby was her grandson. The process had taken several weeks, but Samuel Vogler was now Beth's adopted son. Each Sunday when she returned to the mission to help in the nursery, little Samuel came with her, enabling her to keep an eye on him while helping with the other children who were still awaiting adoption. And each time she visited the mission, she knelt in prayer to thank the Lord who had made it possible for her to have another blessed chance to raise a son to manhood.

# Chapter Twenty-Seven

**Fall, 1868 - Majestic Saloon**
**Perryville, Oklahoma/Indian Territory**

Back in 1866, after Henry's two year absence from the Circle S during the war, the old foreman of the Circle S had moved on, and a new foreman, Hiram Mullins, had taken his place. Lean and leathery, Mullins had all the signs of a man who had spent his life riding a horse and herding recalcitrant steers. He was short, bow-legged, and minced no words; that is, what words he spoke. A soggy chaw of tobacco was usually bulging out one of his cheeks, and he did not much care where the resultant brown spittle landed as he expectorated the tobacco juice. The cow hands respected their foreman and, as a rule, stayed in line. If they did not, Mullins had no qualms about firing the offender. Even though he was not the owner of the spread, his word among the cow hands on the ranch was the law.

In 1866, when Henry had ridden north from San Antonio, he had returned to the Circle S to look for work. On that occasion, no words came out of Mullins' mouth. He was simply looking at the hombre who had shown up at the ranch riding a mule and asking for a job. Hiram turned his head slightly and let fly with a large brown globule, then turned his head back to face Henry. The war had decimated the ranks of the physically fit, and most of the young cowboys had either been conscripted or had gone on their own to fight in a war that Hiram Mullins could not understand, was too old to fight in, and didn't care about. With such a shortage of men on the ranch, in truth, Hiram would have hired a three-legged jackrabbit if it had been able to herd cattle.

"Conscripted, eh," said Mullins, after Henry had told him the story of being taken off of the ranch at the hands of the conscription patrol two years ago. In his narrative, Henry was careful not to mention his time with Quantrill's raiders, or the true nature of the cause for the injury to his leg. Mullins continued to eye Henry. "I might give you a chance, but that gimpy leg of yours better not slow you down, 'else you might need to look for other work," said Hiram. Following further minimal discussion, and an attestation by two of the old hands who remembered him and his mule, Henry had been placed on the payroll of the Circle S.

\*\*\*

If he was not assigned to the small group of cowboys who stayed at the ranch on Saturday night after payday to watch over the herd, Henry could be found at the bar in the *Majestic Saloon* drinking part of his wages. In addition to a couple of the other ranch hands at the bar, a woman dressed in the gaudy attire of a lady of the evening also stood by Henry's side, hanging on his arm, encouraging him to finish his drink so that they could retire to a room on the second floor of the establishment.

For the past two years, now that Henry had been working at the Circle S, he had been seen keeping company at the bar with comely blonde Renee Evans on the nights he was able to leave the Circle S. The two of them had developed a rapport, not necessarily based on any true love for each other; more simply, they both seemed to enjoy each other's company. Both were life-hardened and soul-deadened, and neither held any concrete illusions of ever pulling themselves higher on life's social ladder. In spite of their individual cynical outlooks on life, they each held a personal dream. Henry's was that he knew that at some point in his life he would have the opportunity to become rich enough to never work again and never answer to anybody else. He meant to fulfill that dream either honestly or dishonestly if the opportunity arose.

Renee's dream was simpler. She wanted to find a man to take care of her and raise a family. The man's financial standing was not all that important to her, since other than when she had absconded with some of her estranged husband's wealth, she had never had more than ten dollars at any one time in her life. She just wanted to stop making a paltry living on her back for the pleasure of drunken cowboys. Her greatest dream was to be accepted as a wife and mother. Renee Evans saw Henry as a possible means to achieve that simple goal.

Renee Evans was a strong-willed woman. She was physically and mentally tough. Even as young as she was, she did not like being crossed and would do everything in her power to get even with the offender. For example, when she was still Sarah Colson and living in Chicago, she had schemed and planned and finally run from a brutish, wife-beating husband after relieving him of cash and other small assets in order to have the cash, clothes, and means to make her escape. She had changed her name to Renee Evans and travelled under that assumed name until she finally alighted from a stagecoach at Perryville. Just looking around at the run down settlement, Renee Evans knew she had found a home where her husband would never look for her. But the prospects of employment for a woman with no work experience, and the fact that she had assets that were always in demand by amorous, reveling cowboys, had driven her to take an offered position at the *Majestic*. Initially, she had been disgusted with her plight, but as she realized that she had a steady stream of customers and revenue, she swallowed a bit of her pride. Even though she was working in a trade that was held in low esteem by the clergy and the lady folk of the settlement, she kept her inner spirit alive and never gave up her simple dream of companionship and motherhood.

In Henry, Renee had initially seen just another cowboy coming to town to get drunk and take his pleasure with the sporting women. But as she grew to know him better, she could see that he was not as transparent as the other men she had known. No matter how much time she spent with him, Henry did not reveal his inner self, as if he was holding something back. He was a mystery to her, and she liked mysteries. She had only seen the darkness rise in Henry one time, when a drunken cowboy jostled him at the bar and caused him to spill a drink. A trivial happening, but Henry had become so enraged that he punched the drunken cowboy to the floor. Renee thought little about it; just another disagreement between cowboys on a Saturday night at the bar. Nor did she know anything about his background and the truly evil deeds that he had committed, including the wanton murder of a young boy. Over time, she would come to learn that Henry was not the quiet, unassuming fellow she had initially thought he was.

But on this cool, fall, Saturday evening, Renee was once again at Henry's side at the bar in the *Majestic*. The evening was drawing to a close, and the couple finally left the bar and went to Renee's room. It wasn't much of a room really. Rough plank floors, a simple bed with a ruffled spread, colored in a pink and light green floral pattern, a dresser, its top covered in female potion bottles of assorted sizes and shapes, a night stand with an oil lamp, and a chair that faced the only window, which looked out beyond the back of the *Majestic* where Renee watched the sun come up on those mornings when sleep eluded her. A small wardrobe held the meager assortment of hanging clothes of a working girl. A heavy, cast-metal bed pan could be seen under the bed. The window was open slightly to allow the cool fresh air to enter.

The couple lay in the bed, a thin sheen of sweat covering their bodies. As usual, there was no talking in their post-coital bliss. In a moment, Renee left the bed and reached out to the chair to retrieve a light robe. Henry watched dispassionately as Renee's ample, pink breasts rose and fell as she bent to pick up the robe and put it on. She then walked over and closed the window. She was feeling the chill of the night air crossing her damp body. She quickly tied the robe closed, jumped back into the bed, and curled up next to Henry.

Henry's eyes were heavy, and he dozed while Renee continued to talk quietly to him. He wasn't paying much attention, and this was the way most all of their nights ended when they were together. He quietly mumbled, seeming to agree with whatever it was she was talking about.

As morning light crept into the window, Renee was far too excited to sit in her chair and watch the sunrise. Instead, she had roused two of her girlfriends who occupied adjoining rooms. Laughing and shouting they all burst into Renee's room and jumped on the bed where Henry still lay inert. He slowly roused to the excitement, but not yet fully awake, he still did not quite understand their revelry. However, he soon learned the reason.

He did not have any recollection of any serious discussion last night, but apparently there had been some sort of understanding on the part of Renee that he had agreed to be married. Henry remained stunned, trying to keep the flimsy bed sheet covering himself while the three giddy women continued bouncing on the bed. The same thought kept whirling in his head; what the hell had happened last night?

Initially Henry thought if he just sat up and slapped Renee a few times, he might be able to remove her giddy thoughts of marriage. Repressing that plan, he then thought that he could simply run away rather than abandon bachelorhood. In the end, and very much against his nature, he decided that marriage might not be so bad, but he refused to be rushed into it.

News of the pending nuptials spread through the bar and the Circle S, and within two months, Renee had moved out to the Circle S to be with Henry.

***

There was not a great deal of native timber available, but with the consent of the owner of the Circle S, and the help of some of the other cow hands, a crude log-sided shack was hastily constructed where it could not be seen from the main ranch house. Renee moved in immediately upon its completion. In the beginning, she asked Henry nearly every day about setting a date to be married. Henry continually stonewalled her, and before long, Renee slowly came to the realization that Henry was probably never going to marry her. She resigned herself into thinking that maybe it just did not matter anyway. She had a man to take care of her, and on the coldest day of the winter of 1869, Elmer Vogler, another in the continuing line of Voglers born out of wedlock, made his appearance in the small shack on the Circle S Ranch. Two years later, Martin Vogler, with a lusty bawl, joined his brother. Renee Evans loved her little boys with all her heart. Be she ever so locked into harsh poverty and even more humble living conditions, Renee was reasonably happy with her life. She was living her simple dream.

Renee lived under the blissful disillusion that when she went to town for supplies each week, the women of Perryville respected her as a wife and mother, placing her in satisfactory social standing. What she could not know was that the stigma of being a whore did not go away simply by having two babies with the man she lived with. Because she had never married, nothing would change in that regard, but Renee was oblivious to the guarded, disdainful looks from other women.

While the mother of his children was content, Henry was not. He felt trapped and had to stretch every cent to feed the four of them. He greatly disliked being beholden to the owner of the Circle S for his generosity of allowing the family to live on an unused parcel of land. And he was not truly interested in his family. He used Renee for pleasure and took only a mild interest in the raising of the boys, leaving their welfare to their mother's loving and nurturing. But things would take a turn for the better for the couple in the following years.

# Chapter Twenty-Eight

**February 1876 - Summer Prairie Ranch**
**Outside of Tioga, Kansas Territory**

The relentless ferocity of the cold weather would lead one to believe that this winter was never going to end. It had been unusually brutal, with a seemingly constant, howling wind blowing across the Kansas prairie, resulting in many days with a wind chill well below zero. Nearly a foot of snow remained on the ground from a white-out storm that had raged two days before, and the temperatures were well below freezing.

Robert Summers had spoken with his fellow ranchers after church a few days ago. Whenever the group got together, the conversation always centered on three topics. It never failed. The ranchers discussed the price of beef in Kansas City, the weather, and the prospects of the upcoming calving on their ranches. Those were the variables in their profession that would make or break a ranching operation. Rain provided the food for their beef stock, the price of beef on the hoof provided the income, and the calves that were born ensured the replenishment of livestock to sell. As a group, the ranchers always looked forward to calving time, and at this time in February, the calves were dropping in fine numbers.

To date, Robert and Virginia had been happy with this year's production of calves. But the numbing winter storm two days ago, with its continuing frigid wind was a great worry to them. The birthing of calves did not stop on account of the weather. Mother Nature made no proviso for difficult circumstances in birthing of calves. As a result, if the cows did not find shelter for themselves and their calves at the time of birthing, there was a chance that the icy wind could take the lives of the helpless calves, still wet from the birth process.

Worried as he was about his cows and calves, Robert had arisen at first light. As he pulled on his boots in the bedroom, he looked over at his wife, Virginia, as she continued to sleep. He watched for a few seconds as her obviously pregnant stomach rose and fell in her breathing. The couple had been trying for several years to have children of their own. Even though they had adopted Will, the expected baby would be the highlight of their marriage when it was born. He smiled to himself, rose, and went to Will's bedroom. For a few minutes, he watched the small black-haired little boy as he slept. He smiled again as he remembered how the boy had come into their lives.

Will Summers had lived on the Summer Prairie Ranch for two of his five years. The first three years of his life were now a faint lingering memory; a memory of travelling across the prairies, streams, and forest thickets with the native people, the Kansa tribe. The memories of the years with the Kansa people were fine memories of playing games with the other young children of the nomadic tribe and even at a very young age, beginning to learn the ways of nature and the skills of the native hunter and warrior.

Although his faint memories led Will to believe that he was a Kansa, in truth, Will was not an Indian at all. He had been kidnapped as an infant from a Mexican encampment by a roving band of Kansa hunters, who, after a victorious battle with the Mexican group, took the horses and two small children back to their camp to be raised in the native ways; a practice which was, sadly, very common. Will's Castilian features led the Kansa to believe that the boy was white, and therefore, considered to be an asset to the tribe. But another common practice was that slaves in Indian camps were traded by the nomadic people in exchange for something needed by the tribe. In the case of Will, he had subsequently been traded by the Kansa tribe to Robert Summers for two yearling beef calves. Virginia had taken to the boy, named him Will, and raised him as a part of the family. As far as she was concerned, Will was the son that she had been unable to conceive. The feeling was reciprocal, as Will now considered Virginia to be his mother.

The Summers' ranch was a close-knit family that included its seasoned cow hands. In addition, with personal oversight by Virginia, it was a well-run business operation. And because of the large number of deadly, straight-shooting cowhands on the ranch, the Kansa's and the Kiowa's, aside from occasionally rustling a fat steer or two, generally did not bother Summer Prairie Ranch, respecting Robert and Virginia Summers with whom they had bartered in the past.

Robert left Will's bedroom and continued on to the kitchen. He ate a quick, cold breakfast of biscuits and beans left over from the previous night's supper, donned his coat and gloves, and left the ranch house. He was dressed for the cold with a heavy wool coat, lined horse-hide gloves, and a wool hat with ear flaps. He went to the barn and saddled his favorite horse, pulling the cinch snugly to account for the cow pony's heavy winter coat of hair. He intended to ride to a thick grove of scrub trees to look at the cattle that were congregating there to escape the wind. He would be able to check the condition of the new calves as well as their mothers.

Robert shivered a bit as the biting wind crossed his face and entered his coat. His layers of shirts and the coat were no match for the relentless wind. He decided to hurry and get back to the house as soon as possible.

As he rode to the grove of trees, he needed to cross a wide, shallow creek. But as he approached the creek, mixed in with the sound of the whistling wind, he heard the unmistakable sounds of a cow in distress. The repeated bawling sounds of the cow could be heard with intermittent bleating of a calf. Robert reined his horse toward the sound and soon came upon the pair. They were standing in a location where the banks of the creek were higher. At the top of the bank, a lone, dead, windswept tree stood in stark contrast to the open sky. Below the tree, the creek had washed back the bank to reveal clusters of tangled tree roots. It was in this entanglement that the calf had somehow become wedged and trapped; unable to scramble free. Apparently, the careless calf had fallen from the top of the creek bank into the dry roots. The calf's mother stood bawling to the calf, as if she could bid the calf to free itself.

At the sight of Robert approaching on his horse, the cow moved away a few feet, but would not leave her calf. Robert dismounted and walked to the calf, while the vigilant cow watched his every move. Robert studied the situation for a few seconds and could see that two of the calf's legs were trapped in the roots. The legs were so tightly enmeshed that he was not sure he could extract the animal. He began trying to free the calf, but would need to lift it higher to get the legs clear of the roots. Ordinarily, Robert would have little trouble lifting a new calf, but the manner in which the animal was caught would not allow him to lift it high enough. Robert struggled mightily to save the calf, and he began sweating beneath his layers of clothing. On his last attempt to free the calf, he gave it all of the physical effort he could muster; and that is when he felt it. He felt the distinct pain in his chest, and the pain spread to his left arm. He cried out in pain and slumped against the calf, causing the calf to bawl.

A man who had worked around cattle for years should have known better. But Robert failed to heed some basic precautions. He should have roused one of the ranch hands to accompany him that morning, but had not wanted to disturb any of them so early. And because it was Sunday, the ranch hands were not expected to work that morning, also making him hesitate to ask one of them to accompany him. What he also overlooked was the fact that it was always a bad idea to get between a mother cow and her calf.

In great pain, as he slumped against the calf, from the corner of his eye he saw twelve hundred pounds of furious cow charging toward him. In the next instant, the cow's horns had raked him to the side, causing him to fall on his back. The shock of his body harshly striking the frozen ground finished the heart attack, which had started with Robert's exertion in trying to free the calf. The beating of his heart ebbed, pulsated for several seconds and stopped. Robert Summers had succumbed to heart failure.

They found him several hours later. His cow pony stood near the dead man's body, its rump turned into the wind, its reins lying on the ground. Nearby, they found the dead calf, itself a victim of its struggles to be free from the root ball that still had it entrapped. The calf's mother had moved away, somehow knowing that she was no longer needed to look after the calf. The cow stood ten yards away, curiously looking on as Robert's body was lifted and tied onto his horse on a windy, cold, February day.

Virginia Summers would now take over managing Summer Prairie Ranch. After some misgiving on their part, the ranch hands came to admire their strong-willed, fair, and loving "boss lady." In spite of her crushing grief, Virginia was determined to continue to build Summer Prairie Ranch into a highly successful business.

# Chapter Twenty-Nine

**June 1888 - Circle S Ranch**
**Outside Perryville, Oklahoma/Indian Territory**

Henry had now been with the ranch for many years. He had reached the age of forty-eight; well past the usual end of productive years in the life of a cow hand. He was well aware that he could not keep up this life much longer. It was hard, dangerous work and his body was slightly bent with the strenuous routine. Every day when he woke up on the hard, only slightly padded bed platform next to Renee, his leg pained him greatly. As the muscles and tendons stretched and warmed, the pain subsided to simply be bothersome, and he continued to do his share of the work. And because he had no other place to go, Henry had outlasted numerous other cowboys. Many of them had left the ranch during the war years and did not return. Some left to take other work. Others had been injured or even killed in the strenuous work. But Henry had been lucky during his tenure with the ranch.

Two years ago, Hiram Mullins had taken ill to the point that he was not able to eat, nor could he do his job in a satisfactory manner. With an undiagnosed severe stomach ailment, he spent a large part of his time sitting in a chair on the porch of the bunk house. His only nourishment had been a few drams of straight whiskey each day. And as those days had passed, the cowboys had watched their foreman shrivel up and die before their eyes. He had been buried with little ceremony on a small rise in a grove of trees west of the main ranch house.

Much to his surprise, upon the death of Hiram Mullins, Henry Vogler had been made foreman of the Circle S; a position for which he may have been suited based on his experience, but one for which he was sorely lacking in the rudiments of handling the cowhands. Apparently, the owner of the Circle S based his selection of a new foreman on Henry's longevity. Another factor may have been that Henry did not display any distinguishable empathy or sentimentality, traits which the ranch owner thought might interfere with getting the job done as foreman. The fact that Henry had three other mouths to feed only fleetingly crossed the owner's mind.

Just as good cowhands could judge the temperament of a horse or a steer in order to avoid a chance of injury from a foul-tempered critter, they could also judge the character of men. The consensus of the Circle S hands was that they were none too keen on Henry Vogler. There was a dark and somewhat secretive side to Henry that the men had observed when Henry was still a cow hand. It exhibited itself periodically in the form of a violent temper and a seeming lack of scruples. Henry had never allowed himself to become close to any of the other hands. Oh, certainly he was congenial with all of them, but never allowed any of them to be a true friend. Unlike with Hiram Mullins, the men only had conditional trust in their foreman. Henry was astute enough to know that he was not highly regarded by the men, but he simply did not care. He was making a little bit of extra money, had his own shack some distance from the crew's bunk house, did not have to work as hard as the general hands, and enjoyed taking a wayward cow hand to task when necessary. As the cow hands would say only to each other when Henry was out of range of hearing, "He is damn hard to live with!"

\*\*\*

The flies were especially bothersome that summer. Zeke shook his head and switched his short tail from side to side as the flies tried to attack his skin and eyes. Even though he was the ranch foreman, Henry still preferred to ride Zeke, even though he was gently ribbed by the ranch owner regarding his choice of mounts. He sat astride the mule, peering into a corral where a group of three dusty cowhands were unsuccessfully attempting to break a horse. They were taking turns jumping on the back of the bronc, only to quickly find themselves on the ground, lying on their backs looking up at the sky. Eventually, the men would prevail, and the mustang would join the ranch remuda.

Zeke was nearing nineteen years of age. Much of the hair on his forehead and muzzle had turned to white. Just like his owner, he was stiff in the morning, and was not nearly as fast as he had been previously. Henry knew the end of the mule's working days was drawing near, and he had already purchased a young partially-broken two year old mule to take Zeke's place. When he felt the time was right, he would turn Zeke out into the grasslands to live out the rest of his life. Henry could not bear to shoot what he considered to be his most faithful friend. Henry softly kicked Zeke and guided the mule to another corral some distance from the breaking corral. This corral contained four more horses and a mule. This was the stock being held for breaking. Henry had already named the new gray mule Johnny, a name that had come to him one day when he was riding a portion of the ranch boundary. A gelded mule is often referred to as a John Mule, and since Henry's new gray mule had been gelded, Henry thought that Johnny was an appropriate name. Johnny would not be hard to break, as Henry had already had him on a lead with a blanket tied to his back. In a few days he would put a saddle on the mule and lead him around the pen.

Henry patted Zeke on his neck. "What do you think, old boy? Do you think he will ever be able to take your place?" He continued to rub the mule's neck. "No, I don't think so either."

He nudged the mule again and trotted from the corral area. He needed to go check on the hands who were branding spring calves.

# Chapter Thirty

## May 1895 - Circle S Ranch
## Outside Perryville, Oklahoma/Indian Territory

Everywhere a cowboy looked as he rode the grasslands of the ranch, calving was taking place. Usually in the shelter of a grove of trees, or even on the open range, cows were giving birth. More calves meant more money for the ranch and a continuing job for the Circle S hands. Makeshift corrals had been set up at various outlying points on the ranch. The corrals would serve two purposes. Even before the calves were weaned, they had to be branded with the Circle S logo. And the male calves would need to be castrated.

For several weeks these operations had been taking place, with the cowboys driving the cows with their calves to the holding corrals. The calves would be separated from their mothers and driven into the corrals, and this was not a simple matter. Separating the cow from its calf was the job of a good cowboy mounted on a seasoned cutting horse. This gave the individual cowboys a chance to demonstrate their prowess. To cut out the calf, the horse worked back and forth, literally staring down the cow and its calf, until the calf made a panicky mistake and bolted from its mother's side. The cowboy could then drive the calf into the corral with other men closing the gate behind the calf. If necessary, a cowboy would rope an ornery calf and drag it into the pen. When several calves were in the corral, each was roped, wrestled to the ground, held down and branded with one of the irons which had been heated to a red-hot temperature in a nearby mesquite fire. While men held the calf down, it was branded, and if it was a bull calf, it was castrated at the same time. The same operation took place at all the outlying pens.

Johnny was tied to the top rail on the outside back of one of the branding corrals. Henry sat next to the mule on the top rail of the corral fence keeping a tally in his head of how many calves were being branded that day. The same tally was kept at the other corrals, and the total would be passed to the ranch owner. The noise of the operation was nearly deafening. The din was caused by cows milling around the corral bawling to the calves and vice versa. Henry paid no attention to the noise as the cows circled the corral. He was fixated on keeping a correct tally of the number of calves. Suddenly, Johnny moved quickly to the side, tightly pulling the rein which was attached to the top rail. A cow had come around to the back of the corral and aggressively bumped into the mule. The top rail upon which Henry sat jerked beneath him, causing Henry to fall forward, landing on his knees on the ground. A jolt of intense pain shot through Henry's leg. It took some time for him to be able to rise to his feet. The pain had not subsided, but Henry figured that since he could walk, the knee was not rebroken, but it was several days before he could painfully climb up on to Johnny's back and ride again.

The incident in the branding corral, although isolated, served again to remind Henry that he was nearing the end of his usefulness as a ranch hand. He was fifty-five years old, and that was past the normal time of most cow hands calling it quits. The work was simply too hard for an older man, but Henry figured that as long as he was the ranch foreman and did not have to rope and wrestle steers, that he would continue working.

*** 

Life in the small cabin had taken on a routine many years prior. Henry and Renee simply cohabitated the small, crude home. They talked little.  Renee prepared the meals and carried out the other domestic chores.  Henry ate his dinner at night, slept in the same bed with Renee, drank his coffee in the morning while gazing out the cabin window, and then left to look after ranch chores.  He demonstrated little respect for the woman with whom he had lived for twenty years.  He still harbored resentment that he had been trapped into living with Renee, which left him unable to pursue his dream of obtaining wealth and independence.  For her part, Renee still found Henry to be a satisfactory partner.  He provided for her, only occasionally physically abused her, and provided some companionship, albeit meager.  For some strange reason, Renee did not feel that her dream had been shattered.  She simply believed that it was somewhat different than she had imagined in her younger years.

Both Elmer and Martin had moved out of the cabin.  At twenty and eighteen years of age respectively, they had long ago joined the ranch crew and were living in the Circle S bunkhouse with the other ranch hands.  They visited their mother when they had the free time to do so, because although they had moved into the bunk house, they both loved and respected their mother.  They knew she had loved and nurtured them and had withstood a great deal of abuse through the years at the hands of their father.  They had considerably less respect for their father.

# Chapter Thirty-One

**October 1895 - Northern Branch of the Shawnee Cattle Trail
Oklahoma/Indian Territory**

Henry had awakened and turned his head slightly to look upward
through the spokes of the rear wheel of the chuck wagon at the blanket
of stars that shone in the night sky. The Circle S's querulous cook who
was in charge of the chuck wagon lay at the opposite end of the area
beneath the wagon snoring quietly. Only the cook and the foreman were
allowed to sleep under the wagon, a small acknowledgement of their
standing among the ranch crew and a practice that allowed them to stay
relatively dry in the event of a night time rain storm. There was no hint
of rain in the clear night sky of this chilly fall night.

Johnny was hobbled a short distance away, and Henry could hear the
mule tearing the prairie grass and noisily chewing. The herd was quiet,
and off in the distance Henry could make out the silhouette figure of one
of the mounted cowboys walking his horse slowly at the edge of the
herd. As Henry continued to watch the horseman, he was absently
trying to remember how many trail drives he had ridden in his lifetime,
whether they had been to Kansas City or to Dodge City. Each year there
had been at least one, and in the years following a year of heavy calving,
there had sometimes been two drives. He could not remember; the years
all ran together in his head. He rolled over and drifted back to sleep.

In the dim light before the sun peeked over the horizon, Henry's
steaming tin coffee cup sat upon the saddle which lay in the grass next to
the mule. Henry continued brushing the animal, preparing to saddle him
and join the rest of the crew who were also finishing their breakfast and
saddling up. When he had finished, he drank the rest of his coffee,

walked the few yards to hand the cup to the cook, and returned to the mule. He painfully pulled himself into the saddle and began walking Johnny to the edge of the herd. At his signal, the cowhands riding drag began shouting and whistling to put the herd into motion. As the riders passed, the chuck wagon fell in behind, followed by the remuda. Another long day on the cattle drive had begun.

\*\*\*

The sun had now cleared the horizon as the herd continued northward. They had been underway for about three hours when the forward scouts come back to the herd and rode up to Henry. Even as they approached him, Henry could see the reason for their doubling back to the herd. A line of horsemen was motionless, standing to the side of the eventual path of the cattle. As the herd got closer, the lead cowboys turned in their saddles, looking back toward Henry. At least twenty Cherokee braves were now plainly visible. Henry's instructions were quickly carried out. Six steers were cut from the herd, and two of the cow hands drove them toward the Indian line. As the two ranch hands drove the steers forward, the Indian line of riders split, with the two ends riding outward and then approaching to circle the steers. The cowboys stopped their horses and watched momentarily while the steers were surrounded by the Indians, who then continued driving them west. In a few moments, the steers and the Indians were no longer visible. It was not always the Cherokees. Sometimes it was a different tribe, but the outcome was always the same. Rather than risk a greater confrontation with perhaps more serious consequences, a gift of steers was always made to the confronting tribe. The ranchers driving cattle through Indian Territory recognized it as a rent payment for crossing the Indians' land.

Driving the herd across a multitude of creeks and rivers became routine as they made their way northward. Now only four days out of Perryville, Henry had been riding to the side of the herd as it crossed a tributary of the Canadian River. At this particular shallow ford, the banks next to the river were only three feet high; easily scrambled up and down by the animals, whose thrashing hooves knocked the sharp edge off of the top of the banks so that the chuck and supply wagons could also proceed down the bank and up again on the other side.

Everyone thought it had been a freak accident. Inexplicably, as Johnny planted his front legs and slid to the bottom of the river bank, the mule must have hit something solid at the bottom of the slide, jolting him, and causing him to jump unexpectedly, which threw an unprepared Henry from the saddle. But as he tumbled from the saddle, his boot caught in the iron stirrup. As Henry continued downward, the previously injured leg surrendered to the twisting forces placed on the old mended break. The leg snapped under the pressure. Henry was now hanging into the water with the broken leg still attached to the stirrup. Johnny dragged him for several feet, but then stopped. The cook jumped from his wagon, and with the help of another hand, Henry was extricated from the stirrup. But the damage had been done, and it was severe. Carrying Henry back up the bank, the cook and the cow hand could see the blood on Henry's trousers. In that instant, Elmer rode up and dismounted. He was soon followed by Martin. The four men cut Henry's trouser leg, only to find themselves looking at a horribly grotesque compound fracture, with the leg bone protruding at an odd angle through the skin next to Henry's knee. The injury was still bleeding.

There was no such thing as a doctor on a cattle drive, and none of the cow hands knew anything about medicine other than basic remedies for ailing cattle. But the men who were looking down at Henry's injury all knew that if it was a steer or horse with a similar injury, the animal would be shot immediately. None of them said it, but they also knew that the leg would have to be removed.

The cook leaned down over Henry, who was grimacing and perspiring. It was obvious he was in a great deal of pain.

"Henry, I'll try to straighten your leg some, but we need to get you to a doctor. I reckon the closest one would be over at Tulasi." The cook went to the chuck wagon and returned with a stone jug. He poured a tin cup full of the liquor and handed it to Henry.

"You best drink the whole thing down fast," said the cook. Henry followed the advice.

Within twenty minutes, it was obvious from Henry's drooping eyelids that the alcohol was working. With four men holding him still, and while Henry screamed loudly from the pain, the cook pulled Henry's leg downward until it was in a semi-straight position. The leg was then wrapped tightly with cloth bandages. Leather strapping was used to tie tree branches to the sides of the leg to hold it securely. Even so, the pain was nearly more than Henry could stand.

Because Henry could not ride a horse, and the ranch could not possibly lose one of the two wagons, a travois was fashioned from tree branches. The travois was solidly braced with other branches and a canvas sling was lashed between the main poles. Henry was then adequately and tightly strapped into the sling with his head down and his legs at the higher end of the travois. The straps would keep Henry from sliding downward on the travois. It was felt that his leg would not be subjected to the jarring bounces of the poles crossing the rough ground if he travelled in the head-down position. The travois was then attached to Johnny's saddle, and Elmer would lead the mule and travois to Tulasi. The herd continued to move north, and the cowboys watched as their foreman and his son moved northwest.

After two days of tortuous, painful bouncing, a physician in Tulasi took one look at the leg which was already showing signs of blood poisoning, gave Henry a strong sedative, and removed the lower leg.

# Chapter Thirty-Two

**Indian Summer, 1898 - Circle S Ranch**
**Outside Perryville, Oklahoma/Indian Territory**

She had experimented with scores of ingredients, and over the months and years, she now had a number of recipes that she held in her head and which the cow hands seemed to enjoy. At the urging of her sons, following Henry's injury nearly three years ago, and out of a monetary necessity, Renee Evans had asked the ranch owner for work. Probably due to a general grumbling among the cow hands regarding the oft times barely edible creations of the old cook, the owner had given her a chance to do some of the cooking in the bunk house. Before long, the ranch owner heard that the food was appreciated much more by the hands when it was prepared by the foreman's wife. This led to some rather heated discussions between Renee and the old cook. But it was resolved that the older man would continue preparing the meals for the cattle drives, and Renee would do the cooking when the ranch hands were home. On occasion, Renee had been asked to go to the main house to help the family's cook prepare special meals. Through talent and hard work, she had gained the respect of both the cowboys and the ranch owner. She was happy.

Henry had learned to ride again. With the help of a skilled wood worker on the ranch crew, a wooden leg and a special stirrup had been fashioned to allow Henry to mount Johnny. Following the accident, he had lain in bed in Tulasi until he could be transported by wagon to the Circle S. For a considerable time, he did not want to get out of bed, but Renee continued to prod him until finally he would use a set of wooden crutches to walk outdoors and sit on a small bench in the sun. But psychologically, he would never be the same. His old dream haunted him. He would never be a rich man and considered himself to be useless and a failure. Many times he had thought of ending his life, and while sitting on his outdoor bench, he had held his pistol in his hands when Renee was away from the cabin. Not only did he detest the sound of the wooden leg as it loudly thumped on the wooden floor of the cabin as he walked, but he did not wish to have to rely upon the help of Renee and others for his mobility.

It was on one of those days while he was sitting on the bench outside the cabin and holding his pistol in his lap that something unexpected occurred. His elbows rested on his knees, and his face was in his hands. He was once again considering ending his life when he heard the sound of hoof falls and lifted his head to see a rider approaching the cabin. He did not recognize the man until the horse stopped in front of the cabin and the thin, tall rider slowly climbed down and stood smiling at Henry. A slow small smile of recognition crept across Henry's face. "I figured you'd be dead by now," said Henry.

Gospel Billy Rollins took off his hat and wiped his forehead on his sleeve. "Yep, I thought I might be too," he said and then laughed. Then he looked at Henry's leg. "Guess you're aiming to die one piece at a time," he said poking his thumb toward Henry's wooden leg. Then he laughed again.

Henry picked up the pistol in his lap, pointed it at Billy, and said, "Bang!" Then they both laughed.

***

Henry seemed to enjoy having him around, but Renee did not like Billy. He had now been with them for three days, sleeping in the shed by the corral. It wasn't because he was disagreeable or mean; he certainly was not that. And it was not because he was devouring what little food they had in their home, which he was doing. But Renee had been around men long enough to know that Billy was not what he pretended to be. Renee knew that underneath the outward smiles and charm, there was something very wrong with Billy on the inside. He never looked her straight in the eye and was evasive in his conversation whenever she had casually asked him about his plans. He usually stopped talking to Henry when she came around, and it was easy to see that there was something afoot between Henry and Billy. To make matters worse, Martin had begun hanging around the cabin talking with the two men when he was not working. This filled Renee with foreboding. Her youngest son was now in a quiet conversational conspiracy with Henry and Billy.

On this warm spring morning, Henry and Billy sat outside on the bench, sipping their coffee.

"I'm telling you, Henry, I've got it all planned out. It's gonna' work," said Billy. Renee was up at the ranch house, and the men had been talking for over two hours. Billy continued, "I have eight men waiting for us in Kansas City; you know they changed the name last year from City of Kansas."

Henry just nodded.

"But we need Martin to go along because we need another young man to blend in with the soldiers," said Billy, "and I think he wants to go with us."

"I'm not so sure that's such a good idea," said Henry. "I sure as hell hope he keeps his mouth shut. Renee has been sniffing around trying to figure out why you are here."

The reason Billy Rollins had made the trip to search out his old friend had been made clear to Henry over the past two days. Billy had not made much of his life along the Mississippi. Every grandiose plan that he had attempted had come to naught. So, he had reverted to the life of a petty thief and barely pocketed enough to keep up with his gambling debts. He had tried his hand at being a professional gambler, but was not skillful enough to avoid getting called out for cheating on several occasions. During one such incident, he barely escaped with his life after it was discovered that he had been dealing from the bottom of the deck, a deck that had miraculously contained five aces. He fled the small river settlement before he was lynched. He was nearly dead broke all of the time. His threadbare clothing showed its age, he was dirty and unkempt, and he was riding a horse that appeared not to have been fed on a regular basis and was very nearly ready to expire.

But during his numerous travails, Billy was not unlike Henry, in that he had continually dreamed of striking it rich in an endeavor, whether carried out honestly or dishonestly. He was now of the opinion that he had developed a plan to finally gain the wealth he so much desired. And the plan was entirely dishonest, of course. He wanted Henry and Martin to ride north with him to Kansas City to meet with a group of men, and then continue on as a group to carry out the plan.

"I'm still not sure about the plan, Billy. For instance, where are you going to get the Army uniforms?" asked Henry.

Billy chuckled. "You underestimate me, Henry. We already have the uniforms and other items we need. A lightly guarded Army supply depot in St. Louis helped us with those items, along with dynamite, blasting powder, pistols, rifles, ammunition, and other merchandise. We're all set. And that's the gospel," said Billy, smiling.

"Why did you come here to get me when you already have other fellows involved in your scheme?" asked Henry. "I was just doing fine here without you," he said as he rubbed both hands over the top of his head.

"Oh, yeah, you're doing just fine," said Billy, sarcastically. "I suppose that pistol in your lap when I rode up three days ago was there to shoot jackrabbits. Face it, Henry, we're just alike. Neither of us has a dollar to his name, and we're damn near too old to do anything about it. Hell, Henry, I'm over sixty years old; sixty, Henry. But I still have enough piss and vinegar in me for one last try at getting rich. And I intend to take care of that while I still can. And because you saved me from getting myself killed a couple of times, I figured you should share in our future good fortune and come along. And we need another man who can shoot straight and isn't afraid to shoot somebody if necessary. That's why I'm here. Now, I'm leaving in the morning. Are you and Martin going to be ready?" asked Billy.

Henry rubbed his hands back and forth on his thighs for a moment. The thought kept haunting him that he too was approaching sixty years old and did not have more than ten dollars to his name. He looked up at Billy. "I guess I just won't tell Renee anything. It would be better that way. We need to let Martin know tonight. Yeah, we will head out right after Renee goes up to the ranch house in the morning," said Henry.

***

It was their third night on the trail, and they had pitched camp next to a small stream. They had not yet unsaddled their mounts. Billy insisted that they did not unsaddle until darkness, just in case they were being followed in the daylight. Henry did not agree with Billy on this point, but decided not to argue. Martin had a small fire going and was watching as the pot began to boil the water and a small handful of coffee that he had placed in it moments before. He turned his head in the waning light, watching his father feeding Johnny a handful of grass. Martin did not have a great deal of respect for his father. He viewed their relationship strictly as father and son. If anyone would have asked, he could not truthfully say that he loved his father. Henry was a man who was too hard to love. But Martin did love his mother and felt some remorse that he had simply left the Circle S without telling her. But he was determined that he was going with his dad and Billy in order to gain the money to help his mother. At least that is what he told himself.

After a meager dinner, the men had sat sipping their coffee. When Billy had finished, he stood up and threw the remaining drops from his cup, and set the cup on the ground by his bedroll. He then walked over to Johnny, turned to Henry and said, "I'm going to borrow Johnny for a little while. I need to take care of some business over in Tioga. I figure we're about five miles from there." With that, he vaulted into the saddle, wheeled the mule, and trotted off. Henry and Martin just looked at each other, wondering about the sudden absence of Billy.

"Goddam it, Billy; now what the hell are you up to? Get back here with my mule," shouted Henry.

Billy paid no attention and kept riding.

"What kind of trouble is he getting into now?" mumbled Henry.

Henry did not sleep well that night. He had serious misgivings about the purpose of their travel. But as many times as he had mulled the plan over in his head, he still believed that it could work. In addition, his leg was giving him some pain. Three days of riding had been more than he had done for quite some time, and the continual bumping of his leg had caused the flare-up of pain. As a result, he was up before dawn and had started the coffee. He had lard melting in a pan and would soon throw hardtack biscuits into the hot fat to make them more palatable.

Martin and Henry sopped up the last of the grease from the breakfast pan and were chewing the biscuits when Billy rode slowly into the camp. He was riding a horse and leading Johnny and two other horses. Henry studied the three horses for a moment, and then he vaguely remembered having previously seen the brand affixed to the hip of each horse.

"God dammit, Billy; where did you get those horses?" asked Henry.

"Now, now, don't fret about where I got these fine-looking animals. Somebody owed them to me, that's all, and I collected," said Billy.

Henry looked at their brands one more time. "You got them from that ranch we went to years ago, didn't you?" said Henry. "You're going to have every lawman in the territory looking for us. I don't fancy sitting in a jail waiting for a rope around my neck or spending the rest of my life inside of a jail just because you went and decided to be a horse thief."

"Yeah, yeah. I took them from that uppity ranch fellow who left us without clothes and on foot some years back. I figured that place owed us. Now, I believe that we ought to just continue moseying on north at a good pace, so if you two are ready, I'll lead on."

If it appeared that Billy was in a hurry, he was; he had reason to put distance between himself and the Summer Prairie Ranch. It wasn't just the horse theft that had occurred. It was something far more serious.

# Chapter Thirty-Three

**Eight Hours Earlier - Summer Prairie Ranch**
**Outside Tioga, Kansas**

Lupe Vera had lived on the Summer Prairie Ranch for nearly twenty-five years. She had followed the love of her life, a young vaquero who had charmed her away from her parents those many years ago, promising her a better life in the United States. The couple had eloped, travelling from Monterrey to Nuevo Laredo where they were married. They then travelled for many days, finally coming upon the beautiful ranch in the Kansas Territory. He had taken a job on the Summer Prairie Ranch, and the Summers had hired her to be a maid and nanny for Will and later for Claire May, the daughter who had been born to Virginia Summers not long after the unfortunate death of Robert Summers. The love of Lupe's life was later killed by a rutting bull when he carelessly got between the bull and a cow that the bull was pursuing. The vaquero had spurred his horse, but the bull charged both the horse and rider, and the vaquero had been killed when he was thrown from the horse and trampled. Lupe stayed on at the ranch and became an integral part of the Summers family. In the absence of her mother, when she was busy with ranch chores, Claire May had been Lupe's constant companion. The little girl had loved her nanny, and even now, when she was grown, Claire May considered Lupe to be a special friend and confidant, thinking of her as an older sister.

Lupe had gone to bed with a stomach ache. She thought little of it, but later during the night, she knew that she must leave her warm bed and venture outdoors to the outhouse. In her nightgown and a light shawl, she lit a small oil lantern, quietly slipped down a rear staircase from her second floor room and went out the back door of the house. She had snuffed her lantern as she was returning to the house as her eyes had adjusted to the dark, and she was able to see by the light of the stars and the moon. In that dim light, she suddenly saw a strange horse tied to the outside of the horse corral. But she quickly determined that it was not a horse. In the dim light, she could see the long ears of a mule. Stopping where she was hidden by a porch support, she continued to peer through the darkness and soon saw the silhouette of a man inside the corral. The man, who had neither seen nor heard her, was swinging a rope above his head. She remained hidden and continued to watch while the man roped and tied one of the Summer Ranch horses to the corral fence. He then roped another horse and tied it next to the first one. He did this one more time until he had three horses captured, led them out of the corral, and tied them next to the mule. Now Lupe knew what the man was doing.

Lupe set the unlit lantern on the ground. She walked quietly to within ten paces of the man, who had removed the saddle and bridle from his mule and put it on one of the Summers' horses. "Mister, those are not your horses," said Lupe. "You need to put them back."

She had clearly startled Billy Rollins. He jerked around to face the woman. When he saw that it was an unarmed woman, he only knew that he needed to get away as quickly as possible. He struck Lupe with his fist, and before she fell, he hit her again. Lupe fell backwards and as she fell, her neck violently struck one of the corral rails, making a horrible popping sound. Her head then snapped upward just before the small woman hit the ground. Billy looked at the fallen woman for only a second, then quickly mounted the saddled horse and quietly led the two other horses and the mule away from the ranch.

Four hours later in the dim light prior to sunrise, a ranch hand discovered Lupe Vera, still lying in the same position as when she had fallen to the ground. He quickly ran to the ranch house door and banged on it, shouting for Mrs. Summers. Virginia had been in the kitchen of the house, getting ready to pour her first cup of coffee of the morning. She rushed to the door, followed the ranch hand, and gently lifted Lupe's head. She was drifting in and out of consciousness and as Virginia leaned down to look more closely at Lupe, she heard the words "riding a gray mule" come from Lupe's mouth. Virginia took Lupe's hand to check her pulse, and after a few seconds, began sobbing. Lupe Vera had died at the hand of Gospel Billy Rollins.

Two more hours passed. Lupe had been carried to a porch at the back of the house where, away from the eyes of the ranch hands, Virginia and a house maid would properly dress her for burial. At the bunk house, ranch hands had already begun building a wooden coffin for Lupe.

No matter how they tried, no one could console Claire May. She stood wailing and swaying back and forth shifting from one leg to the other as she watched her mother and the maid placing shoes on Lupe's inert feet. Virginia knew exactly how Claire May felt, because she had experienced the death of her husband. Hence, she knew that time was really the only true antidote for grief. But every minute or so, Virginia walked over and hugged her daughter, stroking the girl's hair. Then she returned to her work of preparing Lupe. Twenty-two year old Claire May watched in horror as four cowboys carried the wooden box to the porch and gently placed Lupe's body in the box. Will Summers stood well away from the porch watching. He struggled to hold back his own tears as he watched his sister and the ranch hands.

As the sun moved toward its western resting place in the late afternoon, the Summers family and several of the ranch hands circled the open grave. Virginia Summers stoically said a few words, asking her God to take the soul of their good friend Lupe Vera. After throwing a handful of dirt into the open grave, Virginia, Will, and Claire May Summers walked slowly back to the ranch house.

***

Two days after the family had buried Lupe Vera, Will Summers walked past the partially open bedroom door of his sister. He saw various items laid out on Claire May's bed and saw her standing in the middle of the room looking at the items, seemingly in thought. He knocked gently on her door and entered the room.

"What are you doing Claire May?" Will asked.

"Will, just go away and leave me please," she responded.

Will stood for a moment, looking at the assortment of riding clothes on Claire May's bed. He suddenly realized what his sister was doing.

"You're going after him, aren't you?" said Will.

"Dang it, Will. Why do you have to be so nosy?" She looked in her brother's eyes. "Yes, I'm going after him. Other than you, Lupe was my best friend in the whole world. No outlaw horse thief is going to come here and kill my best friend. Now go away and leave me alone. And if you tell mother I will scalp you, I swear I will," said Claire May.

Will did not leave. He only walked back and closed the bedroom door and turned to face his sister. "Claire May," he said, "I understand your feelings. I loved Lupe too. But I certainly don't want to see my sister killed by outlaws. You can't go. And that's that! Besides, the only clue you have is that maybe the outlaw was riding a mule. That's not much to go on. And you sure as heck don't know anything about tracking this criminal; you going after this man would be fool-hardy, to say the least."

Claire May Summers was no wilting flower. Besides being a very pretty young woman, she was born with the backbone of her mother, was physically strong, could outride most men, and could shoot the eye out of a prairie dog at twenty-five yards. She was a smart woman, and when her dander was up, she was a force to be reckoned with. The ranch hands on the Summer Prairie Ranch had learned a long time ago not to mess with the boss's daughter, especially if they had foolishly attempted to flirt with the attractive young woman. They had a healthy respect for her, as did Will. Will also knew that when Claire May said she was going to do something, it was right near impossible to get her to change her mind. Still, he was determined to dissuade his sister.

"Claire May, if you don't give up this foolish idea, I will tell mother." After the words left his mouth, Will realized how futile and juvenile they sounded. Claire May had turned her back on him and continued sorting the items lying on the bed.

Several more futile words and minutes passed, and Will moved and sat down in a chair next to the bed. He idly scratched at a couple of chigger bites on his arm as he thought through the situation. He figured that even if he told their mother what Claire May was planning, aside from hog-tying her, Claire May would find a way to light out after Lupe's killer. Mentally, he resigned.

"All right, if you insist on chasing this guy, you can head out. But I'm going with you. And we're going to take Jeb McCoy with us," said Will.

Jeb McCoy was an old trusted hand and the best man on the ranch with a gun, and he could track a trail that was long cold. By cowboy standards, Jeb was a grizzled old man. He had been fifteen years of age when he had served in the Union Army at the battle in the wilderness during the Civil War. He was certainly not afraid of trouble and would do everything he could to protect his boss's children.

Will continued, "Oh, and one more thing; we can't tell Mother any-thing about this. I'll leave word with one of the hands to let Mom know later in the day, after we've gone."

Claire May smiled, walked over, and kissed her brother on the cheek. "We'll leave tomorrow night," she said. Will looked at his smiling sister, shook his head from side to side, and walked out of her room. He always marveled at how his sister could somehow always manage to get her way.

# Chapter Thirty-Four

## October 1898 - Outside Olathe, Kansas

Henry was leery of the whole lot of them. He looked around the group as all the men were busy breaking camp and saddling their horses, and apart from Billy, he did not trust any of them. He knew a couple of the men from his boyhood days in the Kansas City Bottoms, but the rest of them were low-life acquaintances of Billy's. Not a one of them had ever held a meaningful job for any length of time in their pitiful lives. Aside from being men who had spent their lives in the city, they were all various levels of criminals who had spent nearly as much time behind bars as they had as free men. They were dirty, smelly, and wore clothes that, except for occasional rain water, may never have been washed. The men were poorly mounted; not that it mattered a great deal, since none of them were skilled horsemen. Their horses ranged from near invalid to the three fine horses Billy had stolen in Kansas. Four of the men had to double up on horses. Another horse was used to carry the supplies and dynamite. All of the men carried side arms, but there were only a few rifles among the group. According to Billy's plan, the dynamite would eliminate a great number of the guns that they would face.

Billy had never forgotten a cold, rainy day near Fort Riley, Kansas, many years ago, when he and Henry had been working on the rail line to the fort. He remembered the sight of the payroll train arriving at the fort on its run from the U.S. mint. That train would drop off payrolls at all of the forts along the rail line as it headed from east to west. At Fort Riley, it would turn south to stop at other Army frontier facilities to pay the military. It was Billy's intent that the train would never cross the Missouri River at Kansas City. The gang intended to blow up the train east of Independence, Missouri, and make their escape into Kansas, split the loot, then break up and scatter.

For the past two days, the men had gone over the plan of action enough times that each man knew exactly what his part was to be in the hold-up. Billy and Henry were confident that the men knew what was expected of them. Still, that did not put Henry's mind at ease. Not only was he worried about the hold-up, but he was inwardly regretting having allowed his son, Martin, to accompany him.

## Chapter Thirty-Five

**October 1898 - Paola, Kansas**

Jeb McCoy had lived up to his reputation. The Summer Prairie Ranch trio had made progress in tracking the killer of Lupe Vera. They had tracked the outlaw to a previously used, cold camp where he had joined two other persons. The Summers group was now following three men on horseback. But after four nights on the trail, and in the middle of an unseasonably warm, drenching rain storm, they had decided to head into town and get a hot meal and rest for the night at the Paola Hotel. While Claire May soaked in a hot bath, the two men made some inquiries around town.

"Yep, I shod that mule a few days ago; gray mule, it was, and the owner seemed to be in a hurry to get back out of town. He had a wooden leg, that one did. I put shoes on the mule and another skinny fellow's horse who rode in here with him," said the blacksmith, after he spat a brown tobacco glob on the dirt floor of his shop. "Never seen them before and don't reckon I'll ever see them again, bein' they was in such a hurry. Didn't much like the looks of those two. They had another fellow with them, but he just waited outside. Heard the stockier fellow call the other one, Billy, I believe. I'll grain your horses up tonight, and they'll be ready for you in the morning."

Will and Jeb shook the smithy's hand and headed back to the hotel where they each purchased a beer at the bar and settled at one of the tables. "So he was here," said Will.

Jeb sucked the froth from the top of the beer mug. "I reckon he was, Will. But, don't forget that he was not alone. I hope there's no more than the three of them."

An hour and a half later, after Will and Jeb had cleaned up, they joined Claire May in the dining room of the hotel. Three grease-speckled, empty plates sat in front of them. "That had to be one of the best steaks I've eaten in a long time," said Jeb. Three fingers of bourbon reflected an amber light from glasses in front of Claire May and Jeb. Will's fingers idly tapped around the rim of the nearly-full beer mug in front of him. The trio was full and relaxed.

"I think we are going to be real happy we aren't on the trail tonight. Take a look out that window," said Will. They watched as the rain poured down relentlessly.

The hard rain persisted for another twenty minutes while the trio chatted and sipped their drinks. Suddenly, Jeb said, "Listen," and he cocked his head to one side. They listened. The rain had stopped, and the sound they heard was something much more ominous. At first it had been strangely quiet, and no outdoor sounds were heard. But what Jeb had heard sounded like a faint hissing sound. Then it grew steadily louder. The sound changed from the hissing sound to a low-pitched whine that was slowly growing in intensity. The wind then came up, revealing dust devils and tumbleweeds racing down the street outside. The sound had now become a roar which was steadily getting louder. The two men and the woman had lived on the prairie long enough to know the sound of the devil himself approaching. They jumped up from the table, and Will went to the bartender.

"Have you got a root cellar around here, or a wine cellar?" Will asked.

By now, the bartender could hear the roaring sound too. "No cellar, mister, but you can join me here behind the bar. It's built about as sturdy as anything else in this town," he said.

Jeb, Claire May, and Will scrambled around behind the bar and wedged themselves between the bar and the wall behind it. The bartender hurriedly joined them. Within twenty seconds, the roar was deafening. It sounded like an approaching freight train at full throttle was coming through the front door of the hotel. The windows, through which they had been peering only minutes before, loudly exploded sending shards of glass in every direction. The floor of the building began shaking. Bottles behind the bar crashed to the floor sending more glass flying. They clutched onto each other and prayed, as the tornado ripped off the roof and tore the building apart, toppling the back wall of the bar over onto the trio.

Within fifteen minutes it was over. The tornado continued spiraling a path of death and destruction as it made its way to the east, the wind died down, and a gentle rain continued for a short time thereafter.

# Chapter Thirty-Six

**October 1898 - East of Independence, Missouri**
**Encampment on the Little Blue River**

The tornado had passed far to the south of them, but the torrential rain had forced the outlaw band to seek high ground. They were camped on a tree-shrouded rise overlooking the Little Blue. Even on the higher ground, their camp was a sloppy, muddy refuge. From their vantage point, they could see the swollen river as it passed beneath the train trestle bridge made of sturdy timbers. It was that bridge they planned to cross the next morning to place dynamite charges some distance to the east of the bridge. They intended to make their escape from the holdup by crossing the trestle again heading west, blow up the bridge behind them, and continue fleeing to the west to make good their escape.

The morning dawned cool and crisp with an unobscured sun that promised to dry out the saturated ground. The mounted men moved slowly down the rise until they reached the rail line. They dismounted and led the somewhat skittish horses across the bridge. For the next hour, they went over the plan once more, while two of the men placed the dynamite charges under the rails. While that activity took place, two other men placed dynamite charges on the pilings beneath the tracks on the trestle bridge. After both tasks had been completed, wires were strung from the blasting caps to the rack bar blasting machine hidden in a dense grove of trees along with the horses.

Martin Vogler and another man had now donned their stolen Army uniforms. Their jobs would be to lie hidden next to the train rails and rush to the baggage car immediately after the blast. In the resulting confusion of the blast and train derailment, they were to enter the baggage car and kill any survivors left in the car so the gang would meet with no resistance as they entered the car. Their uniforms would ensure that they would not be shot by any remaining union soldiers. The rest of the gang would storm the Army soldiers who were riding the train to guard the payroll. It was hoped that the majority of the guards would have already died in the blast and derailment. With all preparations completed, there was nothing left to do but wait for the train.

The previous day, Billy had ridden into Independence and after making some discreet inquiries, mostly at the rail of several saloons, he had learned that the monthly train from the east, which everyone seemed to know as being the Army payroll train, was due at this point sometime after noon. As the sun reached its high point of the day, Henry watched as his son and the other man who was wearing an Army uniform took their places, hiding in some high weeds near the tracks. Seeing his son smiling at him as he lay down in the brush, Henry now knew he was making a regrettable mistake, but it was too late to back out. A crow alit next to the tracks near Martin and the other hiding man. The ebony bird strode a few paces and let out a loud cawing cry. Henry shuddered at the evil omen and sorrow temporarily overcame his heart.

They did not have to wait long before they heard the pounding noise of the wheels of the 4-4-0 Baldwin; the sound of steel pounding steel that travelled for miles through the rails. The gang, hidden in the trees, was mounted. Only the man operating the blaster remained on the ground by his electrical generating box with his horse securely tethered nearby. The steam engine, pulling its short string of cars, charged toward the waiting bandits. When the train's engine reached a point seventy-five yards from the dynamite, the man connected the one loose wire to its terminal and depressed the plunger of the blaster. The explosion was deafening, sent a shock wave outward, and then seemed to hang in the air. Ballast rocks and wooden shards from the ties became deadly missiles as they whistled through the air. The train rails broke their connective plates and bent straight up, then subsequently turned and bent to the sides. In seconds, sparks began shooting from beneath the drive wheels of the locomotive as the engineer vainly attempted to reverse the wheels. The tortured machinery screamed in protest as the two steel surfaces abraded each other. The gang members clung tightly to the reins of their animals, doing their best to control the terrified beasts.

The forward motion of the train would not be stopped. The forward bogey wheels soon hit the torn rails, causing the wheel platform to rise in the air, flinging it to the side, and guiding the drive wheels from the rails. Momentum carried the engine down the raised rail bed at such an angle that the powerful locomotive rolled over onto its side. The boiler, now weakened as it crashed on its side, blew up, breaking the locomotive into three sections. The rail cars followed the locomotive. The car behind the tender contained the bulk of the Army guards. Most of them were killed in the rail car as it was crushed while toppling down the rail embankment. The coupler behind the troop car broke, leaving the baggage car and two other cars to remain on the track, but still rolling to the bent rails. The baggage car hit the upturned rails, breaking its forward truck and dropping the car onto the rails as it came to rest. It was a strange sight; the front of the rail car missing its front wheels and sitting just to the side of the rails, while the rear of the car remained on the rails, still sitting on its rear truck and wheels. It was several seconds before the shock of what they had just seen faded and sent the outlaws into action.

While the outlaws began streaming from the trees, Martin and the other uniform-clad gang member ran to the baggage car. The end door of the car was ajar, and they kicked it in. Three guards lay on the floor, trying to get to their feet. Martin and the other outlaw shot them, killing them instantly. An older, civilian baggage clerk lay moaning on the slanted floor of the car. He was unarmed. Martin opened the large side door of the baggage car, and he and the other outlaw quickly reloaded their rifles and pistols. Then they grabbed the legs of the baggage clerk, dragged him to the door and rolled him out to fall to the ground below. The clerk remained where he landed. He was in too much pain to move.

A gun battle had broken out behind the baggage car. Unbeknownst to the outlaw gang, the car behind the baggage car had also contained a group of Army guards, and they were not about to lose the payroll without a fight. A fusillade of shots was fired by both sides, many times with no clear target in sight through the thick gunpowder smoke. One by one, though, the gang was seen toppling from the saddles of their horses in the midst of the deadly accurate fire from the Army troopers. But the soldiers were not without loss. They were killed at nearly the same rate as the outlaws by the lead bullets as they easily pierced the thin sides of the train car sending lead balls and sharp wooden shards into the troopers. Henry and Billy had taken up flank positions on their mounts, virtually unseen by the occupants of the rail car and, therefore, not in the direct line of fire. They kept up a steady angled fire into the rail car.

At some point during the height of the battle, Martin and the other uniform-clad outlaw ventured too close to the open door of the baggage car. Mistaking them for union soldiers, they were subjected to a hail of outlaw gunfire, killing them both. Martin Vogler, the spurious son of Henry Vogler and Renee Evans took his last mortal breath while lying on the floor of a railroad baggage car he was helping to rob.

The battle continued to rage for nearly half an hour. Henry and Billy were still firing when there was an eerie quiet. A small white flag tied to the end of a rifle barrel was waving from the window of the rail car.

On a gentle breeze, the remnants of the smoke were clearing. Bloody bodies of both men and horses were strewn where they had fallen in the gunfire. The sides of two horses lying on the ground still heaved, but they would die very soon. Other horses had run from the battle and were grazing as a group in the grass fifty yards from the train. From across the length of the rail car, Henry and Billy looked at each other. There was no expression on either of their faces. They gazed at the dead men lying in various positions next to and near the rail car. The gang members had all been killed or mortally wounded. Henry and Billy now surmised that they were the only survivors of the gang. Turning to the rail car, Billy moved his horse to where he could see in the rail car window openings.

"Come on out of there," he said.

"I, I'll try," was the answer.

It took a couple minutes, but a young Army Corporal soon appeared at the door of the car. His trouser leg was bloody, as well as his shirt in the upper left shoulder area. His face was nearly black from the burned gunpowder. It was not readily apparent whether he was wounded or had simply been hit by the blood of his fellow soldiers during the fight. He was unarmed, and he was in shock as evidenced by his pale demeanor. "You killed 'em all, mister," he said quietly.

Henry motioned to a spot on the ground. "Sit over there, and if you move, we will kill you. You understand?"

The soldier nodded, stumbled, and finally fell at the spot that Henry had indicated.

Billy and Henry moved their horses to the door of the baggage car. From there, Henry could see his fallen son.

"C'mon, Henry. The cash boxes are just sitting there waiting for us," said Billy as he dismounted. He climbed into the open door and immediately threw a heavy cash box out the door to land on the ground. Henry had not taken his eyes off of his son.

"Check to see if Martin is dead, Billy," said Henry.

Billy leaned down and examined Martin. "He's dead, Henry."

The tragic enormity of what he had done soon pushed Henry into a sullen depression. In addition, as he watched Billy struggle to throw another box to the ground, a red hot rage was building inside of him. The man who was partially to blame for the death of his son, and who who had lured him away from the Circle S was in the baggage car. The inner rage had now taken over Henry's reasoning. He knew what he was going to do.

"That's enough, Billy. We need to get out of here, and we can only carry two of the boxes," said Henry. Billy stood in the doorway of the rail car. He was looking directly at Henry and could see a strange, fearsome look in the eyes of his friend. Billy was going to object, and his mouth began to form words, but nothing came out. Billy then watched in horror as Henry drew his pistol, quickly aimed, and fired the gun. Billy did not immediately fall, but he grasped his side in surprise and pain.

"This is all your fault, Billy," screamed Henry. "Why did you have to find me? My son is dead, and it's your damn fault." Henry's face was bright red as he shouted. He took aim and fired again and this time, Billy fell from the door of the rail car, landing on the ground next to the inert baggage clerk.

Henry looked down at Billy and then nudged Johnny, turning him to face the Army trooper. "Soldier, come here," said Henry. The soldier rose from the ground and complied.

As ordered at gunpoint by Henry, the young soldier went into the baggage car and retrieved the body of Martin Vogler and carried it to a grassy area in the same tree grove in which the outlaws had hidden.

Using a shovel from the locomotive's tools, the soldier dug a shallow grave and buried Martin. He then retrieved one of the outlaw's horses, and following Henry's instructions, he lashed two of the cash boxes to the saddle of that horse. Henry retrieved a rifle from the horse's scabbard, checked it for ammunition, and put it in his own scabbard on Johnny's saddle.

He then led the soldier over to the trees again and showed him the blasting machine. "Take those two wires off those posts. You see those other two wires there? Put one of the wires on one of the posts." Henry watched as the soldier followed his instructions.

"Now, I'm going across the bridge leading this here horse. And when I get to the other side, you are going to attach the remaining wire to that other terminal and push the plunger down. Now move on over there where I can keep an eye on you. I'm going to sit sideways on my saddle with this here Sharps in my hands with a bead on you. If you move, I will shoot you. When I get across, you blow that bridge. If you don't, I'll come back across and shoot you. You got that?"

The young soldier just stared at Henry with his mouth open. "Y, Y, Yessir," he said.

"One more thing, soldier; nobody knows if you are dead or alive. You might want to just think about grabbing a couple of those horses and loading some of that money for yourself and then disappear," said Henry.

Henry remained twisted in his saddle with the rifle at his shoulder as he crossed the trestle. He rode up on the hill side and stopped to watch the soldier. In a moment, the bridge erupted in a thundering explosion which collapsed the rails and timbers into a heap of debris on each river bank, while some of the timbers floated slowly down the river. Henry smiled ruefully as he watched the young soldier strip off his uniform and exchange it with the clothes of one of the outlaws. The soldier then tied two of the cash boxes to one horse, mounted another, and rode east. Henry kicked Johnny and rode south.

Contrary to what they might have thought, Henry and the soldier were not the only survivors of the holdup. The lives of two other men at the scene had been spared.

# Chapter Thirty-Seven

**East of Independence, Missouri**
**Site of Train Robbery**

It was late afternoon, with a dull red sun not yet to the western horizon. The robbery scene was an ugly array of dead horses and men. Lying next to the baggage car, he was so badly bruised, that nearly every part of his body ached, but he was alive. The baggage clerk tried to stretch his legs while remaining on the ground. He then turned on his side in preparation for rising to his feet. But as he did so, he froze and made no further movement for fear of being heard and noticed. He had thought that he was the only survivor of the train robbery. Instead, he was both mesmerized and curious as he watched the skinny man crawling on his belly in the direction of the grazing horses. The man stopped and rested several times, but ultimately, he was able to drag himself upright by grasping the stirrup of one of the horses. It was then that the baggage clerk saw the blood stains on the man's clothing. He continued to watch as the man struggled to mount the horse and was finally able to gain the saddle and ride slowly away to the east. Gospel Billy Rollins was severely injured, but he was not dead. No, indeed; though wounded, he was making his escape and heading back to the Mississippi River.

When the outlaw was nearly out of sight, the baggage clerk regained his feet. He peered into the baggage car, then turned, and achingly walked to the grazing horses. He picked up the reins of one of the horses, climbed into the saddle, and began riding at a fast walk, urging the horse when necessary to keep up the pace. Upon reaching Independence in the early evening, he stopped outside the marshal's office, paused momentarily to catch his breath, dismounted, and tied the horse to the hitch rack. He hurried into the lawman's office where the night deputy was on duty. After telling the deputy the horrific story, the deputy trotted from the office and soon returned with the marshal. The baggage clerk repeated the story for the marshal, and also added that a man who appeared to have a wooden leg had been sitting astride a gray mule that stood only two feet from him when the man looked into the baggage car. He also told the marshal that this man had shot an accomplice and had ridden away with two of the payroll boxes. The three men quickly walked to the telegraph office where the marshal sent several urgent telegrams; recipients were the U.S. Army at Fort Leavenworth, the Union Pacific Railroad, who then sent wires to the Pinkerton Detective Agency, and the U.S. Marshalls' offices in Kansas, Nebraska, Oklahoma, and Texas. Each of the marshals then sent wires to the local sheriffs' offices in their jurisdictions. A web of law enforcement was being spun to catch the ring leader of the gang who had brutally held up the payroll train.

\*\*\*

Henry's camp was well outside the settlement of Paola. It was hidden in a thickly wooded draw where a passerby would not be aware of the camp's existence. Even the smoke from a small campfire could not be seen in the thick canopy of vegetation. He had left the camp earlier in the day after hiding the payroll boxes and securely tying and staking the pack horse. He entered Paola for only one reason. He could not travel with two payroll boxes tied to a pack horse. He would need to hide part of the loot and transfer the remainder of it to two large saddlebags that he could then carry on the pack horse without arousing suspicion.

The mercantile owner, who had been busy with a hammer and nails completing repairs to his storm-ravaged hardware store, paused in his work when the stranger entered his store. He watched as Henry counted out the three silver eagles on the store's counter and then put the few supplies he had selected into the new saddlebags. Henry picked up the saddlebags and the shovel he had purchased and turned to walk out the door. The merchant was curious, but knew it was none of his business how the customer had lost his leg, as he watched Henry leave the store. From the front window of the store, he observed the customer as he lifted himself into the mule's saddle, secured the saddle bags and shovel across the pommel of the saddle, picked up the reins, and rode away. The store owner shrugged and returned to his place behind the counter of the store.

Just off the main street of Paola, Jeb McCoy sat on the front porch of the Paola Hotel. That is, he sat on the half of what was left of the front porch. Roughly one-third of the hotel had been blown away in the storm, but with the few remaining rooms, the hotel staff had quickly worked on some much-needed patch jobs, reopened the bar, managed to serve some meager meals, and cleaned up those few rooms which could be rented by paying customers.

Jeb was simply passing time whittling a piece of wood that he had found in a scrap pile behind the hotel. He had just come from the rooms of Will and Claire May Summers. Their scrapes and bruises were healing nicely, but the sprains would require a few more days' rest. When Jeb and the two Summers siblings had taken refuge behind the hotel bar, it was the bar that had saved their lives. Although portions of a wall had fallen on them, the bulk of the fallen timbers had been held from reaching them by the stoutly built bar. Will and Claire May had been injured more seriously than Jeb. As it was, they would be able to resume their trip home in a few more days. At that moment, if Jeb had lifted his head from his whittling, he might have seen the one-legged rider on a mule walking down Main Street to leave town; the very same man they had been pursuing prior to the tornadic storm.

After carefully watching to ensure that no one was following him, Henry returned to his camp. He then divided the cash, taking a portion of the paper currency and some of the coins and securing them in his saddlebags. He then consolidated the rest of the money in one of the boxes. Using the shovel he had purchased, he buried the two payroll boxes with the rest of the loot, and then threw the shovel in the underbrush. He stayed in his camp that night and left for the Circle S the next morning.

# Chapter Thirty-Eight

**Four days later - Circle S Ranch**
**Oklahoma Territory**

Renee Evans was returning to the cabin from the ranch house, where she had finished cleaning up after serving dinner to the ranch owner and his family. She rounded the corner of the cabin and was startled to see two animals tied up outside the cabin. She immediately recognized Johnny, but the other horse had a brand affixed which was unfamiliar to Renee. She stood still for a moment, thinking that Henry and Martin had finally returned. She desperately wished to see her son, but was not excited to see Henry. Just as she was about to continue to the door of the cabin, Elmer came riding to the front of the cabin, dismounted, and tied his horse next to the others. He walked over to his mother and glanced over at the mule.

"Is he back?" asked Elmer.

His mother looked at him and shrugged her shoulders. "I haven't been in the cabin yet," she responded.

Elmer and Renee entered the cabin to find Henry sitting asleep at the table, his head resting on his arms. An empty whisky bottle lay on its side on the table near Henry's arms. A cork lay next to the bottle. A set of fat leather saddle bags was slung over a chair next to the table. Henry's mouth hung open as he quietly snored.

It started with an innocent question. After looking around the cabin, Renee and Elmer roused Henry. He lifted his head and looked first at Renee and then at Elmer. His eyes were glassy and red. With an even tone in her voice, Renee asked Henry a question to which she was deathly afraid that she already knew the answer.

"Henry, where is Martin?" asked Renee.

Several seconds passed before Henry answered in a low gravelly voice, "He's dead."

Renee had not clearly heard him, so with a quavering voice which rose in pitch she asked, "What did you say?"

Henry looked at her again and sat more upright in the chair. "I told you, he's dead."

Her lips pursed and her small hands clenched into fists at her sides. "How did my son die, Henry; how did he die?"

"He was killed in the holdup."

"What holdup, Henry. What in God's name have you done?"

The black core inside of Henry was beginning to rise. The alcohol was contributing to removing any inhibition Henry may have had to remaining civil in his discussion with Renee and Elmer. "God dammit Renee, we held up a train and robbed the payroll." Henry stood, opened one side of the saddlebags and dumped out all of the coins. With the silver and double eagle coins in the pile, there was, indeed, a small fortune. Henry then opened the other side and drew out a handful of bills and threw them on the table. "There. There's more money than you ever had in your life, so stop yapping at me. Martin got killed making sure you had enough money to be respectable and to stop kowtowing to the ranch owner. You should be happy, Renee. For almost getting myself killed and all the trouble I've been through to get this money, you ought to give me a little respect." As he said this, Henry waved his arms and his face took on an evil, dark-red hue.

For several seconds, Renee stared incredulously at the man standing in front of her. "For a few dollars, you and that no account Billy have killed my son." Renee's fists were still clenched, and she spoke through gritted teeth. The tears were now flowing from her eyes.

Henry began shouting. "Shut up woman; just shut up! I don't want to hear anything more about me killing Martin. I didn't kill him. He just got himself killed in the holdup, that's all."

Henry was still standing. In his anger, he was quivering slightly, but he turned back to the table and began pushing the coins into a pile to dump them back into the saddlebags.

Quietly and unseen, Renee moved to the fireplace. She picked up the heavy iron rod that was used to lift pots from the cooking frame in the fireplace. She moved quickly and before Henry could react, she struck him across one shoulder and his neck with the rod. She screamed, "You killed Martin, and I'm going to kill you."

The impact of Renee's blow was not powerful enough to hurt Henry. As Renee began to raise the rod again, Henry turned quickly and grabbed the end of the rod and jerked it from Renee's hands. He then struck her with it, and she slumped to the floor. He heard a noise behind him and spun around. As he turned, he pulled his pistol before Elmer could draw his own gun. The evil anger in Henry had not subsided, and his eyes glared at his son, whose hand rested on his own holstered gun.

"Elmer, I don't want to kill you," said Henry. "Pull that pistol out with two fingers and set it on the table. Then back up against that wall. If you don't do what I say, I will kill you where you stand," said Henry. "I swear I will do it."

Elmer's hand relaxed, and he did as he was told. The look in his father's eyes confirmed a growing feeling within Elmer that he would have to bide his time until another day when he would avenge the death of his brother and the ill treatment of his mother at the hands of the maniacal man who faced him.

"You and your mother are stupid fools." He motioned to the saddlebags on the table. "That's only part of the loot, and I'm going to go get the rest of it. But I won't be coming back here when I get it."

Elmer was inwardly ashamed of himself. He was thinking that he should have killed his father a moment ago. He said, "In your warped mind you may think that we are fools for not being happy that you killed Martin to get that money. But I don't think so. You can't even think straight, old man. Hell, we didn't even want you to come back here at all. Mother was happy when you were gone. But here you are, telling us that you got my brother killed in some goddam train holdup. Every lawman in the country will be looking for you. Yes, old man, there is a fool in this room, but it is not my mother nor me. So why don't you just get the hell out of here. We don't want you here anyway," said Elmer. He slowly walked over and bent down and cradled his mother's head in his arms.

Henry left the money on the table, picked up the saddlebags, and turned and walked out the cabin door. Henry then mounted Johnny and rode away without looking back.

Elmer looked down at his mother and pushed the hair to the side of her face. Renee was regaining her senses and opened her eyes and looked into her son's eyes for a few seconds. There was a fiery glow in her eyes, as haltingly, in a quiet voice, she said to Elmer, "He killed Martin. I am going to kill that man."

# Chapter Thirty-Nine

**November 1898 - Paola, Kansas**

The three horses and the pack horse were saddled and loaded. The four horses stood quietly dozing with their heads down while tied to the hitch rack in front of the livery stable. Claire May, Will, and Jeb had paid their hotel bill and profusely thanked the hotel owner for his help during the aftermath of the storm. They had been at the hotel for over a week and were anxious to start back home. They had had their breakfast and were now heading to the livery stable to get their horses.

"I'm sure glad to see you folks again. I'll bet you're eager to get back on home. Them horses are ready to go. Hope you don't run into no more trouble," said the livery owner.

"We appreciate you looking after our horses," said Will. "How much do we owe you?"

"Ahh, I guess three dollars ought to cover the cost of the hay. Yep, three dollars, and we'll be even."

Will counted out the money and prepared to climb in his saddle.

"Say," said the livery owner. "You remember that fellow you were asking about; the one with the wooden leg that was riding the gray mule?"

Will and Jeb quickly turned to face the livery owner.

He could see he had the men's' attention. "Well, I'll be doggone if he didn't show up here again. It was about two days after the storm, early in the morning. I saw his mule hitched up by the mercantile, and I saw him again when he came out of the store. He appeared to be carrying a new set of saddlebags and a shovel. Just thought it was interesting, that's all; a bit odd, but interesting."

"Did you see which way he went?" asked Jeb.

"Not really. He just walked the mule on out of town," said the livery owner.

"Much obliged mister," said Claire May.

The livery owner watched as the four horses left town.

*** 

After clearing town, Jeb turned his horse to the east with the pack horse following. Will and Claire May looked at each other and spurred their horses into a fast walk to follow the old tracker.

"If he came into town during the morning, I'm guessing he camped over at the stream," said Jeb.

When they got to the stream, Jeb said, "You two wander up and down the side of the stream over there, and I'll move up this way."

Jeb knew that if a man was trying to hide out, he would not have camped in plain sight, and within twenty minutes of searching amidst more dense vegetation, he found what he was looking for. "Over here," he shouted to Will and Claire May.

In addition to evidence of a camp, Jeb showed them the other items he had found. Apart from a slight patina of rust, they could see that the shovel was near new. In addition, the rains had washed away the dirt from the top of a hastily buried metal box. On the side of the box were the letters, "US." Upon opening it, they discovered it was empty. They had no way of knowing there was yet a second box which had been more carefully hidden.

Jeb pointed to the ground where the mud was now drying. "Look at these holes here in the ground," he said. "Footprints have washed out in the rain, but these smaller holes are deeper. I'm thinking that these holes were made by the outlaw's wooden leg."

"Well, we've got ourselves a real mystery now," said Will. Jeb squatted on his heels, staring at the metal box.

"If I had to guess, I would say this fellow stole something that didn't belong to him. Just like our horses," said Jeb. He continued to study the area, but soon rose to his feet. "By the look of those fire ashes, I'd say he was here after the storm, but hasn't been back for a while. We ain't going to see him here, so let's go on home."

After another day on the trail they made camp for the night. The camp was well hidden in a stand of trees and brush, where it could not be seen by anyone passing by. They figured that two more days of riding would bring them home. They had a small fire heating the coffee pot and the lard in a pan to fry up some potatoes, onions, and salted-beef cuts. The smells were making Will's mouth water. It had been a long time since breakfast. Jeb was doing the cooking, and as the pan sputtered, he spread a few pinches of pepper into the fry pan. He then replaced the wooden top on the small salt and pepper box and stowed it back into the supply pack. Both of the men had been quiet up until now, when Will finally spoke.

"Well, which way do you think he went, Jeb?" asked Will.

Jeb stirred the frying pan before he responded. "Don't rightly know for sure. But the small signs I saw make me think he is moving south. I guess there are too many pieces missing in this puzzle."

\*\*\*

The day began to get lighter, but it had dawned gray and cold, with a stubborn ground fog hovering above the prairie grass. Claire May shivered slightly as she was rolling her bedroll and thinking about what she was needing to do. If it just wasn't so darn cold, she thought to herself. She walked away from the campfire that Jeb was coaxing back to life and rounded a bend in the creek to be out of sight of the men. The trees and shrubbery thinned in this location. Stripping off her riding trousers, she shivered and settled herself into some tall grass to take care of her personal business. As she squatted, she was able to gaze out to her west. A clearing in the trees and bushes allowed her to see a considerable distance. She completed her toilet and hitched up her trousers. She then walked over to the stream, bent down, and splashed the cold clear water onto her hands and face. She shivered again. Standing, she dried her face and hands with the scrap of cloth she had brought with her. While drying her face, she turned and looked back to the west through the slowly clearing fog. Suddenly, she started. In the distance, she could see a man riding slowly to the north. She quickly scrambled behind a nearby stand of oaks. As the misty fog parted and then seemingly closed back upon itself several times, she was finally able to get a better view of the rider. While still in the distance, she could see that the man appeared to be half asleep and was slouched into the saddle. Claire May drew a quick gasp. The man was riding a gray mule.

Claire May slipped backwards through the dense brush where she had hidden and quickly ran back to the campfire. She quietly told Will and Jeb what she had seen. Both men retrieved their rifles and walked slowly to the west, reaching the edge of the trees. Jeb looked back, and then up. He wanted to make sure that the fog was hiding the smoke from their fire. Both men crept forward on their hands and knees and waited. After a few moments, they, too, saw the man on the mule as he passed and continued north.

Rushing back to the camp, the trio soon had their horses saddled. They left the pack horse hobbled and began the chase. Their intent was to stay close to the stream, where the footfalls of the horses would be quieter in the grass. They would get in front of the rider to confront him on the trail. After they had gone a sufficient distance, they turned westward to the trail and waited.

A characteristic of fog is that it sometimes makes sounds travel farther than normal. Henry Vogler had heard the sounds of the horses ridden by Will, Claire May, and Jeb. He stopped Johnny and listened. He did not see anything in the fog, but he knew what was happening. He had two choices; he could flee or confront the unseen riders. He made up his mind.

"How much longer do you think, Jeb?" whispered Will. They had turned and were facing south, waiting for their quarry. Jeb did not answer, shrugging his shoulders instead. He peered intently into the fog. To himself, he thought that something was wrong. He should have heard or seen the mule rider by now. And a moment later, he did not hear Henry Vogler walk up behind the three horses.

Suddenly there was a shout. "Drop the guns and don't turn around or I will kill you." Even as he shouted the warning, Henry still did not know the identity of the strangers to whom he aimed his rifle.

"Dammit," was the only response from Jeb McCoy. He had been bested and he did not like it one bit. But there was nothing for the trio to do except to drop their rifles.

"Now the gun belts," said Henry. The belts were dropped on the ground next to the horses.

"Now get down from your horses," said Henry.

They did as they were told. "Start walking that way," said Henry as he pointed to the east. As they walked, Will, Jeb, and Claire May watched helplessly as Henry picked up, examined, and stuffed one of the Summers' pistols into his belt. When the trio was some distance from the horses, Henry began to mount one of the Summer Prairie horses. But as he did so, he stopped and stared at the brand on the horse's hip. He remembered the brand, and now he knew who these people were. He climbed into the saddle of the horse, swinging his wooden leg across the back of the horse, then letting it swing free of the stirrup. He sat still in the saddle thinking for a moment. He was not sure why this ranch group was following him. The only reason he could think of was for Billy Rollins stealing horses from the ranch. But since that was a hanging offense, he decided that he just did not want this group following him any longer. Maneuvering the horse, he was now in front of the other two horses, and he quickly fired two shots to their heads, instantly killing both animals.

He then walked his horse back and forth across the remaining discarded guns, allowing the weight of the horse and rider to bend the gun mechanisms and drive the guns into the moist ground.

Henry walked his horse to where the group was standing. "All right, now all three of you, strip down to your union suits. You too, lady," said Henry.

"Now just a minute, mister," said Claire May.

Henry pulled the pistol from his belt and fired it. The bullet thudded into the ground next to Claire May.

"Now get to peeling," said Henry maleficently.

"What's the damn point in us shucking our clothes?" asked Jeb.

"Well, if you think you gotta know, some of your ranch folks did the same thing to me and a partner some years ago. I figure this is just payback. How's it feel to stand around in your underwear with a gun aimed at you? Fun, ain't it," he said.

Henry kept looking at Will while he eyed Claire May. "What's this filly to you, mister? Is she your wife?" asked Henry.

"She's my sister. But that ain't no business of yours. You're in a heap of trouble, mister. Every lawman in the country is looking for you for killing our Lupe and for stealing our horses," said Will.

Henry became alert. "What's that you say? Who's this Lupe person?"

"She was one of the people that live on our ranch, and you killed her," said Will.

"Is that so?" said Henry. "Now just when was I supposed to have done such a thing?"

"You know damn well when it happened; about two months ago," answered Will. "And you were riding the same gray mule."

Henry sat still for a moment. Then he remembered back to a late night when Billy Rollins had come into camp with the Summers' horses. Billy had been riding Johnny and must have killed somebody on the ranch. My God, he thought; can my luck get any worse?

"For what it's worth, mister, I didn't kill anybody on your ranch. Now you, missy," he said as he pointed the pistol at Claire May. "Gather up them clothes and start walking up that trail." Henry and the other men watched as Claire May, in her short riding bloomers, cotton camisole, and boots, picked up the clothing and began walking.

"Now if you want to see your sister again, mister, I would advise you to just sit tight for a couple hours and see what happens. Otherwise, she's liable to get hurt." Henry fired the pistol again, with the bullet landing at the ground close by Will. "Do we understand each other?" asked Henry.

"Yes, we understand," said Will. "But I'm going to enjoy seeing you hang, mister."

Henry scoffed, wheeled the horse, and followed Claire May as she walked into the fog.

When they could no longer hear the horse walking away from them, both men ran to where the discarded guns lay in the mud. They pried them out of the dirt, only to find that just one of the rifles appeared to be operable, but it would need to be thoroughly cleaned before it could be fired safely. Dejectedly, the two men walked back into the woods to their camp site.

"Well, at least he did not find the pack horse," said Jeb.

"The hell with the horse, Jeb! What are we going to do about Claire May?" asked Will.

Jeb was already going through the supplies, discarding what was essential and what would have to stay behind. He tossed a spare shirt to Will, and he donned the only other spare shirt himself. They had brought no other spare clothing. "We're going after her, Will. But we have to be a little patient and lag behind. We're going to have to ride two up on the pack horse, and with only one long gun, we're at a real disadvantage. Now help me break camp," said Jeb.

When they had hastily left camp earlier in the morning, many of the supplies had been left at the camp site. They had their bedrolls, some food, and ammunition. Both men soon wished they still had their coats and trousers as they were already very cold.

Two hours after Henry had abducted Claire May, Jeb and Will set out after her. Their only horse was carrying two men and some of the supplies, a much heavier load than normal, so the men could not tax the horse at more than a swift walk for fear of injuring the animal.

***

Henry had led Claire May back to where he had previously tied Johnny. He dismounted from the horse, picked up Johnny's reins and climbed onto the mule's saddle.

Looking down at Claire May, who was visibly shivering from the cold, he said gruffly, "Put your clothes on."

Claire May hastily dressed.

"Leave those other clothes there, get on the horse, and start riding."

Claire May was truly frightened. To the best of her knowledge, the man who was holding her at gunpoint was a killer and a horse thief. She had no idea how this was all going to come out, but she had a horrible premonition that the outlaw would soon decide to kill her. And yet, it never left her mind that this was the same man who had killed her best friend, Lupe. If given the chance, she would certainly turn the tables on the killer and gladly watch him die at her hand.

Henry rode just to the rear and to the side of Claire May's horse. They were traveling at a fast walk.

"How come you said you did not kill my friend, Lupe?" asked Claire May.

Henry did not answer for a moment, but finally said, "I didn't kill her. Hell, I don't even know her or how she got killed. It wasn't any of my doings."

"Well, if you didn't kill her, who did. Before she died, she said she saw your mule there the night she was killed," said Claire May.

"I'm telling you, it wasn't me. It was my mule, all right, but I wasn't riding him. A man I used to call my friend had borrowed my animal, and I didn't know why until he came back to our camp with a couple of your horses. Hell, I didn't even steal your horses except that time years ago when you weren't even born yet," said Henry.

Claire May did not know what Henry meant by that remark, as she had never heard the story about the horse thief stealing horses from the ranch many years before.

For several minutes neither of them spoke a word. Then, he said something so quietly that he was sure Claire May would not hear. But her sense of hearing was much keener than he thought, and she heard Henry say under his breath, "I'd never kill another woman." Claire May was not sure whether to believe him or not and wondered exactly what he had meant by that remark.

They rode on for at least another hour. Little was said between them, but Claire May continued to think about what Henry had said. She now figured that the outlaw must have once killed a woman. Otherwise why would he have said what he did? She was not exactly sure when she made up her mind, but she decided that there must be some weight in what the outlaw had unintentionally divulged. With that in mind, in an instant, she violently kicked her horse and wrenched the reins to the right while she continued to kick the horse to make her escape. She bent low over the neck of the horse, slashing the ends of the reins back to the horse's flank, yelling at the horse to urge it on. She listened as the horse gasped for breath and galloped. She was expecting a rifle shot at any second. It did not come. Nor did she hear any other sounds of pursuit. She risked a glimpse back. What she saw elated her. The outlaw was standing still in the middle of the trail, simply watching her gallop away. She continued to speed away. When at last she looked back over her shoulder, she could barely make out the figure of the outlaw on the mule as he loped away into the distance.

Henry was headed to his old camp to dig up the payroll box that he had carefully buried weeks earlier. He did not intend to harm any of the Summers ranch people. He only wanted to be left alone. He would get the remainder of his payroll loot and make his way to Chicago. Where no one knew him, he was sure that he could disappear in the multitude of people in that city.

***

Claire May had stopped her horse to let it catch its breath. She faced north and could no longer see the outlaw. She was certain he was gone. She walked her horse to the location where she had discarded the men's clothing, dismounted, and gathered up the clothes. She held them as she remounted and headed back to where Will and Jeb had been left. But she was surprised later when she spied her brother and Jeb, doubled up on the pack horse riding toward her. She was so happy to see them that she began to giggle as they rode up.

"Now there's something you don't see every day. Two grown men in their union suits riding down the trail," she said to them and laughed again.

Will jumped down from the horse and walked over to her. "It's not nice to laugh at men in their underwear," he said, and then he also laughed.

"Are you all right?" asked Will.

"Yes, I'm fine. He just let me leave," said Claire May as she dismounted. "Put your pants on, you two, or I'll start laughing again." She grinned as she threw them their pants and watched the two men slip their boots off to get their trousers on.

They soon remounted, with Claire May up behind Will, and headed back to their camp. It was now late afternoon, the horses were tired, and they would stay for the night.

Later, as the fire burned low, Claire May asked, "What do you think we should do now, Will. That outlaw just keeps getting farther and farther away."

Out of earshot, Will and Jeb had already discussed their next course of action. They knew what they were going to do. "We'll talk about it in the morning, Claire May," said Will as he rolled over with his back to the fire.

***

Claire May was so mad she could spit rocks. She was riding south at a brisk trot, heading for home. Three hours ago, she had punched her brother in the nose, making it bleed. She would have done the same to Jeb McCoy, but thought better of it. The reason for her anger was that the two men had verbally ganged up on her after breakfast and told her in no uncertain terms that she was to go on home and report what was happening to her mother.

There was no doubt that Virginia Summers was worried sick over the disappearance of her two children, but she was also very aware of the stubborn personalities of Will and Claire May. And after questioning several of the ranch hands, she also knew that Jeb McCoy was with them, providing her with some consolation. But it did not completely remove the anxiety that she felt for her children in their absence.

So, it was with a great deal of relief to Virginia when two days later, she spotted her daughter trotting her horse down the lane to the ranch house. Claire May dismounted, and with tears in her eyes, Virginia embraced her daughter. But Claire May would not escape a severe verbal dressing down from her mother. That began outdoors, moved indoors, and lasted for nearly thirty minutes. When Virginia had finally satisfied her wrath, she patiently listened to the entire narrative of events from the mouth of Claire May, who continued to talk about it all through dinner that evening.

After dinner, Virginia began giving orders to the ranch staff. It became clear to Claire May that her mother intended to pursue the outlaw and find her son. And the next heated discussion then began.

"I have no intention of leaving my son and Jeb alone with one horse and one rifle to face that outlaw," said Virginia. "I'm leaving in the morning with horses and supplies, and you, Claire May, will stay home."

While Virginia made preparations, mother and daughter lashed out at each other the entire time Virginia was packing her duffel. In the end, once again, Claire May broke down her mother's will. The two women would start out in the morning to catch up with Will and Jeb.

Virginia shook her head from side to side, looked at her daughter, and said, "Go find Buster Wilson and tell him to pack for several days. I want him to go with us in the morning. Now, I'm going to bed, and you need to do the same thing. There's going to be some long days ahead of us," she said, and walked toward her bedroom after giving more instructions to the staff to make preparations for their early morning departure.

At dawn the next day, Virginia Summers sat on the front porch draining the last dregs from her coffee cup as she watched Buster Wilson, another trusted ranch hand, bring six horses to the hitch rack. Three were saddled and would be ridden by herself, Claire May, and Buster. Another was already carrying the loaded pack tree, and the other two were spares. After final preparations were made, the three set out on their mission to find Will, Jeb, and the outlaw.

She knew that Claire May, Will, and Jeb had parted in northern Kansas, so Virginia was taking the most direct trail to reach the northeast corner of the state. She also knew that she would be crossing land that was occupied by the Kansa Indians. Their people were at peace with the white settlers, but Virginia also knew that on every cattle drive from her ranch to Kansas City, an "unofficial toll" was paid to the Kansa's in exchange for crossing their land. On cattle drives the toll was in the form of three steers given to the tribe, but since she was not driving cattle, there had been a purpose in her having Buster bring extra horses.

Sure enough, in the afternoon of their second day on the trail, they were met by a small Kansa hunting party. Virginia allowed Buster to converse with the Indians, as the natives did not hold women in the same regard as men. She and Claire May kept their rifles across their saddle pommels, each with one hand on her gun. The dealings went agonizingly slow, with each party using broken language to attempt to have the other understand their position. As Virginia sat in the saddle listening to the negotiations, she soon realized that the Indians wanted both of the spare horses. But she continued listening while the conversation took a different course. After a moment, Buster turned and pointed to Virginia, saying, "Mrs. Summers, Mrs. Summers." It was as if a light went on in the Indians' faces. They had dealt with cattle drovers from the Summers' ranch for many years, but they had never seen Mrs. Summers. They moved their ponies closer to have a better look at Virginia and Claire May while talking among themselves.

Again in broken language, Buster soon had them understand that they were moving north to try to find Mrs. Summers' son, Will, and needed the second spare horse for Will to ride. A deal was soon consummated, and one of the spare horses was given to the Indian hunting party.

More conversation took place before the Indians turned their ponies and trotted away, leading the horse that had been given to them. Virginia and Claire May returned their rifles to their scabbards.

As they again headed north, Virginia asked Buster, "What was that you were talking about just before the Indians left?"

Buster looked at his boss for a second or two, and then said, "I'm not completely sure what they said. But I think the one fellow was trying to tell me that two other white folks came through here a day or two ago. He said it was a woman with a younger man. They rode up close enough to have a look at them, but did not stop them because it looked like they did not have anything that the Indians wanted. At least I think that's what he said."

"No concern of ours, I guess," said Virginia. "Just the same, I wonder who they were."

\*\*\*

In the late afternoon, the woman and man had turned from the trail to camp near a stream and among some trees where they would be out of the wind. The day had been cold, and the woman was tired. Moreover, she was painfully chafed to the point that she had burning blisters. A warm fire radiated heat, and the man and woman both held their hands close to the fire. Their horses were hobbled close by. A coffee pot was warming, and they would eat hard tack softened by the coffee for their supper.

"Elmer, I don't rightly know if I can go on," said Renee. "I'm not used to riding this long, and my bottom end is in real pain," she said.

"I'm sure you will be all right, mother, and I don't mind camping here for a day to let you rest up. I can shoot a duck over in that slough next to the stream in the morning so we have some fresh meat. Ducks always have a good coat of fat on them, and we can use that for a lotion for your blisters. It's the best I can think of," he said. "We'll get back on the trail in another day or so."

Using some dead tree branches, Elmer Vogler propped up their ponchos to make a small shelter with the back closed and the opening toward the fire. They would stay reasonably warm through the night.

They said little as they ate, but as they readied for sleep, Renee winced as she rolled on her side and said, "Once again that no account Henry is causing me pain in my backside."

***

It was a cool damp morning, and they had been on the trail for only an hour at most. Buster had heard the shot and turned his attention to the direction of the sound. He stopped his horse and pointed. Virginia and Claire May rode up close to him.

"You probably heard that shot, too," said Buster. He pointed into the trees, saying, "There's somebody camped in those trees over there, Mrs. Summers."

Virginia and Claire May peered intently into the trees and saw the wispy camp fire smoke vapors in the branches and then could see two horses grazing among the vegetation.

"It can't be Will and Jeb," said Virginia. "They only have one horse."

"Don't rightly think it's our outlaw man neither. There ain't no mule in there," said Jeb. "Mrs. Summers, why don't you and Claire May keep your rifles handy, and we'll go pay them a social call."

Virginia and Claire May retrieved their rifles, kept them at ready, and the three of them walked their horses toward the encampment.

"Hello in the camp," shouted Buster.

Elmer had just walked back to the camp, his rifle in one hand and a green-headed mallard in the other. "Hello yourself," he shouted. "C'mon in."

When they reached the edge of the camp, Buster, Virginia, and Claire May dismounted and walked to Elmer. Renee rose from where she was sitting and turned to face the visitors. As she did so, a slight grimace of pain crossed her face.

"My name's Buster Wilson, and this is Mrs. Summers and her daughter, Claire May." Buster stuck out his hand and waited for Elmer to shake hands.

Elmer looked briefly at the trio and came to the conclusion by their looks that they did not appear to be a threat to him and his mother. He stuck out his hand to shake with Buster. "I'm Elmer, and this is my mother, Renee Evans." For the time being, he let the strangers assume that his name was also Evans. "Glad to meet you. I've got some coffee there, if you want some."

Virginia studied the man and woman for a few seconds. "I'm sorry, but we can't stay. We need to be heading on to meet my son up near Kansas City," she said. She paused a few more seconds, thinking before she decided to continue talking. "But we are also looking for a man that caused some trouble on our ranch. We believe he is riding a gray mule and that he has a wooden leg."

Virginia's eyes flicked quickly toward the woman as she heard a small gasp from Renee Evans. The thought instantly occurred to Virginia that perhaps Elmer and Renee Evans knew something about the outlaw they were pursuing. "Mrs. Evans, have you and your son seen that man?"

Elmer slightly stammered when he said, "No. No, we haven't." He had also heard his mother's slight breath intake. But he covered it by saying, "We've been riding a spell, and you see, my mother is in a bit of pain. We are going north to visit an ailing aunt, and my mother isn't used to riding this much, and she's contracted some saddle blisters." He held up the duck in his hand and said, "Reckon we'll use a little duck fat to ease her discomfort."

Virginia studied the two a bit more and felt that they might be telling the truth. "Where you coming from?" she said as she studied the brand on the strangers' horses.

"Circle S ranch; down in Oklahoma territory," answered Elmer.

The brand, which had the letter "S" inside a circle, matched the ranch name, thought Virginia.

"Mighty long ways," said Virginia as she eyed Renee. She continued, "Have you got any oats for your horses?"

Elmer looked at her quizzically, thinking that she wanted the oats for her own horses. "Yes, we have a small bag," said Elmer.

"Good," said Virginia. "Take a little bit of those oats and grind the husks off of them. Then get rid of that chaff and take the seeds and grind them up with a little bit of water to make a paste. Put that paste on the blisters and don't ride for another day. That should help some," said Virginia.

Buster was getting restless. He stuck out his hand again and shook with Elmer. "We'd best be moving on. Hope your mother gets to feeling better," said Buster. He moved over to his horse and mounted.

"Much obliged for the advice," said Elmer.

Virginia and Claire May mounted their animals, and Virginia waved as the three walked their horses from the camp.

When they were well clear of the Evans camp, Virginia turned to Buster. "What do you make of them, Buster? I have a hunch they know something about that outlaw," she said.

"Oh, you saw it too, eh. Yeah, the woman may have had saddle sores all right, but I'm thinking she also knew something else she wasn't telling. It just may be that we aren't shed of those two quite yet."

"What do you mean, Buster?" asked Claire May.

"Now don't be reading anything into what I say, Claire May," said Buster. "I just have a funny feeling about those two, that's all."

Virginia and Claire May looked at each other, but neither responded to Buster's remark. They all urged their horses into a fast walk.

## Chapter Forty

**Late November 1898 - South of Lawrence, Kansas**

Overnight the temperature had approached freezing again. Henry woke up cold, stiff, and sore. His leg was bothering him again, but since he had no other means to walk, he had reattached the wooden leg, agonizing with each painful step. He boiled a bit of coffee and gnawed on some jerky as he watched Johnny tearing at the brown prairie grass.

He had slept poorly. Aside from being cold, he had had a horrific nightmare. Henry knew where he was and knew he would pass by Lawrence, Kansas, today. Last night in a dream, his subconscious had recalled in vivid detail what had happened nearly thirty-five years ago when he had been riding with Quantrill's raiders. In the dream, he had killed a boy in cold blood, an innocent child, and he had participated in the killing of other residents of Lawrence, which woke him from the dream. Returning to sleep, the dream continued with him getting shot in the leg and the horrible pain of later having the leg amputated. He had awakened again and decided that he would forgo any further attempt to sleep.

Soon, he packed up the camp and saddled the mule. His stomach was sour and ached as he moved north. As he passed west of Lawrence, he peered to the east. None of the town looked familiar except for the church spires. He remembered seeing them years ago when they had ridden into the town and burned most of it to the ground. He shivered as a cold breeze crept beneath the collar of his coat.

Just as he thought he would soon be away from Lawrence, Johnny began to favor one leg. The mule was not lame, but seemed to step more lightly on one of his front legs. Henry dismounted and walked to the side of the mule and picked up his leg.

"Dammit!" said Henry as he looked at the hoof. Johnny had thrown a shoe, and on closer examination, the hoof had developed a slight crack, which necessitated fastening a new shoe to the hoof or risk further damage to the hoof. Henry had no choice; he needed to go into Lawrence and find a blacksmith. He turned the mule to the east and slowly walked him into town. As he continued toward Lawrence, he glanced over his shoulder and was surprised to see a horse and rider approaching at a lope. Henry rested his hand on his pistol as the rider approached. To Henry's surprise, the rider did not stop. But as he loped past, the rider waved, and at that moment Henry saw the metal star pinned to the coat of the rider. Henry waved back at the disappearing rider and shuddered involuntarily.

Henry found the livery stable, and as he turned into the livery, he noticed that the lawman who had passed him on the trail was across the street, still astride his horse, talking jovially to another rider. The lawman gave a brief glance in Henry's direction, then turned and continued his conversation with his friend. Henry gave instructions to the smithy, lifted his saddle bags and rifle from the saddle, and found a hay bale where he could sit and wait for Johnny while keeping a watchful eye on the street. He watched as the lawman turned his horse and continued down the street. Henry let out a deep breath, rose, and walked to a nearby café to get a hot lunch.

Several hours later, the old clerk at the telegraph office, put on his coat and walked a few buildings down the street to the sheriff's office. He entered the lawman's office and found one of the deputy's on duty. He was the same man who had ridden quickly by Henry Vogler that morning. The deputy was sitting at his desk and had just taken the first bite of the steaming meat loaf sharing a plate with mashed potatoes and boiled cabbage. He was of the opinion that the small corner café nearby had the best meat loaf in Lawrence, and he was savoring the mouthful, masticating it with gusto. The telegraph clerk laid the sealed telegram on the deputy's desk as they exchanged pleasantries. He told the deputy that the telegram was about some outlaw who was wanted by several jurisdictions. The deputy thanked him for bringing the telegram, but also said that he would get to it after he finished his dinner. The clerk watched the deputy for a few seconds before his mouth began watering. He bid the deputy a good night and quickly left the sheriff's office to get his own supper at the café. The deputy continued eating.

Another half hour passed before the deputy finally emitted a rather loud belch and picked up the telegram envelope, which he slowly sliced open with a small pocket knife. Not a learned man, his brows furrowed as he struggled through the reading that described the crimes and description of a wanted outlaw. The telegram also made mention of the authorities to contact if the outlaw was sighted. He then slowly read the telegram two more times before jumping up and running out the door of his office. He walked quickly up the street and entered the livery where the smithy was cleaning stalls to end his day.

"Where's that man that came in here with the mule this morning?"

"He left right after lunch," said the Smithy.

"Well, dammit. The sheriff is going to have me for breakfast when he gets back in the morning," said the crestfallen deputy before turning and walking back to the office. He slowly reread the telegram. Then, he left the office and went to the telegraph office. He followed the instructions in the telegram, telling the telegraph clerk what to write. Wires were sent to the U.S. Army, the Union Pacific Railroad, The Pinkerton Detective Agency, and the U.S. Marshall in Kansas City. Without the authorization of the sheriff, who would not return to town until morning, the deputy could take no further action.

\*\*\*

Renee Evans was not the only individual suffering saddle sores. Earlier in the day, and miles to the north, Jeb McCoy and Will Summers had traded places every couple of hours with one of them sitting in the saddle which had been retrieved from one of the horses killed by Henry Vogler, while the other man sat behind the saddle on the wider rump of the horse. The rear accommodations on the horse were certainly not comfortable for very long, the wide girth of the horse causing sore inner thigh muscles for the rider. It was once again time to trade riding positions, and the two men had dismounted. While stretching their muscles, Jeb studied more closely the trail of the outlaw they were pursuing.

"Lookee here," said Jeb as he bent down and retrieved something that had been on the ground. When he stood up, he was holding a horseshoe. Then Jeb began walking, stopped, and knelt on one knee, pointing to the ground. Will walked up and kneeled down beside him. "That outlaw's mule threw a shoe. See how this horseshoe is a little smaller and elongated? And see how the track now shows an animal with three shoe tracks and one unshod hoof? That's going to slow down that outlaw, and that's a stroke of luck for us." Jeb and Will stood up and peered intently up the trail. In the distance, they saw what they were looking for. Smoke on the horizon meant that there was a town, and where there was a town there was always a blacksmith.

They remounted the horse and urged it into a fast walk. Will was riding on the horse's rump. "I swear this goddam horse is going to kill me," he said.

Jeb continually peered at the ground as they rode. He turned the horse slightly as they neared the town of Lawrence. But after another minute, he stopped the horse.

"He's in town there," said Jeb. "He has to get that mule reshod."

Impatient as usual, Will said, "Well, what are we waiting for? Let's go get the bastard."

But Jeb did not move the horse.

"C'mon Jeb, let's go," said Will.

For a brief moment neither man spoke. It was clear that Jeb was weighing out his options until finally he spoke. "I want this sumbitch just as bad as you do, Will. But I don't aim to die trying. Hell, we don't even know his name. Think about this. We are two men with one horse and one gun and very little ammunition. We can't go up against a well-armed outlaw who is bound to be on the lookout for anybody suspicious. I've got another plan."

"OK, so what's your plan?" asked Will.

"We're going over yonder on that rise in that stand of trees and camp for a while," said Jeb. "From there, we're going to keep an eye on the road coming out of that town."

They drank their fill from a creek at the base of the hill and began their vigil of watching the road. That afternoon, Will was catching a short nap while Jeb kept watch. Later, Jeb nudged Will with his elbow and pointed in the direction of the road. While remaining hidden, both men watched the outlaw as he rode the same gray mule out of town and turned again to the north.

Will turned to Jeb and asked, "What are we going to do now, Jeb?"

Jeb just smiled and clapped Will on the shoulder. "Well youngster, we are going to pitch camp and wait for reinforcements." Will just looked at Jeb for a few seconds and thought, youngster indeed. Jeb was not that much older than him. But rather than protest, he decided that he was so tired of riding that he finally just shrugged his shoulders and helped Jeb set up their camp.

***

Jeb McCoy's reasoning proved correct. Although they spent another very cold night on the ground, the morning sun promised to bring the temperature up as the day progressed. From their vantage point, they watched the road approaching from the south and the travelers entering and leaving Lawrence. Jeb whittled as he watched Will Summers pacing the camp site. He chuckled at the impatience of youth. He turned his head, looked south, and then looked back at Will.

"Look over yonder, Will," said Jeb as he pointed to the south trail.

Will strained his eyes and finally saw what Jeb was pointing out. He immediately began walking quickly toward the trail, waving his arms as he walked.

Virginia Summers urged her horse into a trot and rode to greet her son. She was followed by Claire May. When the women dismounted, Virginia hugged and kissed her son on his bearded cheek and began walking along with Will back to the camp site. All the while they walked, Virginia sternly lectured her son. Will took it in stride. He figured he was owed a bit of verbal chastisement from his mother. While his mother continued, Will stole a look back at his sister, who was visibly struggling to keep a straight face, which almost made Will laugh. It was good to see his mother and sister again. But when she reached the camp site, Virginia Summers did not play favorites. She lit in on Jeb McCoy, allowing her ire to make the threat that Jeb would be fired as soon as he got back to the ranch.

But Will spoke up for Jeb. "Now mother; you can't blame Jeb for us running off. I sort of forced him to come with us. Shoot, we would have gone after Lupe's killer even if Jeb had refused."

Virginia knew that was probably true. With two strong-willed children, she had had opportunities in the past to pick up the pieces after other Will and Claire May ventures. Her steely eyes looked back and forth at her children and at Jeb McCoy. Finally she said, "Hmmph. Well, Jeb, I appreciate you looking after these two. Lord knows they need looking after." She bent to fill a coffee cup, then straightened and turned away.

The cold temperatures had kept the bread and butter fresh, and after retrieving it from the pack horse, Jeb and Will ravenously ate their share while the two women and Buster looked on. After they had eaten, Jeb McCoy told the group of the progress of the outlaw.

"He has a full half day's lead on us and is still heading north. He appears to be following the cattle trail toward Kansas City," said Jeb.

"Well, what are we waiting for?" said Virginia. She turned and retrieved rifles, pistols, and ammunition from the pack horse and handed them to Will and Jeb. From atop the pack tree, Buster hauled down a saddle, and Will quickly saddled the spare horse. Then, Jeb and Buster tightened the ropes on the pack tree. With everyone now mounted and sufficiently armed, the Summer Prairie Ranch group was once again on the trail of Henry Vogler.

# Chapter Forty-One

## Late November - Burlington, Iowa
## CB&Q/Union Pacific Railroad Roundhouse

The man pacing the floor of the roundhouse lunch room looked sorely out of place, as did the man who accompanied him.  They were distinguished by their fine wool suits, along with their coats and beaver-nap derby hats.  Their open coats revealed watch chains attached to their vests.  They were obviously out of their element in the dirt-stained, poorly-lit hangout of the off-duty train crews.  The two men had arrived early that morning, riding in a special car attached to a Union Pacific train.  That train car had been detached from the train and sat alone on a nearby siding reserved for just such a purpose.  As the man continued pacing, his companion had taken a seat at one of the rough board tables and was sipping a bit of steaming coffee from a scarred and dented tin coffee mug.

On the opposite side of the table sat a very nervous Nick Wentz, a railroad detective based in Burlington.  At his home the night before, he had received a frantic telephone call from the Burlington Station Master telling him to meet two gentlemen when their train arrived this morning.  When he had told his wife, Helen, about the call, there was a bit of foreboding when he kissed her good-bye before leaving the house to meet the train.  He now wished that he had not installed that new-fangled telephone in their house, but the station master had insisted some months ago that with the telephone, he could reach Nick whenever necessary.  Apparently it had been necessary last night.

Nick did not know the nature of the business of the two gentlemen with whom he presently shared the lunch room.  Upon his arrival, Nick had been told that all discussion would wait for the arrival of the sheriff. But Nick did know that the pacing gentleman was a railroad vice president, and the other gentleman was a Pinkerton detective. Nick had seen the bulge under the shoulder area of the man's suit coat, which told him that the man was armed. All three men were waiting for the fourth man to arrive, and the railroad executive again extracted his pocket watch from his vest to view the time. It was only two minutes after their scheduled meeting time, and just as the railroad man, with a contemptuous look, had snapped the watch cover closed and returned it to its pocket, the outer door of the roundhouse opened.

"Howdy gents," said the new man, who wore a silver star attached to his coat. He was Nathan Wolf, the local county sheriff, whose reputation had spread far and wide in southeast Iowa and western Illinois. Des Moines County, where Burlington was located, was known by every ne'er do well for several counties around, as well as in the Illinois counties across the river. It was known as a county to stay clear of if crime was your ilk, or risk the wrath of the diligent, no-nonsense, young sheriff who took prisoners and asked often-painful questions later. Nathan did not appear to be much older than Nick. He was tall with a square and muscular build, and was ruggedly handsome; he was a force to be reckoned with. He and Nick Wentz were best of friends, and when Nathan entered the room, Nick began to feel more comfortable.

Nathan Wolf was only thirty years old, but he was street wise and knew the ways of criminals. His good looks drew women like bees to honey. There were at least three young ladies in town who were interested in making Nathan's single life a thing of the past. But Nathan Wolf was more interested in being a peace officer and solving crimes than settling down on a permanent basis. He figured that there would always be time for marriage and a family later.

Nathan smiled as he shook hands with the two strangers. "My name is Wallace Ferguson," said the railroad executive. "I'm the Vice President in charge of security with the Union Pacific Railroad, and this here is Caleb Munson, a Pinkerton man," he said nodding to the detective.

Wolf eyed the men and their expensive clothing. "Pleased to meet you," he said.

A few pleasantries were exchanged and coffee mugs filled before Wallace Ferguson abruptly began talking business.

Looking at Nick and then Nathan, Ferguson said, "Now you may not know it, but you two boys have acquired a fine reputation with our railroad. The way you handled that case of the murder of Charlie Mason last year is still talked about at the home office. When anyone harms a railroad detective, we want swift justice. And you boys did a cracker-jack job of bringing that killer to the gallows."

Nick and Nathan looked at each other and both had a slight hint of a smile on their faces. But for Nick's part, it was a bittersweet smile. The murder of his good friend Charlie Mason had impacted his own family in such a negative manner. Solving the case had implicated his mother-in-law; a sad ending to the case.

Although Nathan and Nick still wondered what the Mason murder case had to do with the reason for the visit by Mr. Ferguson, they wisely kept their mouths shut and continued to listen to the railroad man.

"Some weeks back you undoubtedly heard about the train holdup down around Independence, Missouri." He paused and watched Nick and Nathan both nod their heads. You also may have heard that there were a couple of survivors in the gun battle after the outlaws blew up the train. Well, I take that back; there were three survivors that we know of. One of them was the baggage clerk in the payroll car, another was one of the outlaws who stole the money from the train, and the third was a soldier who was guarding the payroll. Turns out he took some of the money, too, and hightailed it away from there."

Nick and Nathan looked at each other again. They had both heard about the outlaw escaping and the baggage clerk surviving, but this was the first they had heard of the surviving soldier.

"That damn soldier is not my concern. He is the Army's problem and still is. They'll eventually find him and hang him," said Ferguson.

Nathan sipped from his coffee mug and spoke up. "Mr. Ferguson, what's all this got to do with me."

Ferguson held up his hand, palm out. "Give me just a second, Sheriff, I'm getting to it."

Almost simultaneously, Wolf and Munson each took a noisy slurp of their respective coffees. At the sound, Ferguson's face showed a slight look of disapproval.

"We are not much farther along in our investigation than we were some weeks back," said Ferguson. "Hell, we still don't know the outlaw's name or where he's from. All we know is that he rides a mule and has a wooden leg."

Wolf thought about interrupting Ferguson again, but then thought better of it.

"After the holdup, our baggage clerk gave us some good information, and we immediately made that available to the U.S. Marshalls and Pinkertons. For a while, we heard nothing. Damn incompetence, I say." He turned to Munson, "No offense, Munson. Just the way I feel, that's all."

Caleb Munson remained silent as Ferguson continued, "But recently, this outlaw has been sighted down in southern Kansas and then most recently near Lawrence, Kansas, where he should have been captured. But a damn fool deputy sheriff there let him slip through his fingers.

Anyway, we are certain that he is still coming north, but we don't know why."

Wolf got up from the table and walked over to the coffee-spill encrusted coffee pot and refilled his mug. He turned around and faced Ferguson while he carefully sipped the hot steaming liquid. Ferguson looked at him and then at Nick Wentz.

Ferguson continued, "All right now, Sheriff, here's where you come into the picture."

Wolf walked back to the table and sat down.

"I just told you that we have had no luck in bringing our robber to justice," said Ferguson. "He is a moving target, and neither local law enforcement nor Pinkertons have been able to catch up with him. But your reputation at headquarters prompted me to suggest to our board of directors that we get you and Wentz involved. My boss and the board approved it, and I'm here to get you started."

Nathan and Nick looked at each other. Nathan quietly chuckled before he said, "Just what is it you are starting, Mr. Ferguson."

Ferguson glared back at Nathan, thinking to himself that this young sheriff was just a bit too impertinent for his liking. But he continued, "Well, I thought that was rather obvious, Sheriff. We are turning you and Wentz loose to track down our outlaw and either shoot him or bring him back to hang."

Inwardly, Nick Wentz was delighted. He would be working an exciting case with Nathan Wolf; it would be a lot more exciting than rousting hobos out of boxcars in the Burlington rail yard. He wondered what Nathan was thinking as he watched him slowly take another sip of his coffee.

"Kinda out of my jurisdiction, don't you think, Mr. Ferguson? I'm only a local sheriff, and I work for the county officials in Burlington," said Wolf, and he smiled at Ferguson.

Ferguson returned the smile. "That's all taken care of Sheriff. As of today, you have been granted a leave of absence by your county folks, and you are on the Union Pacific payroll with a ten per cent increase in pay."

Wolf stood up from the table quickly. "Now just a minute here; you can't just force me to go looking for a killer without even asking me about it." Wolf's face showed his irritation.

"And I failed to mention that if you two are successful, both of you will receive a bonus of $500 from the railroad when you bring in the outlaw," Ferguson added.

As a general rule, for the danger to which they are exposed, and other reasons, most lawmen are underpaid. They gravitate to the job because they have a strong sense of right and wrong and wish to bring down the unlawful. Therefore, the promise of additional money to carry out a job that sounded challenging, immediately ensnared Nathan Wolf. In truth, he thought, he probably would not have objected even if there had been no mention of a bonus. His bluster was only meant to show Ferguson that he would have preferred to have been consulted beforehand, and that he did not much cotton to the pompous attitude of the railroad man.

For the next hour, Wentz and Wolf were briefed by Detective Munson, who was periodically interrupted in his briefing by Wallace Ferguson. They were told that the outlaw was still moving north, but there were indications that he had made camp in Jefferson County, still in Kansas. At the end of the briefing, the railroad detective and the sheriff knew all that was available about the elusive outlaw. They would leave as soon as possible to take up the hunt.

\*\*\*

Two days after their briefing in Burlington, Nick Wentz walked up the narrow aisle of the passenger car, catching himself on the wooden upright back of several seats as the rail car swayed left and right as it sped through the late afternoon, making its way west. He had been in the stock car giving a cupful of oats to his and Nathan's horses and the pack horse. When he was satisfied that the animals were properly taken care of, he returned to the passenger car.

Nathan Wolf had his hat pulled down over his eyes, and his legs were crossed and stretched out in front of his seat. Nick knew Nathan was not sleeping and playfully kicked his friend's boot so that Wolf would draw in his legs to let Nick pass and sit in the adjacent seat facing him.

"Everything all right back there?" Wolf asked without sitting up.

"Yep, they're just munching away. They don't seem to mind the ride."

Two days ago, after a great deal of head scratching, the two lawmen had started out by train from Burlington. They had reasoned that because the outlaw had been moving north, they might be able to intersect his path as he continued north, or if he had changed his course to the east. Either way, they planned to find his trail and run him down. The train had followed the old Mormon Trail, but in Lamoni, Iowa, they had off-loaded their horses and boarded a different train, which, only a few hours ago had crossed into Missouri. The following afternoon, they would arrive in St. Joseph. And from there, they hoped to perhaps meet up with the outlaw by moving south to intercept the fugitive.

The train began slowing. The engine would take on water and fuel in Unionville, Missouri. As he pushed up his hat, Nathan Wolf slowly drew his legs in and sat up in the hard seat. Both he and Nick idly watched out the car window as the train crept slowly into Unionville. As they neared the water and coaling location, they crept by another passenger train waiting on a siding. That train would move on its journey east as soon as their train passed. In the light of the oil lanterns in the passenger cars, Nick and Nathan could see the faces of the passengers in the other train looking back at them as they passed. They soon reached the coaling location, and the passengers were allowed to step off the train for the few minutes it would require to replenish the water and fuel. The two lawmen stepped down to stretch their legs. They watched over the tops of the rail cars as the water pipe was lowered from its tower and water began rushing into the engine's water tank that was built into the tender car. At the same time, coal clattered down a pipe from its over-head hopper into the same car. Nick went into the train station and sent a hurried telegram to the railroad detective at the St. Joseph, Missouri, station, telling him of their pending arrival, and then he walked back to where Nathan was standing.

Hearing a shrill whistle, Nick and Nathan turned and watched the previously waiting train roll out of the siding and begin moving east down the same rails on which they had just arrived. They continued to watch as the train gained speed and grew smaller in view. The receding sounds of the departing train had triggered their private thoughts of home, and prompted them to wonder what would happen when they finally confronted the killer they were pursuing.

With the watering and coaling completed, their conductor whistled for all the passengers to re-board. In only a few minutes, the lawmen again had settled down in their seats as their train continued to the southwest.

# Chapter Forty-Two

## November 27, 1898 - Northwest of Lawrence, Kansas

It was pure vengeance and hate that drove Renee Evans and her son, Elmer Vogler. For Renee, vengeance was for killing her son, and for Elmer, it was anger for the loss of his brother. Henry had acted with a wanton disregard for the love and safety of Martin Vogler. They meant to exact revenge on the man who had caused Martin's death and who had made their lives miserable for so many years. They were determined that Henry Vogler would die at their hands.

Renee was surprised that her painful saddle sores were no longer causing the intense discomfort that had plagued her only days before. She had been able to continue their trek the day after treating herself with the ground oatmeal paste. She had also used a spare shirt to afford herself some extra padding on her saddle.

The weather had cooperated during their trip, allowing the pair to easily see the occasional mule track as they continued north. They were afraid that they had lost Henry's track at Lawrence, but after speaking to the livery stable owner, and an hour spent searching both north and south on the trail, they once again followed the tracks moving north.

After Lawrence, the trail had narrowed to the width of a wagon. The wider cattle trail they had been following now turned to the east to enter Kansas City, but Henry's trail, mixed in with the tracks of other horses, continued north. Two days after resuming their travels, Renee and Elmer were at the top of a long hill. They could see far into the distance, and from their vantage point, they could see the group of riders ahead of them moving north. Because of the distance, they could only determine that the group was made up of five riders and a pack horse. They also knew that as long as the group was not coming toward them, there would not be any trouble. After two more days, Renee and Elmer were convinced that Henry's tracks were leading them to the Missouri River.

# Chapter Forty-Three

**November 28, 1898 - Wathena, Kansas**

Their horses were hobbled and contentedly grazing not far from the campfire. Renee Evans and her son were taking turns sipping from the last whisky bottle they had packed when they had left home days ago.

"Elmer, do you think we will ever see that skunk again? I'm so tired of sleeping on the ground, and I gotta tell you, if we don't catch up to him in another day or two, I'm inclined to head on back home before the worst of winter sets in," said Renee. Elmer's face seemed to be glowing as he sat near the fire, staring at the dancing flames that reflected on his face. He turned to his mother, staring at her for a moment. She did, indeed, appear to be fatigued and seemed to be losing her zeal to pursue the man who had been responsible for the death of her son and Elmer's brother. He, too, was inclined to give up the chase in another day or two.

"I don't know, Ma. I'm so sick of thinking about that son of a bitch that if you decided to pull out in another day or two, I wouldn't give you any fight."

***

Only three miles away, in Elwood, Kansas, Virginia Summers finished up her bath in the Elwood Hotel. Claire May sat on a small stool next to the tub, waiting to use the same bath. Will and Jeb were downstairs in the hotel resting themselves on stools at the hotel bar.

"I think we're getting really close, Jeb," said Will.

He had good reason to say this as the two men sipped the strong amber-colored bourbon from their glasses. Late in the afternoon, the group had approached the Elwood ferry operator at the Missouri River crossing. He was closing down for the day, and told the group they would have to wait until the following morning to cross the river. But on a hunch, Jeb McCoy had asked the ferry operator if he had recently taken a one-legged man riding a mule across the river. The answer had been positive. He had taken the man across the river the previous day.

"Wasn't hard to remember," said the ferryman as he spit a glob of tobacco juice downwind to the side. "Don't get too many one-legged gents riding mules passing through here," he said, and then he laughed, causing a drop of tobacco juice to dribble from the corner of his lips. When queried further, he had recommended that the group bed down at the hotel where they were now staying.

"I hope you're right," said Jeb. "But right now, I'm going upstairs and fall into a nice soft bed. It'll sure be nice after all those nights on the ground." His boot heels clomped the wood floor as he walked from the hotel bar.

***

Only a few miles to the east, across the Missouri River, in St. Joseph, Missouri, Henry Vogler downed his third rye whisky in the bar of a run-down hotel not far from the livery stable where Johnny dozed on three legs; his fourth hoof turned up in a resting position.

As he sat at the bar, Henry was feeling the warming sensation of the whisky in his stomach. His mind wandered as he contemplated his future plans. He was going to Chicago to start a new life, and he was anticipating the chance to return to a life of crime. In his short-sighted view of the world around him, he was of the opinion that stealing from others was a whole lot easier than toiling at honest work. He smiled as he thought that honest work was for suckers. He smiled again when he thought of all the money that he was still carrying in his saddlebags, safely stashed in his hotel room. It was time that he went to bed, but he decided on one more drink. After the glass was set in front of him on the bar, he thought again of how he was escaping the long arm of the law. He was sure that he had made good his disappearance, especially since he had observed no one following him. As with everything else in his useless life, he had no idea how wrong he was.

# Chapter Forty-Four

**November 29, 1898 - St. Joseph, Missouri**

Nick and Nathan watched as other passengers exited the cars and were greeted by friends and family. Nick felt a pang of loneliness for his sweet wife, Helen, as he watched couples meet and kiss each other. The two men walked back and stood to the side of the livery car as the large side panel of the car was unhooked and lowered, making an inclined ramp so the animals could be walked down from the car above. The men walked up the ramp, gathered up their gear, and saddled their horses. They walked the horses down the ramp and continued leading the horses to the nearby depot hitch rack.

Even before they could take their first steps after tying the horses, a young man walked briskly out of the depot door and said, "Are either one of you Nick Wentz?"

Nick looked at the man and said, "I'm Nick Wentz."

"Wonderful," was the reply. "And you must be Sheriff Wolf," he said, extending his hand, which both Nick and Nathan shook.

"I'm Tadd Springer," said the younger man. "I'm with the Union Pacific Railroad, stationed here in St. Joseph. I'm afraid I've got some rather bad news for you," he said. Nathan looked carefully at Springer, thinking that if he was the local railroad detective, then the railroad must be hiring detectives at an awfully young age. Springer had the appearance of an eighteen year old.

"OK," said Nick. "What's the news?"

"Well, I came here to the depot about noon to check the progress of your train, and by chance, I asked the ticket clerk whether he had sold a ticket to anyone matching the description of your outlaw. Turns out that he sold a ticket to a man with one leg who checked a mule into the livery car."

Nick and Nathan looked at Springer, thinking that he was going to continue. But the younger man just stood looking at them with a grin on his face. Finally, Nathan spoke up, "Now where do you suppose that outlaw may have been heading?"

"Oh, pardon me," said Springer. "Yes, you see the ticket he bought was on this morning's eastbound. He bought a ticket to Hannibal. Your train and the outlaw's train must have passed each other someplace along the line," said Springer. "Isn't that odd?"

"Goddamit!" blurted Nathan.

"Why didn't the station master see our outlaw? We sent telegrams and wanted posters out to all the stations," said Nick.

Tadd Springer looked down at the ground for a moment before answering. "Well, you see, our station master is an older gentleman, and he doesn't always get around to going through the posters."

Sure enough, when the men entered the station master's office, a stack of wanted posters lay under other papers in the man's desk mailbox. The station master was not on the premises. He had already departed for the day.

In a very irritated tone, Nathan Wolf asked, "OK, Springer, what time does the next eastbound leave?"

"I'm afraid that the next eastbound does not leave until ten a.m. tomorrow," said Springer.

Nathan shook his head back and forth. "Make sure you have room for us and our horses on that train," he said to Springer. "Let's go Nick; I need a drink."

The two detectives sat in the bar at the *Pony Express Hotel* after delivering their mounts to the nearby livery stable. They each nursed a beer and waited for the sandwiches which they had ordered.

"I can't believe the luck of this damn outlaw," said Nick. "He has managed to slip through the law at every turn. I'm not sure we are ever going to get him."

Nathan did not turn his head to look at his friend as he quietly said, "We'll get him, Nick. We'll get him."

# Chapter Forty-Five

**November 30, 1898 - St. Joseph, Missouri**

By nine a.m., Nick Wentz and Nathan Wolf had loaded their horses into the livery car. The eastbound train sat on its track, the large black 4-4-0 engine periodically chuffing its excess steam. The sheriff and detective stood to one side of the depot waiting room, occasionally making small talk while they watched other passengers buying tickets or patiently waiting as they sat on the hard wooden benches. Nathan Wolf was tired of waiting and was just about to go outdoors and walk along the station platform, even though the outdoor temperature was quite cold that morning. Just as he was about to turn and leave, he and Nick watched as the ticket clerk came from behind his counter and walked toward them.

"Mr. Wentz," said the clerk. "I thought you gentlemen might want to know that two other parties have asked about the one-legged outlaw you gentlemen are pursuing."

The clerk immediately had the lawmen's attention.

"Who might that be, sir?" asked Nathan.

"Well, they were two different groups of folks. One group is over there in that corner," he said as he pointed to the Summer Prairie Ranch group. "There is a lady there with her daughter and son, and two acquaintances. She said they are her ranch hands. They came in very early this morning and asked about the outlaw before they purchased their tickets. They also bought livery space for their animals," he said.

Nick and Nathan looked closely at the ranch group. Just by looking at the members of the group, the lawmen formed a quick opinion that they were not outlaws.

"The other group is in the opposite corner. They appear to be a mother and son, and they were here about two hours after the other group. They also wanted to know if we had seen the outlaw. And when I told them the man had been here yesterday and took the eastbound train, they bought their tickets and livery space."

The lawmen looked at the mother and son. Renee Evans and Elmer Vogler sat quietly passing the time watching the other passengers. Their eyes roamed the room and rested briefly on the two lawmen and the clerk who were looking back at them.

Nick and Nathan studied the mother and son for a moment. And although the dress of the two individuals revealed them not to be wealthy, the lawmen again drew the conclusion that they did not have the look of outlaws. But the lawmen were now very curious. They wondered what the connection could be between these two groups and the outlaw. They aimed to find out once the train got underway.

A man dressed in the uniform of a train conductor entered the station waiting room. He announced loudly that those passengers waiting for the eastbound train should now get aboard.

As the lawmen approached the train, Nathan broke away and told Nick that he was going to check on the horses. He entered the livery car, first checking his and Nick's mounts, and then moving down the line of partitioned stalls. In the dim light of the car's interior, he carefully examined each of the rear flanks of the horses, paying close attention to the brand on each horse. As he turned to leave the car, it lurched, causing him to steady himself on one of the stall partitions. The train had gotten underway. He made his way out of the end door of the car and crossed into the next two passenger cars until he found Nick. But before he sat down, he looked around the car, noting where the other passengers were sitting. There would be time to have a conversation with the other folks who had shown an interest in the outlaw he and Nick were pursuing.

Neither lawman had had breakfast, aside from the coffee they had drunk at the St. Joseph station. So when the conductor came through the car and announced that lunch was being served in the dining car, Nick and Nathan remembered how hungry they were. They were in the first seating of diners, which also included the Summers Ranch group. The lawmen devoured the roast beef and boiled potatoes followed by a sweet bread pudding. When they finished, they remained in the dining car drinking hot, strong coffee. Jeb McCoy and Buster Wilson were seated at the table across the aisle from Virginia, Claire May, and Will Summers. The group had nearly finished eating when Nathan and Nick walked to their table. After begging their pardon and asking to speak with them for a few moments, the lawmen were invited to join them. Nick sat with the ranch hands while Nathan joined the Summers family. The two lawmen identified themselves, showing the group their badges and explaining that they were from Iowa. After the introductions, Nathan got to the point with Virginia Summers.

"I beg your pardon for my being so blunt, Mrs. Summers, but I am curious as to why you asked the St. Joe railroad clerk about a one-legged outlaw. You see, my partner and I are also after this fellow."

In the course of their conversation, Virginia revealed that following the death of her husband she had assumed ownership of the Summer Prairie Ranch in Kansas. Nathan knew that she was probably telling the truth, as the brands on six of the horses in the livery car had carried an "SP" brand.

"We are chasing this outlaw, Sheriff, because he killed a woman who worked on our ranch," said Virginia. "This woman meant a great deal to all of us, and we aim to either kill the outlaw or see him hanged. In addition to being a killer, he also stole several of our horses. I believe both of those offenses are punishable by hanging, are they not?" Nathan was rather taken aback by the blunt talk of Mrs. Summers, yet he immediately liked the woman for her character.

Virginia Summers had no way of knowing that it had actually been Billy Rollins who had killed Lupe Vera and stolen the horses; not Henry Vogler. She only knew that it had been a man riding a mule who had killed Lupe. She also knew from the encampments of the outlaw that he had only one leg. She had put these two pieces of information together, thereby erroneously chasing the wrong man. Nor could the lawmen know that the Summers group was pursuing the wrong man. But at this point, it did not really matter. It was an established fact that the outlaw they were pursing was a killer and a train robber.

Nathan Wolf admired the will of Mrs. Summers and smiled slightly as he replied, "Yes, ma'am, I believe they are." As he said this, he glanced at Claire May, who seemed to be studying the lawman with a slight smile on her face.

Nathan continued, "But why not let the law take care of capturing this fellow, Mrs. Summers?"

"Where we live, Sheriff, there is no lawman within a hundred miles. Ranchers in our area have to carry out our own form of frontier justice. I'm sure you can understand that." She gave Nathan a strong, knowing look as she took a sip of her coffee. "Might I ask why you are so far from home and pursuing the same man?"

Nathan looked at Mrs. Summers and her two children for a few seconds and then explained that the outlaw had been part of a gang that had blown up a payroll train and killed quite a number of soldiers who had been guarding the train. He then told them that the Union Pacific Railroad had hired him to accompany Nick Wentz, the railroad detective, in pursuit of the train robber/killer.

All the while Nathan Wolf had been speaking, Claire May watched the handsome Iowa sheriff. She found herself fascinated by the lawman.

"Sheriff Wolf, I believe our goals appear to be the same," said Virginia Summers. "Thus, I hope that you will allow us to accompany you in your search and watch the conclusion of our mutual quest. Would you please allow us to do so?"

Nathan replied slowly. "I mean no disrespect, ma'am, but you must understand that there is great danger inherent with bringing murderers to justice. For your own safety, I wish you would reconsider."

"I'm well aware of the danger, Sheriff, and I assure you that we will not hinder you in any way as you carry out your duties. We wish merely to observe as the final curtain is brought down on the outlaw," countered Virginia.

Nathan then looked at Mrs. Summer's pretty daughter, Claire May. She was actually grinning coyly at the sheriff. He turned his eyes to Will Summers and saw that he was watching his sister, a smile on his face. Nathan grasped the significance of the look of the young man and his sister. His face turned a slight pink hue.

Turning his eyes back to Virginia, he said, "It would be a pleasure to have you along, ma'am."

"Wonderful; then it's settled," said Virginia as she rose from the dining table. "I think we shall now return to our seats in the coach car. It was a pleasure speaking with you, Sheriff."

The look on Claire May's face during Nathan's conversation with Virginia Summers had not been overlooked by the other table. Jeb and Buster rose to follow Mrs. Summers. Both were grinning, and Jeb good-naturedly elbowed Buster as they walked away.

After the group was gone, Nick slapped his friend on the top of the shoulder. "Well now, Mr. Sheriff. I believe that little ranch filly has an eyeball on the good sheriff. What do you think?" said Nick with a big grin on his face.

"Want that grin wiped off, pal?" said Nathan.

Nick just laughed.

"Now shut up, 'cause we've got more work to do," said Nathan as the passengers assigned to the second lunch seating were now beginning to enter the car. Renee Evans and Elmer were in the second seating. The two lawmen went back to their table and sat down, where they were able to furtively watch the blonde woman and her son as they ate.

Renee Evans was now sure that the two men sitting a few tables away from them were lawmen. She had seen the star pinned to the shirt of one of the men when his coat swung open and revealed it. While she had done nothing to bring on the attention of any lawman, it still made her nervous just the same. Many years ago, when she lived the life of a saloon girl, it seemed that lawmen were always meddling in her life. She did not know why, she just did not trust or like lawmen. She had quietly told Elmer that the two men sitting and drinking coffee were lawmen. Elmer turned slowly and caught Nick Wentz looking back at him.

He turned back to his mother and said, "Ain't no concern of ours, Ma. We ain't done anything wrong."

But just as they were finishing their meal, the two lawmen came over to their table.

Nathan put on his most pleasant persona. "I beg your pardon, ma'am. My name is Nathan Wolf, and I am sheriff of a town up in Iowa. This here is Nick Wentz. He's a railroad detective. I wonder if we might have a word with you."

Renee swallowed. "Suit yourself."

The lawmen sat down at the table. "May I ask your name, ma'am?" said Nick.

Renee hesitated but then said, "My name is Evans, Renee Evans. This is my son Elmer."

"Pleased to meet you," said Nathan. "Where abouts are you folks from?"

"Oklahoma. Oklahoma Territory. We live on a ranch down there called the Circle S."

Nathan then knew that this woman and her son were at least telling some of the truth as verified by the circle brands on three of the horses in the livery car. The brands each had an "S" in the center of a circle.

In much the same manner that they would elicit information from a cooperative witness to a crime, Nick and Nathan cajoled more facts from the mother and son. Within fifteen minutes of talking, the lawmen knew that this couple was following the same outlaw that they were pursuing. They continued until they found out why.

But Renee and Elmer did not tell the whole story. They told the lawmen that they were after the outlaw because he had been responsible for the death of another of the woman's sons. That son, named Martin had died needlessly in a train holdup. They also told Nathan and Nick that the outlaw had beaten Renee up numerous times. And finally, they said that they intended to see the man dead; whether at the hands of a hangman or by their hands. What they failed to mention was that they had in their possession part of the very loot taken from that payroll train.

"Well, I'm mighty glad we have had a chance to meet," said Nathan. "Because you are the first people we have run across who actually know who the outlaw is. Perhaps you could tell us his name."

"His name is Vogler, Henry Vogler," said Renee.

"How old is Mr. Vogler, Miss Evans?" asked Nick.

"I don't know for certain," said Renee. "But I'm guessing that he might be pretty near sixty years old."

Continually trying to gain the trust of Renee and Elmer, Nathan said, "You'd think a man would know better by the time he is that old, wouldn't you?"

"He ain't nothin' but a road apple, mister. He ain't got any sense and abused my mother for years and got my brother killed," said Elmer. "We aim to set things straight."

With that piece of information, Nathan now surmised that Vogler probably lived with Renee, and that there was a real possibility that Vogler was Elmer's father.

"Indeed. Well, it was mighty nice of you to talk with us. You be careful now on the rest of your trip," said Nathan as he got up to leave. He and Nick shook Elmer's hand and walked back to the passenger car. They glanced briefly at the Summers' as they returned to their seats.

Quietly, Nick said, "Well ain't that the damnedest thing you ever heard? A mother and her son tracking this outlaw half the way across the country to kill him. Now that's somebody who I would not like to cross."

"My guess is that there's a real strong bond between that woman and her sons, especially since the old man did nothing but beat on her and her boys all the time. And this Henry Vogler fella tore out a piece of that woman's heart when he killed one of the things she cherished most in her life, one of her sons," said Nathan.

"I'm beginning to wonder who is going to get to this son of a bitch first," said Nick. "I have a suspicion that this Vogler fellow will never come to trial."

# Chapter Forty-Six

**Late afternoon - November 30, 1898**
**West of Macon, Missouri**

The slowing of the train roused Nick and Nathan from their naps. They would be stopping in Macon for fuel and water. The conductor came through the car and advised them that those passengers who wished could leave the train to stretch their legs or take care of any personal business. The train would be stopping for nearly thirty minutes.

Nick and Nathan stood at the side of the train. The weather was still cold enough for their breath to be seen as they stood watching horses being unloaded from the livery car while other animals stood by their owners waiting to be on loaded. It was not long before the conductor began shouting for passengers to board the train.

Apparently, the same announcement had been made inside the passenger depot, because the doors opened, and an unusually large crowd of people began leaving the warmth of the depot interior to make their way toward the train.

"Guess we better get back on board, Nathan," said Nick, and he turned to walk toward the steps up to the passenger car.

Nathan did not move. His mind was working on what he was seeing. Something was just not right. Then he knew. There were too many people moving toward the train. He caught the conductor as he was passing by.

"Sir, just a minute please. Can you tell me why there are so many people getting on the train here?" asked Nathan.

The conductor began to laugh. "Oh yeah, I can tell you. You see that engine and tender over yonder there on that siding?"

Nathan turned to see where the conductor was pointing. "Yes, I see it?" Nick had come back to join Nathan and was listening to the conversation.

"Well, that was yesterday's eastbound train. That old engine decided it wasn't going to go any further and blew a hole clean through its boiler. It was lucky that it made it into Macon."

As he looked, Nathan could see what appeared to be a jagged hole in the side of the boiler tank of the engine.

"So all those people that were on that train had to find themselves a hotel room for the night and jump on our train today to continue their journeys. Gonna be a full train, that's for sure. You boys better get on board and find your seats."

The conductor began to walk away, but Nick and Nathan both caught hold of one of the conductor's arms.

"Sir, my name is Nick Wentz. I am a railroad detective for the Union Pacific Railroad." Nick opened a wallet and showed the conductor his badge. "I want you to hold this train. Do not let it roll until I tell you. Do you understand?"

"Nathan, I'm going into the livery car. I would suggest you go with the conductor and walk the passenger cars looking for our man," said Nick, and he sprinted down the side of the train until he entered the livery car.

In the meantime, Nathan and the conductor went through the three passenger cars and the dining car. When they passed Virginia Summers, Nathan leaned down and whispered to her. "Ma'am, you need to be ready to leave the train when I tell you." He then walked on, leaving Virginia Summers with a bewildered look on her face.

When Nathan and the conductor were done, they stepped back off of the train and met Nick who was running to meet them.

Out of breath, Nick said, "Nothing but horses, Nathan. There are no mules in that livery car."

Under his breath, Nathan said, "He got off here."

Turning to the conductor, Nick asked, "Were you on duty on that eastbound train yesterday?"

By now the conductor was bewildered. "No, no, I was not. The other conductor is in the depot. He is waiting for the next westbound to head back to St. Joe. Say, what's this all about, anyway?"

Nathan and Nick turned to go into the station. Nick turned back and said, "Remember, don't let the train roll until I tell you."

They found the off-duty conductor reading a paper as he sat by the warm pot-bellied stove in the waiting room. The lawmen introduced themselves and began asking questions.

"Were you the conductor on that eastbound train yesterday that broke down?" asked Nick.

"Sure was," said the conductor. "We were darn lucky to get this far. I thought sure that engine was going to blow sky high after it started leaking. And the damn fool engineer just kept it rolling. Guess he must have known what he was doing because we made it here just before it blew."

"Do you remember seeing a one-legged man leave the train?" asked Nathan.

"Darn right I do. That fellow was a pain in my backside," said the conductor. "He growled and complained while we were rolling, and when we finally got here, he wanted to get his animal off the livery car before anybody else. Mighty glad to see that one leave."

"Was he riding a horse?" asked Nick.

"Shoot no," said the conductor. "He was riding a mule."

Nick and Nathan looked at each other, and then Nathan asked, "Do you have any idea which way he headed when he left here?"

"Sure, he went down to the end of the rail yard there and turned north."

The lawmen shook hands with the off-duty conductor and went back outside and walked to the train. They found the conductor swinging his arms and stamping his feet to stay warm as he stood next to the train.

"We need to get some livestock off of the livery car, and then we will be on our way," said Nick. And while he went with the conductor to get the baggage clerk to open the livery car, Nathan went into the passenger car, leaned down to Virginia Summers and quietly said, "Let's go ma'am. We're getting back on the trail." He turned and walked away while the Summer Prairie Ranch folks gathered up their gear.

While they waited at the livery car, Nathan explained to Virginia Summers that the outlaw, named Henry Vogler, had departed the train after it had broken down and was heading north on his mule.

It was not long before their mounts were unloaded and everyone was once again moving north. The whistle blew on the eastbound train, and it began moving.

***

The train had scarcely moved more than five hundred yards when it abruptly slowed, with the drive wheels screeching against the steel rails.

Renee Evans had been sitting and idly watching two young children running up and down the aisle of their passenger car. She had not looked out the window of the coach until the children's mother grabbed the children and made them sit in their seats. At that moment, Renee looked out the window to see a group of horsemen and two women riding slowly away from the train. She recognized them and immediately jumped out of her seat, reached up, and pulled the emergency stop cord. As soon as he saw his mother jump up, Elmer also sprang up and followed her. Then, as the train came to a hastened stop, Renee met the conductor as she hurried to the livery car. "We have to get off, now," said Renee, as she crossed to the livery car.

"What is the meaning of this?" huffed the conductor.

"I don't have time to explain," said Renee. "Just let us get our horses off the train."

"Now see here," said the conductor. He said nothing further as he stared at the barrel of Elmer's pistol.

"Sir, we mean no harm," said Elmer. "But we must get off the train." He still held his pistol at the ready.

Thirty minutes later, the ramp was again raised and fastened to the side of the livery car. Standing beside the car, the conductor faced toward the engine and waved. A whistle was heard from the engine in answer to the wave, and the train began rolling once more. The conductor hopped up onto the steps of the rail car, stood looking over his shoulder, and watched the man and woman ride away from the train.

*** 

On good mounts, the lawmen and Summers group made nearly thirty miles each day, stopping to camp when the daylight waned. The group stopped periodically to let the horses blow and drink, to stretch their legs, and to take care of personal business. As dusk descended, they camped for the night just south of Kirksville. Because it was so cold, Will insisted that his mother and Claire May ride into town and stay at a hotel. The men would come by in the morning, and the women would then join them at that time.

"Make sure you are ready, mother. We will come through on the main street, and we'll be looking for you," said Will.

His mother and sister waved back as they rode into town.

The night was cold, and the heat from the crackling fire felt good. A skim of ice had to be broken on the stream surface to get water and to allow the horses to drink. As they sat by their fire, the lawmen and the Summers group could see another campfire a quarter of a mile south of them.

"Who else do you suppose is out on the road when it's this cold?" asked Buster Wilson.

The lawmen didn't say anything; that is, until Buster repeated his question.

Nathan then told Buster, Will, and Jeb about meeting Renee Evans and her son, Elmer.

"Do you mean to say that the outlaw's wife and his son are camped over yonder?" asked Will.

Nathan answered affirmatively and told the group how he had seen the pair dogging them all that afternoon.

"Well that beats all," said Jeb. "A wife tracking down her own husband to kill him."

"Well," said Nathan. "I didn't get the idea that the outlaw was legally married to Renee Evans. After all, she told me that the outlaw's name is Vogler; same as her son, but apparently Evans is her last name."

"I guess I'll just have to think on that, then," said Jeb. After a moment, he said, "Just the same, I wouldn't like to think about me being the man that a woman comes all the way from Oklahoma to kill. Now that's a woman with purpose!"

The other men chuckled. "My thoughts exactly," said Will.

"Yessir," Buster quietly said, and then took a swig of warm coffee.

# Chapter Forty-Seven

**December 1, 1898**
**Just South of the Iowa Border**

The rain had held off during the night, but there were sporadic sprinkles of rain mixed with occasional sleet as the lawmen and the Summer's group rode into Kirksville to locate Virginia and Claire May. They made one brief stop at the telegraph office where Nick and Nathan wired two telegrams. The group then rode out of Kirksville. The outlaw's trail had skirted the town on the east, and they soon found it again and turned once again to the north.

But the following day, December 2, the trail was lost for a short time. After a search, Jeb rejoined the group. "He's turned east on the main trail."

Nick turned to Nathan and said, "It's the trail used by the Mormons, isn't it Nathan?"

"Yep," said Nathan. "Same trail we took when we left home."

"Where do you suppose this outlaw is going to land," said Nick. "He can't travel forever. I've always heard that a mule can out walk a horse and carry a heavier load while he does it, but even a mule can't go forever. He must be headed somewhere."

After noon, the skies cleared a bit, leaving light clouds that rapidly changed shapes as they quickly scudded across the sky. The sun shone through the scattered clouds, giving some relief from the cold breeze.

Virginia rode beside her daughter, some distance behind the two lawmen.

"I swear, Claire May. You haven't taken your eyes off of that Sheriff since we began this fool-hardy trip. You're acting like a little puppy dog, and I don't believe he has the slightest interest in you," said Virginia. And then she made a tsking sound with her tongue as she shook her head, but she was also smiling as she spoke.

"Don't be so sure, mother. I've caught him looking at me a few times, too. Anyway, you have to admit, he's very handsome," said Claire May as she trained her eyes on Nathan Wolf's back as he rode up ahead.

"Granted, he's handsome, Claire May. But I don't think he has an interest in you. Besides, he lives clear up here in Iowa."

To Virginia's surprise, Claire May spurred her horse, left her mother's side, and rode up beside Nathan Wolf. "Mind if I ride along with you, Sheriff?" said Claire May as she reined in to walk beside Nathan's horse.

Nathan Wolf looked over at Claire May, slightly embarrassed. Then he looked back at Nick, who was riding on his other side. Nick just chuckled and said, "I'll catch up with you later, Sheriff." He then peeled his horse off to the side and waited for Virginia Summers, joining her as she came up beside him.

"Tell me about your sheriff friend, Mr. Wentz," said Virginia. Nick laughed good-naturedly and began telling her about his best friend. By the time he was finished, Virginia Summers felt more at ease about her daughter's infatuation with the lawman from Iowa. Keeping her thoughts to herself, she still did not think there was a romantic interest on the part of the lawman. But affairs of the heart are not always worn in plain sight on one's sleeve.

# Chapter Forty-Eight

**December 4, 1898**
**Donnellson, Iowa-Fourteen Miles West of Fort Madison**

They had decided to stop in the early afternoon. Almost all of their horses needed attention to their shoes, and the animals also needed a night out of the weather to get a good feed at the blacksmith's livery. The group would bed down in the hotel for the night. They were enjoying an early dinner at a small cafe facing the main street of the small town.

The lawmen were devouring their second pieces of apple pie while seated at the table with Virginia, Claire May, and Will. Characteristic of cowboys, Jeb and Buster had gone next door to a bar, where they were enjoying hot roast beef sandwiches slathered in gravy, along with a cold beer.

The sound of clattering hooves on the hard-packed street brought the eyes of the indoor diners to the window facing the street. The sound grew louder and mixed with that of creaking leather and jingling metal. At a fast walk, a group of mounted Army soldiers, led by a stern-looking officer, moved down the main street and quickly picked up their gait upon reaching the end of the street at the edge of town.

"I suppose they have somewhere important to go," said the waitress as she cleared dishes from the Summers' table. "Those damn-fool soldiers from Fort Madison come clanging through here about every other day," she said. "I thought they took care of the Indians a long time ago." She shook her head as she walked back to the kitchen.

In another hour, Virginia and Claire May had made their purchases at the general store. Buster had his arms full as they began to make their way down the street. It was all he could do to hang onto the bacon, canned goods, hard rolls, coffee, and dried beef. He went on down to the livery with the purchases to load them in the provision bags carried by their pack horse. The rest of the group made their way to the hotel lobby to relax before bed.

They had been chatting in the hotel lobby for thirty minutes when they heard the return of the Army patrol. It was now heading east to return to Fort Madison. They only looked up for a second, then returned to their conversation. But in the dim twilight, Will had seen it.

"Mother, the Army has that woman and man who have been following us," he said. "There they go. Take a look."

Virginia, Claire May, and the lawmen stood and moved closer to the window. Sure enough, Renee Evans and Elmer Vogler rode amidst the mounted soldiers as they passed through town in the deepening shadows. It appeared that they were being escorted, but whether it was voluntary or under duress was not known.

"I wonder if there was more to their story that they weren't telling us," said Will.

***

In the early morning of that same day, a telegram had been received at Fort Madison. The wire was somewhat vague, of course, as it had been paraphrased from the wire sent by Nick Wentz while in Donnellson. The nub of the message alluded to the fact that the wanted outlaw, Henry Vogler, was on the trail heading east in the direction of the fort. True to military bureaucratic procedures, a captain who was given the wire at the fort decided that he must confer with a senior officer who at the time was out on patrol to the north. Hence, nothing was done until the senior officer returned, and by that time, Henry Vogler had departed that trail. The patrol did not find Henry Vogler, but they stumbled upon another Vogler.

An hour ago, Renee Evans and Elmer had dismounted and were walking their horses to give them a breather. The Army patrol came clattering toward them and stopped, following the order of the captain who was their leader.

Captain Benjamin Wardlaw was a veteran of ten years in the Army. He was a product of a merchant class family; not poor, but certainly not rich. Years ago when his family had petitioned for a West Point appointment for Benjamin, they were denied. Instead, he was appointed a sergeant, a position in which he had nearly failed before finally getting the hang of army life. He had worked himself up to his present officer status, not by virtue of his intelligence, but more because of his ability to read a situation, and read people. His ability to discern what his commanding officers needed before they asked for it had stood him in good stead, enabling him to advance through the ranks.

Wardlaw had stopped his patrol with the sole intention of asking the man and woman whom he found walking their horses whether or not they may have by chance seen the one-legged outlaw. The response from Renee and Elmer had been negative; they claimed not to have seen the man. But the subsequent conversation piqued the captain's curiosity. Specifically, why were these people travelling, and where did they live, and where were they going?

"I beg your pardon, madam," Wardlaw said to Renee. "Where are you folks from?" he asked.

"Oklahoma Territory," said Elmer.

"If I might ask, what are you doing here in Iowa?"

The old excuse they had used before came to light again. They told the captain that they were on their way to visit relatives. And when asked where the relatives lived, Elmer was stumped. His knowledge of geography was a bit limited.

"Chicago," Renee hurriedly interjected. Her knowledge of locations was also limited, but she had once had a friend in a bar where she had worked who had been from Chicago. She only knew it was up north and hoped the answer satisfied the Army Captain. Apparently it did, as the captain merely nodded his head in response.

But the final question was the one that prompted the trip to Fort Madison.

"Folks, we have jurisdiction for the protection of travelling citizens in this area. For my recollection, would you please be so kind as to tell me your names?" said the captain as he continued to look at Renee.

"Renee Evans and this is my son, Elmer," she said.

The captain was doing his best to read between the lines and get to the bottom of why a woman and her son were travelling alone and so far from home. He decided to press on. On a hunch, he turned to Elmer and said, "Cowboy, what is your surname?"

Elmer was not even sure what surname meant, but he figured it must be his last name. He was being pressed for an answer by the no-nonsense Army officer and did not know how to answer. He was trying to weigh the consequences of lying to the Army officer who kept staring at him. What could happen to him if he were found to be lying? On the other hand, what would be the harm if he told the truth? By now, the Army knew the name of his father. He did not know how to answer and stood flummoxed.

"Come, come, sir. You must certainly know your name. What is your family name; your last name. What is it?"

Elmer looked at his mother, then decided to come clean. "Vogler, Elmer Vogler."

Captain Wardlaw's lower lip pushed upward in a frown. The name Vogler was all the information that Captain Wardlaw needed. At a signal from the captain, two troopers bore forward with pistols drawn, pointing at Renee and Elmer.

To Elmer, Captain Wardlaw said, "Sir, if you would please hand me your pistol." Elmer did as he was told, and five minutes later, he and Renee began riding with the Army patrol to Fort Madison.

## Chapter Forty-Nine

**December 5, 1898 - Northeast of Donnellson, Iowa**

The group sat unmoving in the intersection of the two roads and watched as Jeb McCoy and Buster Wilson cast back and forth along the trail, only to return to the group and repeat the slow process. Soon, Jeb repeated the process on the second road. Before long, he shouted.

"Over here," he said as he waved to the group. As they joined him, he said, "He's turned north. Here's one of the mule tracks, and there are others further up the trail." Following his lead, the lawmen and the Summers group turned and headed north.

Henry Vogler had indeed changed direction. Furtively asking directions when he could, he knew exactly where he was headed. Years ago, when he had worked as a railroad laborer in Kansas, he had had the opportunity to learn a great deal about the lives of some of the fellow railroad workers. Those workers came from all over the country, all with stories of their own. Two of the workers whom he had befriended had come from the Chicago area and had worked on rail lines in Illinois, Iowa, and Kansas. One thing that those workers had told him that he always remembered was that they had done maintenance on the first railroad bridge to cross the Mississippi, which had been built between Illinois and Iowa in a place between Rock Island in Illinois and Davenport in Iowa. Remembering that story, Henry had decided some time ago that rather than looking for other river crossing points, he would use the Davenport bridge to cross the Mississippi.

\*\*\*

"Make sure he gets a good rubdown and plenty of oats," said Henry to the stable owner as he unbuckled the saddle girth and pulled the saddle from Johnny's back. The mule let out a contented sigh as it curiously turned its head to survey its surroundings. The animal was still damp from the intermittent snow flurries that had been falling as they had entered Davenport. So far, there had not been much of an accumulation on the ground, but the weather remained threatening, with a dark gray overcast sky. Henry had decided that he would like to spend the night in a warm hotel rather than another cold night on the ground and had made his way to the Davenport livery stable in mid-afternoon. He was going to get a bath and a shave and then have a hot dinner sharpened by whiskey.

Later, as he sat soaking in the hot water of his bath in the *Rock View Hotel*, he relaxed and thought about the money that he was still carrying in the leather saddle bags in his hotel room. He daydreamed about what he thought might become of his life when he reached the big city. He even thought that he might just want to become respectable instead of following his inclination to return to the life of a criminal. He certainly had enough money to live a normal life.

But he felt absolutely no regret as he idly thought back on the egregious crimes that he had committed in his life. Robbing others of their valuables, and even killing people, meant little to him except for the furtherance of his own warped goals. There was only one chapter in his life that he mildly regretted, and that was the injury to his great aunt, and the disappointment that he had seen in the face of his mother before he tore off her cherished necklace and left the two women in what seemed like a lifetime ago. He often wondered how life had treated his mother, but he was never man enough to find her and apologize to her. Years ago in San Antonio, he had come close to asking for her forgiveness, but the guilt in his heart would not allow it. Instead, he had left behind his mother's gold locket necklace, and with only slight remorse, he had travelled away from San Antonio without speaking to her. A chill swept over him, and he shrugged his shoulders, then reached to the floor at the side of the tub and lifted the whiskey bottle to his mouth.

***

"Buster, I don't believe I have ever been this cold in my life," said Jeb. "My damn fingers are just liable to fall off." Jeb McCoy had one hand in the pocket of his coat, and the other was holding his reins. He alternated his hands in an attempt to keep at least one warm. Buster looked over at his friend after keeping his eyes on the tracks they were following. Then he looked back at the other four members of their group. He could see that Virginia Summers and Claire May were hunched over in their saddles to block some of the cold northern breeze. Nick Wentz and Nathan Wolf had their eyes focused straight ahead watching their surroundings as the trail wended through wooded areas.

Buster turned back to the front and quietly said to his friend, "Those Yankee lawmen don't seem to be very cold. Guess that's because they hail from these parts. Too damn cold for me, though."

While traversing the high ground, their group had seen the Mississippi River from a distance as they passed Muscatine. While they were tempted to enter the town and stop, the trail of the outlaw was fresh and had bypassed the town and continued northeast, following a riverside trail. They kept moving.

***

If there is such a thing as a man being an example of a paradox, Nathan Wolf was such a man. He was not necessarily the man he appeared to be. To others, he might seem to be just an ordinary man; maybe not even overly intelligent. It was this appearance that had ensnared so many criminals who thought that Wolf could be easily outsmarted. Each time that happened, the outlaw had been proven wrong; in some instances dead wrong. Wolf was highly successful as a lawman; his record spoke volumes of his skill and tenacity, which enabled him to hunt down, apprehend, and bring to justice those worthless members of society who preyed on the innocent. His skill included his ability to out-think his quarry by imagining what the criminal's next move might be. He could literally will himself to think like a criminal. So far in this latest journey, he had been unable to figure out the outlaw's destination, and it was frustrating him. But at the moment, as his eyes appeared to be following the passing landscape, his mind was elsewhere. His scrambled thoughts had organized themselves at last. Imagining himself to be in the boots of his quarry, he had suddenly had an epiphany. It was as if he were in a trance. Caught in the moment, he was now staring at the back of his horse's neck as he slowly drew up the reins and stopped the animal.

Nick noticed his friend stopping and dropped back to join him. The others in the group soon joined them.

"Nathan, what's the matter?" asked Nick.

They all heard him say it, even though he said it very quietly. "Chicago. The son of a bitch is headed for Chicago," said Nathan.

"What makes you think he is heading for Chicago, Mr. Wolf?" asked Virginia.

Nathan raised his head and looked at the faces peering curiously at him. "Because if I were our outlaw, I would be headed there. That town is so damn big that a man could get permanently lost in that mass of humanity."

Turning to Virginia and Claire May, Wolf said, "From what I hear, crime is rampant in that city, and it's no place for a woman to go trying to track a criminal. There are people there who would kill you to get your shoes. It's a place where this Vogler fellow would fit right in."

Turning to Nick, he said, "Nick, think back on our trail. For days, Vogler has travelled north and east, angling toward the Mississippi. I believe he aims to cross the river. But he passed by Burlington, then Muscatine. I think he aims to cross at Davenport."

"But why Davenport, Nathan?" asked Nick. Then Nick suddenly said, "Wait a minute, wait a minute; I think I can answer my own question. It's exactly straight east from there to Chicago, isn't it?"

"Yep, it sure is. And I'll tell you what; again, if I was him, I would catch a train in Rock Island and ride the rest of the way to Chicago in comfort."

Groans and words of discouragement came from the rest of the group.

Finally, Virginia asked, "Do you think we should give up, Mr. Wolf?"

Nathan thought for a few seconds before he answered. "No, I don't think we should just yet. I have a hunch that he is just as cold and miserable as we are and would like to rest up for a day or so. If he is going to cross the river in Davenport, then I think we should keep going at least that far. If he gets a train ticket in Rock Island, then I think we can give it up. We could never find him in Chicago."

Virginia nodded her head. "I'm inclined to agree with you, Mr. Wolf."

"We still have a problem, though," said Nathan. "In order to catch him, we need to keep travelling through the night in case he is there waiting to cross the river tomorrow. Jeb, can you and Buster keep tracking him in the dark?"

"I don't think he is going to need much tracking. Traffic is light on this road, and as you pointed out, the road leads to Davenport. I think we could fire up one of those small oil lamps you brought on the pack horse and walk the road a bit to make sure we see a track now and then. I'm a bit worried about these snow flurries, though. If we get any amount of snow, we might lose the trail."

Showing her frustration at the thought of losing the outlaw, and the fact that she was very cold, Claire May said, "I don't know about you men, but I don't care to camp out tonight in this cold and snow. I think we should go on to this Davenport town. At least there might be a place where we could get warm."

"I guess I would second that," said Virginia. "I'm for pressing on."

"Guess that settles it, Nathan," said Nick. "Jeb, see if you can find us a trail."

The light was fading as the group turned their horses and resumed their walk to Davenport. In the waning daylight, each member of the party was lost in his or her own quiet thoughts.

***

After the light had finally faded to a deep gray, quiet darkness, the group would periodically stop, while Jeb McCoy used a flint, steel, and waxed cotton to light one of the small oil lamps. He would then walk ahead of the group, trudging forward, bent at the waist, until he found the mule tracks; whereupon he would blow out the lamp, cap it, and remount his horse. They rode in this manner all night. The entire group and their animals were exhausted. When possible, they would doze in their swaying saddles with their reins looped on their saddle horn and their hands in their pockets. The horses needed no prodding. Horses are herd animals, and they simply followed the lead animal, which was ridden by Jeb.

Claire May's teeth chattered from the effects of the cold. She looked over at her mother, who was riding next to her and saw that Virginia's eyes were closed. As she looked at her mother more closely, she could not help but feel admiration for her. It was an easy feeling on the part of Claire May. After the death of her father, her mother had assumed the physically demanding role of the ranch manager, along with raising two children. Virginia was an exemplary role model for her children, being strict and strong when needed, and nurturing her children as only a mother can at other times. She had had numerous frank discussions with Will and Claire May, which resulted in two young adults of whom she was very proud. She was confident that when the time came, the Summer Prairie Ranch would be in good hands, the hands of her children. She had raised them to know the tenets of Christianity; to know that there was some good in every man, but to stop evil when it was confronted, and that was what this journey was proving. Evil had invaded their ranch in the form of a murderer and thief, and that could not be tolerated. Her mother intended to see the journey to its end.

Claire May smiled slightly and then quietly spurred her horse forward until she was riding to the side of Nathan Wolf. She turned and faced him and said quietly, "Are you awake Mr. Wolf?"

Nathan had heard the horse coming up beside him and had smiled inwardly. "Yes, ma'am, I am awake. Too cold to have a snooze, I'm afraid," he said. "How are you holding up?"

"I don't believe I have ever been this cold in my life, even when we have one of our big Kansas winter blizzards."

She changed the subject. "Mr. Wolf, I don't believe you have ever mentioned your wife."

From conversations she had overheard from the men, Claire May was reasonably sure that Nathan Wolf was not married. She just wanted to manipulate their talk in that direction.

"No, no, I haven't," said Wolf, not yet being pulled into the gentle snare.

Claire May thought for a minute, then knew he was playing her a bit.

"Well, sometimes, I suppose, that if a man doesn't appreciate the wife that he has, he just avoids talking ill of her, isn't that right Mr. Wolf?"

Nathan couldn't help it. He chuckled. "Yep, I suppose that could be true."

Claire May was losing her patience and finally just came to the point. "Mr. Wolf, are you married or not?"

"Miss Summers, I am not, nor have I ever been, married," said Nathan, and he smiled as he returned Claire May's gaze. He found himself looking at her a bit longer than he probably should have, but he was also beginning to really like this young woman who was perhaps just a bit forward and not afraid to speak her mind. She was also "not hard to look at."

They rode in silence for a few more minutes until Claire May again turned to Nathan and said, "Do you have a special lady waiting for you back there in Burlington?"

Wolf held his face intact. He did not want her to see him smiling. He was enjoying this conversation. "Not unless you count the little black and white lady that lives under my porch."

"What?" said a startled Claire May.

Wolf chuckled. "Yep, and that old cat has lived there for years, and she now has five kittens I've been feeding too."

Claire May now laughed. "Why Mr. Wolf, I believe you have been toying with me, haven't you?"

"I may have, Miss Summers, I may have. And please stop calling me Mr. Wolf. My name is Nathan."

"It's a nice strong name. I like it. And if you please, my name is Claire May."

"Yes, ma'am, it is," said Nathan. She playfully snapped at him with the ends of her reins, then smiled and looked straight ahead.

"Why have you never married, Nathan," she asked.

"Guess I never gave it much thought," said Wolf. "Never figured I needed to be married."

"Maybe you ought to give that a bit more thought, Nathan," she said.

"Perhaps so, Claire May, perhaps so," he said.

Sometimes it is easier for two lovers to bring their feelings to the surface under the cover of darkness, a darkness that might hide a slight hurt or look of disapproval in the eyes or face of the other person. Nathan and Claire May needn't have that fear nor did they need the darkness. They were both confident individuals, and they were falling in love. As they walked their horses in the cold darkness over the course of the next few hours, they quietly talked and told each other about their lives, hopes, and dreams.

# Chapter Fifty

**Early Morning - December 6, 1898**
**Davenport, Iowa**

Each step that he took caused intense pain to radiate in his brain. Henry Vogler was hung over and rued the fact that he had drunk so much that he had been lured from the hotel last night.

Bigger city, more sophisticated whores, he thought, recalling his actions last night. She had taken him to her crib after closing time at the hotel bar. The night was not satisfactory; the alcohol hindering his ability to the point that he became enraged, physically slapping the poor woman who had nothing to do with his lack of prowess. He then verbally abused the prostitute before stumbling back to the hotel. He climbed the hotel stairs to his room, falling twice as he made his way to the second floor. He had managed to get the door to his room open, looked under the bed to confirm that his saddlebags were still there, and passed out on the bed.

This morning, he was walking in spite of the intense pain in his head, because he thought the cold fresh air would do him some good and untangle the cobwebs in his brain. Instead, he was just cold and in alcohol-induced pain as he continued on to the livery stable. He planned to saddle Johnny and bring him back to the hotel. Next, he intended to eat something and get back on the trail. He caught himself in thought. What trail, he thought, and smiled. The previous day, he had learned that the next eastbound train to pass through Davenport would not arrive for another two days. He also learned that there would be a train headed to Chicago today from Rock Island, across the river. That train originated in southern Illinois and would reach Rock Island later in the day.

Henry intended to meet and board that train. He thought to himself, I'm going over that damn bridge and then get a ticket to ride a train in comfort to Chicago. No more sleeping on the ground for me.

He found the mule in the livery stable, munching contentedly on the hay that had been placed in the stall.

"Hello, Johnny. Did you get a good feed?" he said as he stroked the mule's neck. "My only friend, aren't you boy? We are going to cross the river today, and I'm going to get you on a train and take you to Chicago with me. How's that sound, eh?"

He continued to talk to the mule as he bridled, then saddled him. He paid the livery manager and rode back to the hotel, tying Johnny to a hitch rack in front of the hotel. He then went into the hotel to get some biscuits and gravy and a cup of coffee. It would not be long before he and the mule would cross the Mississippi.

***

They had seen the lights of the city over an hour ago. As they approached Davenport, Nick rode on ahead. It only took him a couple minutes to find the livery stable. He spoke to the livery manager, then quickly rode back to join the group.

"Livery manager said he was there and just paid him. He thinks he may have been going back to the hotel since he mentioned something about breakfast." As he pointed, Nick continued, "The livery man said the hotel is down the street and around that corner and then down another street, maybe a mile or so away. It's called the *Rock View Hotel*, but he also said that he wasn't sure that was where Vogler was headed."

The lawmen were the first to pull their pistols and examine them, making sure that all chambers were loaded. The others did the same, and then holstered their hand guns. Then followed a check of their long guns. Satisfied, they kept their rifles in their arms and began to walk their horses, following the directions provided by the livery manager.

But they had advanced no farther than a few yards when a great clattering of horses' hooves and rattling of equipment rose behind them. They stopped and turned to see a squad of Army cavalry rapidly approaching them. The soldiers were led by the same stoic officer whom they had seen leading a patrol through Donnellson. Lagging behind the soldiers were Renee Evans and Elmer Vogler. When the patrol stopped, the two remained several yards to the rear of the patrol. Steam vapors rolled from the nostrils of the Army horses as they caught their breath.

Apparently, the Army had gotten to the bottom of the stories that had been told to them at Fort Madison by Renee and Elmer, absolving them of any connection to the crimes of Henry Vogler and had reluctantly allowed the two of them to follow the patrol from a safe distance to the rear as it made its way to Davenport in darkness.

With the patrol standing by, the Army officer walked his horse over to where the lawmen and Summers group were watching. He looked at Virginia Summers and touched the brim of his hat. "Ma'am," he said as he did the same while glancing at Claire May.

"Which one of you is Wentz?" asked the Army officer.

After Nick answered, the officer said, "My name is Wardlaw, Captain Ben Wardlaw."

Nick introduced the others in their group.

"Didn't know that we had a sheriff following this outlaw too," said Wardlaw.

Nathan did not reply, and let Nick do the talking for the group.

"Now as I understand it," said Wardlaw as he spoke to Nick, "the railroad has you boys tracking down this Vogler fellow; is that right?"

Nick nodded. "That's right, Captain, and Mr. Wolf, who is the Des Moines County Sheriff, is working temporarily with me and the railroad on this case."

"OK, I understand that, but what in the world are all these other folks doing here?" he asked as he looked at Virginia Summers.

Virginia spoke up. "Let's just say, Captain, that I and my fellow ranch folks have a vested interest in seeing this outlaw brought to justice."

"Well, I'm pretty damn tired of chasing an outlaw, even though he killed Army personnel. I don't figure this is Army work. As far as I'm concerned, the Army only wants to see this son-of-a-bitch hung, and I'm here to oversee the Army's interests." Wardlaw touched his hat brim again, and said, "Beg your pardon, ma'am, for my language."

Virginia remained silent. She had decided that she did not particularly care for this pompous Army man.

"Mr. Wentz, the Army will defer to you and Mr. Wolf from here on, and accompany you if you don't mind," said Wardlaw.

Nathan Wolf was not too keen on the Army hanging around and showed a bit of his displeasure when he said, "That's fine with us, Captain. But if you don't mind, please ride to the rear to avoid being shot."

Wardlaw opened his mouth and was about to rebuke Nathan's remark, but then remained silent.

"Now if there is nothing further, we are wasting valuable time."

Nick and Nathan wheeled their horses and began moving again, following the livery manager's directions to the hotel. Directly behind them were Virginia and Claire May, with the rest of the group following. The Army patrol walked to the rear, and they were followed by Renee Evans and Elmer Vogler.

The snow flurries were now thicker. Large, unorganized collections of bundled snowflakes were falling faster, tumbling as they fell, and greatly reducing visibility. At the same time, the snow muffled sounds, making everything seem quieter. There seemed to be no one else on the street aside from the now very large group looking for Henry Vogler. They reached the corner of the street. Nick and Nathan turned the corner, and as they did so, the wind blew the snow aside for just a second or two. But that second or two was long enough for Nathan and Nick to see the man they were seeking mount a long-eared mule in front of the Rock View Hotel.

Maybe he should not have done so, but in his exuberance, Nick shouted at the outlaw, "Vogler, stop. You are under arrest."

Henry turned in his saddle, and through the swirling snow, he saw the group coming his way. He quickly drew his pistol and fired one shot. Behind the lawmen, the Army patrol was coming around the corner when Captain Wardlaw's horse screamed, began to rear, stumbled forward, and fell to the ground writhing from a bullet wound. In the confusion, the Army troopers scattered away from the writhing horse on the ground. Then another shot rang out. It came from the rear of the group. Elmer Vogler had fired at the fleeing outlaw. If his shot had found its mark, Elmer would have killed his father, but the shot missed the intended target.

Henry spurred Johnny and wheeled away from the oncoming group. Nathan and Nick were leading the group and saw the outlaw turn the corner three blocks ahead of them. The curtain of falling snow had closed in again, but the outlaw could easily be followed by the hoof prints in the snow.

Careful not to let their animals slip in the snow accumulating on the street, the two lawmen rounded the corner where Henry had turned and galloped down the street. They continued for several blocks until they came to a set of railroad tracks. Henry's tracks turned abruptly, paralleling the train tracks, and the lawmen followed. But as they kicked their horses, Nick's horse slipped and its legs buckled under. Nick managed to jump free from the horse and quickly grabbed the reins again before the horse could run off. Nathan waited only seconds and then sped off again as soon as Nick had regained his seat. They had lost precious ground.

The snow's intensity diminished momentarily. Once again there were finer flurries, and the lawmen could now see their quarry. He was less than a half mile ahead of them. But while they could see the outlaw, they could also see the path that the rails were taking. This set of rails angled upward to a bridge, the Government Bridge, the earliest railroad bridge across the Mississippi. This particular bridge was the fourth iteration of the bridge that Henry had been told about during his railroad work days, and it had been completed just two years prior. Henry was attempting to cross this bridge into Illinois.

Mules are curious animals. They have a reputation for being innately stubborn, but that is not necessarily true. Frankly, mules have a higher sense of self-preservation than a horse. If a rider so wanted, a horse could be ridden off the side of a cliff to its death. A mule would not allow that. A mule would stop and investigate its path; sometimes putting its nose close to the ground to literally sniff out a situation. If a mule thinks that the path is dangerous and might cause it injury, there is no way the rider of that mule will overcome the will of the animal.

Johnny was now exhibiting those mulish characteristics. In the sporadic snow, the mule could see that the path that its owner wanted to take was going to lead to the top of a high bridge which had no side rails and crossed a large expanse of water. The mule was having none of it. Johnny's legs were braced, and he was not moving while Henry continued to kick the mule and lash it with the free ends of the reins. Johnny let loose with a loud bray to express his displeasure. Henry looked over his shoulder and could see the approaching lawmen, resulting in him kicking the mule ever harder.

Johnny had had enough. He bunched his back and reared his front legs, then thunderously landed his front feet, at the same instant, kicking up his rear legs. Henry had been glancing over his shoulder and was not prepared for the unusual movement of his mount. He rolled forward over the mule's neck and landed on the ground, his saddlebags falling with a thud on the ground beside him. Without his rider, Johnny bolted, finally stopping several yards away where he stood looking back at Henry.

Henry stood and saw the lawmen continuing toward him, now riding slowly between the rails, their horses' heads carried low, being careful not to misstep the ties. More people were strung out behind the lawmen. Carrying his saddlebags, Henry began running across the bridge as fast as his artificial leg would allow. He was determined to cross the river. But as he looked forward, the curtain of snow was drawn opaquely closed once again, and over the water, the visibility was only an arm's length ahead of him, while he could still faintly be seen by his pursuers. A shot rang out behind the lawmen that struck Henry's wooden leg, tearing a splintered piece from the stump. Jeb McCoy's shot was close, but Henry could still manage to awkwardly run.

Suddenly, several shots rang out. Nick and Nathan turned and could see Virginia, Claire May, Will and the ranch hands firing up into the air and frantically waving at them. In a split second opening in the curtain of snow, the women had seen something that the lawmen had not. Nick and Nathan stopped and looked back at the women, and in that very second, they heard it. While they could not see the source of it, through the muffling snow, they heard a whistle, not loud, but they knew the sound well. It was then that they also began to hear the unmistakable rumbling vibrations in the steel rails next to them. They needed no other clue. They wheeled their horses and quickly backtracked to the point where they could guide their horses to solid ground at the side of the tracks. Seconds later they heard the faint, muffled scream. In only a few more seconds, the westbound 2-4-2 Baldwin locomotive pulling twenty-four freight cars and four passenger cars rolled quickly past them.

***

After the last train car had passed them, the lawmen dismounted, dropped the reins of their horses, and began walking up the slope to the bridge. They were nearly a quarter of the way across the bridge when the snow tapered quickly and stopped. The sun soon sent light through the scudding clouds. The weather front carrying the snow would soon move to the east, leaving behind a clear, bright, cold afternoon. The sight the lawmen saw was gruesome. Blood and viscera gave evidence where the impact with the locomotive wheels had occurred and dragged the remains until they fell from the bridge. The men quickly turned and shouted to Jeb and Buster to keep everyone away from the bridge.

Henry Vogler's body had been severed. Only the upper body remained on the bridge between the rails. The lower half of his body was nowhere to be seen. His arms were outstretched and appeared to be reaching for the meager leather pieces hanging precariously on the edge of the bridge ties, all that remained of a pair of saddlebags that had held the product of Henry Vogler's shabby life. The leather strips hanging from the ends of the rail ties swayed slightly in the breeze. Nick watched as Nathan picked up the largest piece of the remains of the saddlebags. As he did so, the few remaining greenbacks that had been trapped in the shredded leather pieces flew up and floated away in the breeze, following the path of the rest of the money that had blown away at the train wheel's impact with the saddlebags. The pieces of paper danced in the breeze and almost daintily floated to the surface of the river where they remained, small monetary vessels slowly moving downstream. Nothing more was left in the bits of leather that Nathan held.

Jeb and Buster were unable to hold everyone back, and Captain Wardlaw along with two Army soldiers soon came to stand next to the lawmen. They were followed by Renee Evans and Elmer Vogler. Renee took one look and quickly turned away. "May he rot in hell," she said, and she and Elmer walked back down the incline and off of the bridge.

Captain Wardlaw removed one glove, lifted his hat, and ran his hand through his hair. He replaced the hat and said, "I guess I will wander over to the telegraph office and then head on back to the fort." He offered his hand and shook with the lawmen. "Ordinarily I would say it was a pleasure meeting you gents, but I'm afraid I might not be able to eat for a day or two after seeing this." He turned and began to walk away. Nathan grinned as he looked at the back of the retreating Army officer.

"Captain," said Nick. The Army man turned back to look at the lawman. "Could you have one of your men find the undertaker and send him up this way?"

"Sure thing," said Wardlaw, and he waved as he turned and walked away.

# Chapter Fifty-One

**December 6, 1898 - Law Office of Samuel Vogler**
**San Antonio, Texas**

She was as slim as she had been in her younger days, still walking with a spry gait and possessing the mental acuity of a younger woman. Her hair, neatly tucked beneath her hat, had lost all of its red hue and was now pale auburn. Her enlarged knuckles showed the effects of arthritis resulting from the years of hand sewing on the beautiful dresses and gowns she had sold in her shop. Those work days were now gone; she was seventy-eight years old. Through her wire-rimmed spectacles, Beth Vogler watched the passersby as she made her way to her grandson's office. She was enjoying the mild weather and looking forward to a late lunch with Sammy.

She pulled on the glass-windowed door and entered the office, where a young law clerk greeted her. "Good afternoon, Mrs. Vogler. My, don't you look pretty today," he said.

"Good afternoon, Tobias. How are you getting along?" asked Beth.

"I'm just fine, Mrs. Vogler. I'll go see if Mr. Vogler is ready," said Tobias as he rose and walked into Samuel's office. He returned within seconds and said, "Sam is with a client, but he should be out soon."

While she waited, Beth glanced back at the office door. A sign was affixed to the door which read, "Samuel H. Vogler, Attorney at Law."

The afternoon sun coming through the beveled edges on the glass door acted as a prism, making a rainbow display on the polished wooden door frame. Beth fixed her eyes on the colors, and her mind drifted back in time.

It had been nearly thirty-five years since Samuel had entered her life as an orphaned infant. With the church's blessing, she had adopted the baby and raised him as her own. And throughout all of those years, she had known in her heart that Samuel was her grandson. When she felt he was old enough to understand, she had told him the story of his father who had left home years ago, but had come back to San Antonio so that Samuel could be born and be taken care of by her. Of course, she had not shared her knowledge of the evil side of the boy's father, and thankfully, Samuel had never asked the sort of probing questions that Beth feared.

Samuel was nothing like his father had been through his younger years. To the contrary, Samuel liked nothing better than reading and learning new and fascinating subjects at school, and every afternoon after school he would come to Beth's shop to enliven her with his tales of school. He was simply a joy to be around. Every day Beth said a prayer of thanks for having been given Samuel to raise.

In addition to his studies, Samuel enjoyed participating in, and even leading, events at his school, and began to take boxing lessons in high school. His sports carried over to his college days at Trinity University. With encouragement from Beth, he continued his education at Baylor School of Law. He had married Elsa, a San Antonio socialite, and was the proud father of a boy and a girl. Beth had no trouble remembering each of these milestones in her grandson's life, and she mused to herself that these events seemed to have blurred by so quickly, giving her pause to remember how terribly old she seemed to be getting. But she was a realist, and while she knew she would enjoy her family during the next few years, she also knew that she would not live to see her great grandchildren grow to maturity. She chuckled to herself. Life was just too short, she thought. But she was at peace with herself, knowing that she had lived a full and rewarding life.

Beth was brought out of her reverie by the sound of Samuel opening his office door. His client came out of the office and was followed by the tall, red-haired attorney. Samuel shook hands with his client and watched as the man left the office.

Samuel then walked over to his grandmother.

"Hello Grandma," said Samuel. "I don't know about you, but I'm pretty darn hungry," he said as he kissed his grandmother on the cheek.

Samuel turned to Tobias and said, "We'll be over at *Pablo's* if anyone really needs to see me."

The law clerk nodded. "Have a nice lunch," he said.

As they sat at a table at their favorite cantina restaurant, Beth once again studied the face of the man she had raised as her own. She always marveled that when she studied Samuel's face, she could see slight resemblances to her late husband Horace and her son Henry. She thought that Samuel was a most handsome man, and she was ever so proud of him.

"How is Elsa, Sammy?" she asked.

"She's fine, grandma. She really has her hands full with the kids. Danny and Kate told me to say hello to you when I left the house this morning," said Samuel.

A mental picture of her two great-grandchildren flashed through Beth's mind, and she smiled at the thought. They brought great joy to Beth when they visited her, or when she was able to visit Samuel's home.

Their lunch was delicious. They both agreed that Pablo made the best enchiladas and tamales of any of their favorite restaurants. As they ate, they talked of family activities and other items of mutual interest.

They sipped their coffee as they waited on their caramel flan dessert. As Beth took another sip of coffee, she quickly put the cup back on the saucer and her hands began to shake slightly. An ominous cold feeling swept over her and she became pale. Unconsciously, her hand went to the gold locket around her neck, and her thumb gently stroked the gold face of the locket.

Samuel looked at Beth and became concerned. "Are you all right, Grandma," he said as he placed his hand on top of hers.

For several seconds, Beth did not respond. Slowly she brought her head up and looked at Samuel. "Yes, Sammy, I'm all right."

But she was not all right. She had always expected that this would happen sometime. But when the dark chill had come over her while sitting with Samuel in the restaurant, at that very instant, she somehow knew, as only a mother might know, that her son Henry had died.

Beth looked into Samuel's eyes, as hers welled up slightly. "I love you, Sammy," she said.

Samuel patted his grandmother's hand and smiled. "I love you too, Grandma," he said.

# Chapter Fifty-Two

**December 7, 1898 - Dining Room, *Rock View Hotel***
**Davenport, Iowa**

The Summers family, the ranch hands, and the lawmen were sipping coffee in the hotel restaurant. Greasy plates on the table in front of them held evidence of scrambled eggs, hash brown potatoes, ham steaks, and gravy. Two baskets on the table held the remaining biscuits. The talk at the table had been subdued, with no mention of the horrific conclusion of their quest to bring an outlaw to justice. Instead, they talked about the weather, local news, and subjects they overheard in the dining room. They had nearly talked themselves out.

Over an hour ago, Claire May and her mother had been dressing in the large hotel room they shared. Their topic of discussion had been entirely different from the later dining room talk.

"Claire May, I have talked until I'm blue in the face. How many times must I tell you that that sheriff has absolutely no interest in you?" Virginia Summers' face was flush as she scolded her daughter. "Furthermore, I fail to see how in the world a long distance romance with a man who lives hundreds of miles away would ever come to anything. Why, the idea is preposterous, and I forbid you to even think of moving from the ranch. Our ranch is the legacy of your father, and it was his wish that it would pass to you and your brother when he was gone. Just how would you propose that Mr. Wolf would fit into a life like ours?" This heated discussion had lasted nearly twenty minutes, with neither side yielding.

"Mother, I am perfectly aware that Mr. Wolf has not shown a great deal of interest in having my future intertwined with his. But how do you suppose he should act, when my mother and brother are watching every move he makes. If I were him, I would certainly be intimidated. But mark my words, Mother, I intend to marry that man, and that will be made perfectly clear to Mr. Wolf before we leave this town. I'm not getting any younger, mother, and I need to get myself married if you expect to ever have any grandchildren." She gave her hair one last pat, and then said, "I am going down to the dining room. I will tell them that you will be along shortly," and she walked from the room out into the hallway. Her steps could be heard fading as she made her way downstairs.

Virginia Summers looked back into the mirror to adjust her own hair. She smiled slightly and shook her head. Claire May reminded her so much of herself when she had been young. She would describe her daughter, whom she loved dearly, as intelligent, impetuous, romantic, and headstrong as an ox. Virginia did not really worry that a long distance romance would blossom and flourish. She felt certain it would not. She preferred to think that her daughter was merely smitten by the handsome sheriff. But she had to admit that if she were twenty-five years younger, she could be attracted to the rugged lawman herself. Her daughter could certainly do worse in a suitor than Mr. Wolf.

As she continued to look into the mirror, she sighed and felt the lump of sadness rise in her throat. She so missed Robert. She wished that he had lived to see the fine young woman and man that his daughter and son had grown to be. She quietly voiced a prayer to Robert and then turned from the mirror and walked out of the room.

The waitress came to the table and refilled coffee cups. Claire May gently told the woman that she did not care for any more and looked across the table at Nathan Wolf. She caught him looking back at her. Nathan placed his napkin next to his plate and rose from the table.

"Miss Summers, I am in need of some fresh air. Would you do the honor of taking a walk with me in the snow this fine sunny day?" asked Nathan.

Somewhat unladylike, Claire May nearly sprung from her chair. "I would be delighted, Nathan," she said.

At the other end of the table, Jeb and Buster exchanged looks and grinned at each other, furtively looking at Claire May. Very quietly, but still able to be overheard, Buster said to Jeb, "I told you so," and they both smiled innocently at Claire May and Virginia.

Claire May turned and glared at the wizened ranch hands. "I declare, Jeb McCoy. I thought you had better manners than to be foolish in front of all these people. You two boys may be excused from the table," she said, but she was smiling and her face was slightly flushed when she said it. She turned and left to go to her room to get her coat.

Buster quickly rose, saying, "Yep, I think I'll wander down to the livery stable and check on the horses; don't you think so, Jeb?"

"Oh, uh, yeah. We best do that," said Jeb and followed his friend away from the table.

In a moment, Claire May returned with her coat, and Nathan helped her put it on. "If you will excuse us, Mrs. Summers," said Nathan. Virginia held a slight smile and merely nodded her head.

It truly was a fine sunny day. Blinding sparkles were reflected from the snow on the ground as the couple walked down the street, peering in store-front windows as they passed the shops. Claire May took Nathan's arm as they walked, chattering about items that took her fancy in the windows. Soon, they came to a store front that was obviously a ladies' dress and millinery shop. The window display contained several beautiful hand-made dresses, but in the position of honor among the dresses was an exquisite, lace-trimmed wedding dress. Claire May had stopped and was gazing longingly in the shop window.

"Oh, Nathan," said Claire May. "Just look at that dress. I have often dreamed of wearing a dress like that on my wedding day. Isn't it the most beautiful thing you have ever seen?"

Nathan studied the gown. "I believe you're right, Claire May. I don't remember ever seeing a dress that pretty. And I believe that you would look quite stunning in that dress."

Claire May jumped into the verbal opening and bent the innuendo ever further. She pulled Nathan's arm, and he obliged by looking directly at her. "Why, Nathan, do you believe that maybe we should talk a bit about the possibility that we should be married?" she asked in her most disarming and demure manner.

Nathan chuckled. He had seen this coming as soon as they had stopped in front of the dress shop. He placed his hand gently on Claire May's cheek and said, "Maybe, Miss Summers; maybe," and then he smiled, and they continued walking.

Claire May was walking on air and did not remember looking into any other stores that they passed. Just before they returned to the hotel, Claire May again turned to Nathan and said, "I would like you to come visit our ranch when the weather gets a bit warmer. Would you like to do that?" she asked.

"Why don't we plan on April first," said Nathan. "I'll be the fool walking down your lane."

Claire May laughed. "You're nobody's fool, Nathan Wolf," and she smiled at him.

The next morning, the Summers group stood on the porch of the hotel and watched as Nathan Wolf and Nick Wentz slowly rode out of Davenport to return to their homes in Burlington. The lawmen turned in their saddles and waved again. Oddly, a large box, securely wrapped in brown paper and sturdy twine, could be seen tied behind Nathan's saddle as he turned for a last time to wave.

"Look for your fool on April first," shouted Nathan, and then spurred his horse into a fast walk.

"What on earth did Mr. Wolf mean by that, Claire May?" asked Virginia.

"He's coming to visit us at the ranch on the first of April, Mother," said Claire May as she smiled at her mother and turned to enter the hotel.

Under her breath, Virginia said, "That girl will be the death of me."

Will, standing nearby, had heard her and said, "Don't die before we catch that train for home this afternoon, Mother," and he laughed as he walked into the hotel.

# Chapter Fifty-Three

**March 10, 1899 - Crystal City, Missouri**
**On the Mississippi**

She enjoyed the slow, but subtle, change in the weather, with the rising temperatures, the evidence of small buds on the trees, and the endless river rising up its banks as the northern snows melted into the father of waters.

Catherine "Cat" Breckmon was an outdoors woman. She was plain, but not unattractive, and wore sturdy men's clothing nearly all of the time. She had lived next to the river for all of her forty years, occupying the same cabin in which her parents had toiled and died. She survived by fishing, trapping, and hunting, and could best any man in those ventures. Her skills with a rifle and a throwing knife were unmatched in her county; not that anyone would know, as she kept to herself at her cabin. She made a living by selling the fish to local merchants and the animal skins to a drummer who came to town once every month. On that occasion, she sold her animal skins and bought what supplies she needed in her solitary life. Each month when she went into town, she conducted her business and skedaddled back home; hence, no one really knew Miss Breckmon save the few merchants she came into contact with during her time in Crystal City.

Cat did not mind living alone. She enjoyed the peace and solitude of sitting on her front porch watching the river with its occasional boat traffic. She had never seen a reason to get married; she never thought she would want anyone else hanging around interfering with her, telling her what to do with her life. But that singular life had taken an unexpected turn some four months ago. She remembered that night vividly.

On that night, she remained awake after having retired for the night. She could hear the wind in the trees, and the gentle rain as it pinged quietly on the tin roof of the cabin. Glowing embers cast a familiar orange glow across the one room cabin. She was beginning to drift off to sleep when she heard the noise. It was the slow footfall of a horse outside the cabin. Then she heard the horse blow. That sound was followed by a faint thud and what sounded like a gasp and cry of pain. Cautiously, she rose from her bed and grabbed her nearby shotgun, quickly making sure that it was loaded. Slowly, she crept to the door, pulled back the wooden bar lock, and opened the door. In the dim light and falling drizzle, she could see nothing in front of the cabin. She moved to one side of the porch and peered around the corner. There was nothing there. She moved to the other side, looked around the corner, and saw the horse. It was not much of a horse. Its head hung low with fatigue, and in the dim light, the ribs of the animal were plainly seen.

The man lay in a heap near the front legs of the horse he had been riding. His clothing could only be described as rags, and those rags were filthy with dirt and dried blood. He appeared to be dead. Cat stepped from the porch, walked to where the man lay, and prodded the body with the barrel of her shotgun. The man's eyelids fluttered, and he looked up at Cat. His mouth moved slightly, but no sound came from it. His eyes closed again. She set the shotgun on the porch and dragged the man into the cabin. He was surprisingly light, and his body felt as if it was nothing but bones. She watched the man for a moment as he lay on the floor. The thought occurred to her to take the man back out into the rain and let the crows work on him the next day, but she did not. Instead, she took some rags and wiped the rain and mud from his body.

Two weeks later, the man could sit upright on the mat in the corner of the cabin where he slept. An old bedpan served as his toilet, and he ate his meals while sitting on his mat. As he gained strength, a twinkle returned to his eyes while he told stories and made pleasant conversation with Cat. From washing the man, she had noticed what appeared to be two bullet wounds, one of which had no exit wound. From the location of that wound, it appeared to her that the path of the bullet may have terminated somewhere next to the man's spine. It was now apparent that with the spinal trauma, he might never walk again, but he was able to drag himself using his arms so that he could sit on the edge of the front porch when the weather allowed. And over the course of time, strangely enough, Cat had come to enjoy the company of the man, and she felt that the man's feelings were mutual.

It was warm on this March morning. Cat was kneeling on a dry spot next to the river. She was washing clothes, especially scrubbing the spot on the man's shirt where his wound often oozed a yellowish red liquid, a practice she had grown used to. She wondered whether the wound would ever completely heal with the bullet remaining in his body. Neither the man nor she was skilled enough to attempt such a life-threatening procedure as removing the lead ball.

She completed the washing and took the basket up to the cabin. She returned to the river in a few minutes where she walked several yards to a small marsh pond created by an indentation in the river bank. The water in the pond was settled, yet continually refreshed by the nearby river. It was here that she obtained their drinking water. The pond was also a favorite gathering place for the bull frogs that kept up a never-ending chorus during the warm months. When she was so inclined, she would use a gig to spear three or four of the larger frogs to harvest their legs for dinner.

As she placed the rim of the bucket under the water to fill it, her eyes wandered to the vegetation that grew around the pond. She often watched the tadpoles and crawdads in the shallow water. But today, her eyes locked on something foreign. It looked out of place there in the shallow water, trapped in the water grass. She reached over and picked it up, examining the greenback. She knew it was money; it said so on its face. But she had never seen a fifty dollar bill. She then looked further, and with a bit of wading, it was not long before she held six of the greenbacks. She hurriedly filled her water bucket and walked quickly back to the cabin. The man was sitting on the porch with his back leaning against the cabin wall, watching her as she nearly ran to him. She placed the bucket on the porch floor and bent down to the man.

"Billy, Billy, look at this." She held the money to him, and he took one of the bills and looked at it.

"Where did you get this, Cat?"

"Down at the pond," she replied. "I reckon it came floating down the river," she said.

The man looked at the rest of the bills, and then looked up at Cat and smiled. "The Lord works in mysterious ways, Cat, and that's the gospel truth."

# Chapter Fifty-Four

**April 1, 1899 - Summer Prairie Ranch**
**Outside of Tioga, Kansas**

Switching trains in Kansas City, he had travelled by rail as far as Paola, Kansas, where he retrieved his horse from the livery car and headed south. Nathan had ridden for three days, finally reaching Tioga, where he asked directions to one of the largest ranches in the area. With a gentle southern breeze against his face, Nathan Wolf turned his horse up the lane to the Summer Prairie Ranch house. He sat still on the horse for a moment, wondering what she was going to say. He needn't have bothered. The screen door of the house opened and Virginia Summers stepped onto the porch.

"It's very good to see you, Mr. Wolf. Come up and sit with me on the porch and tell me all about your trip," she said.

They talked for a few minutes, when finally Nathan asked about Claire May.

"Oh, she'll be along shortly. She was out tending fence when she saw you coming. I'm sure she has had her bath by now and...." Virginia was unable to finish the sentence as the bang of the screen door caught their attention. Claire May dashed across the porch, and as Nathan rose from his chair, Claire May hugged him and kissed him.

"Well, I declare, Claire May," said Virginia as she watched from her chair. But she was smiling as she noticed Nathan's red face.

"I knew you would come, Nathan. I just knew it."

Wolf smiled at Claire May and said, "I've got something for you." He stepped off the porch and retrieved a large box, wrapped in brown paper and twine, from behind his saddle.

"Is that for me?" asked Claire May. "What is it?"

Nathan looked down at the floor for a second and then said, "I'm not telling you what it is. And you can't open it here. You must take it in the house to your room and open it there."

"You mean right now?" she said. He nodded.

A quizzical look crossed her face, but she quickly turned and went into the house. A moment later, Nathan and Virginia heard the shriek of delight.

In a few more minutes, Claire May reappeared on the porch. She was wearing the white wedding dress that she and Nathan had seen in the store window in Davenport, Iowa. When she kissed him this time, she did not let go as quickly. When they did part from their embrace, Nathan turned to Virginia and said, "Mrs. Summers, I would very much like your permission to marry Claire May."

Virginia smiled broadly. "I'm not sure you need my permission. It occurs to me that Claire May has already made her decision. Not much chance of me changing her mind." She stood up and extended her hand. "Welcome to the family, Nathan."

Later that evening, Will joined them at dinner, where the topic of conversation was, of course, the pending wedding. After a lull in the conversation, though, Virginia changed subjects. Turning to Will, she said, "Will, I believe that we should begin thinking about how best to utilize your soon-to-be new brother-in-law." Will began to respond, but just as he was about to speak, Nathan spoke up.

"Mrs. Summers, please don't concern yourself on my account. I will be most happy to help out on the ranch in any way I possibly can. But you see, I have done some planning on my own behalf. I have accepted a job as the new U.S. Marshall for the southeast region of Kansas. I will begin my duties after Claire May and I are married."

Virginia looked intently at Nathan as he continued, "I have been assured that I can maintain an office in Tioga so that I can stay at the ranch at night and those times when I am not needed in the office."

Virginia Summers' smile showed that she was pleased. Nathan Wolf had proven to be enterprising and self-sufficient. She admired that, although she did not like the danger involved in maintaining peace and order in the territory.

Claire May beamed at her future husband, and then said, "Marshall Wolf, I like the sound of that."

## Author's Notes

Readers of books with a Western theme will agree that most of them take a bit of a different course, that of following the "good guys" as they pursue the outlaws. But from the start of my writing *Trail of the Outlaw*, I decided to explore the outlaw's character. Was he born with the proclivity to become an outlaw, or was he a product of his environment? I will leave that answer to the individual reader.

Those of you who have read my previous books, thank you very much. You will undoubtedly remember the demise of Thomas Vogler and the names of two more characters in *Trail of the Outlaw* who appeared in one of my previous books, *Flint Bluff*.

Thank you to those readers who have purchased my books. Your interest keeps me inspired to write. And most of all, I would like to express a special thank you to my wife, Janet, who is my best constructive critic and editor.

# On Sale Now!

**For more information
visit:** www.SpeakingVolumes.us

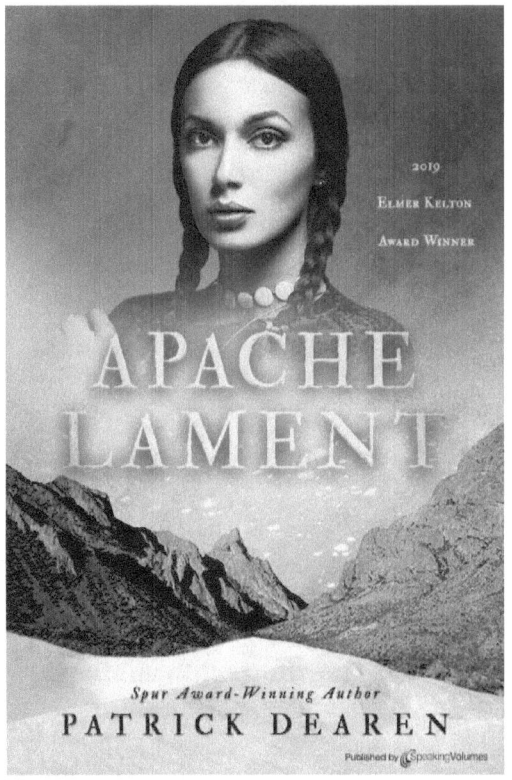

## Sign up for free and bargain books

Join the Speaking Volumes mailing list

Text

# ILOVEBOOKS

**to** 22828 to get started.